Cooper

ERICK S GRAY

BOOTY CALL *69

AUGUSTUS
PUBLISHING

Copyright 2006 by Erick S Gray
ISBN: 0975945343

Edited by Leah Whitney
Design/Photogaphy: Jason Claiborne

Printed in Canada

First printing Augustus Publishing paperback June 2006

AUGUSTUS
PUBLISHING

AugustusPublishing.com
33 Indian Road New York, New York 10034

Some days I try to be strong, need to be strong when I feel the world is against me, people dead set against me—trying to fade a legend I'm soon to be, trying to become that positive brotha from Jamaica Queens. Determination I bleed, I'll breathe my last breath to continue on with my dreams. Y'all can hate, but I'm moving on with better means, got success building in my blood stream. My anger and rage I now press down on a pen, spread my word like a trend, won't let a negative situation eat me from within. With God on my side, I can carry twice the weight, ignore the nay say, and guarantee my fate is for better days. Look into my eyes and you know I'm serious with this, and watch me touch you wit' the pen, have you hooked on my book like a new drug, and daze you wit' some urban love. Keeping my head above the skies, as I hit you with my urban style—creativity burns through my skin, and to let you know, I'm sentenced to life wit' a gift.

First, I thank God for the talents He blessed me with. It's my gift from Him. Now, what I do with it is my gift back to Him. I'm blessed with this. With every book, I'm getting better at it.

Second, I got to give love to my daughter, my true love, heart and soul. Emari Gray, I love you, girl. You know Daddy is in this to win.

Third, I thank God for the parents He blessed me with, Alinda and Spencer Gray; they keep me standing strong with the courage to carry on. They watched me grow, and when I was about to buckle and fold, they were the ones to come along, pray for me and unfold the one they loved and watched grow.

Before I go on, Lauren Hamilton, thank you for your love and support, and coming up with the *69 input to the book. You are a beautiful and creative woman. You know I love you.

I can't forget to show love to my sisters and brothers, Tanya, Terry, Pat and Vincent. We've recently lost one—rest in peace, Corey L. Gray. But as a family, we're still strong, and our younger brother still lives on through us, as we continue to carry on the family name.

Also, I thank Mark Anthony and all he's done for me and the Q-Boro family. You're blessed with Q-Boro, a company meant for such great things. You inspire me and others to keep reaching for their dreams.

Next, I gotta show much love to Augustus Publishing, Anthony Whyte and Jay, my brothers from another mother. Y'all are blessed with business and creative genes. Thanks for giving me the opportunity to get another book out. I see great things in our future; you know we make a mean team.

Linda Williams, you know I have to thank you, too. You're a wonderful woman, always caring, and thank you for always being there to listen. I appreciate and love everything you do for me.

Nakea, my homegirl from Philly—city of brotherly love, thanks for being a friend, a listener, and a great publicist to us all. You, Mark, and the rest all make up an excellent team.

Thanks, Tasha Herman, who also reps South Jamaica, Queens. Thanks for reading my stories beforehand, and showing me support with your input and opinion.

Gale, Ebony, Irvin and family, I miss y'all next door, but I know that God has better things in store for the family. Y'all keep being positive and strong.

My peoples who I've known forever, David Beaumont, K.T, Ryan, Sean, Hasheem, Jamel Rice, my cousin,
Jamel Johnson, Lovey, Michael Thompson, Jerry A.K.A Law, James, Bryant, Lanise and Tania, thanks for holding it down. Gregory G. Goff, rest in peace, and thank you, too.

Shenetta, thanks for gracing your beauty on my new Ghetto Heaven cover. You're a beautiful girl, inside and out. I know you're about to blow up soon, and I felt privileged working next to you for my book cover. Peace, beautiful.

Shavett, you know I had to shout you out in this book, too. You are so cool and down to earth. Keep being you, and keep doing your thang. Never change for anyone.

Okay, this next statement is going to take a minute, so bear with me as I shout out K'wan, Brandon McCalla, Tracy Brown, Ebony Stroman, Denise Campbell, T.N Baker, Kashamba Williams, Ed Mcnair, Hickson, Asante, Thomas Long, Mo Shines, Dejon, Kiniesha Gayle, K. Elliott, Anna J., Joe-Joe, Al-Saadiq Banks, Crystal Lacey, Jihad, Treasure E. Blue, Vonetta Pierce, Danielle Santiago, C. Rene West, Azarel, Shannon Holmes, Ike Capone, Carl Weber, TL Gardner, Gerald K. Malcom, Gayle Jackson Sloan, Dynah Zale, Tu-Shonda Whitaker, Zane, Brenda L Thomas, S.A. Sabuur, Deborah and many more in this game. Let us continue to blow up this genre. If I missed you, I didn't forget about you.

I got to thank Coast 2 Coast and the ARC book club for them online chats. Y'all know I'm always looking forward to them. Thank you for helping to put us authors out there in the market and keeping us on the map.

And last of all, I'm shouting out myself for getting things done. I'm thankful for everything, even for my downs, because it's made me a stronger and better person today. And I thank my fans and readers for showing me that love and support. Thank you.

AUTHOR'S NOTE:

To my Readers and Fans, I appreciate the love and support y'all have shown me over the years, and believe me when I say that I came correct for y'all with Booty Call *69. But before I go on any further, Booty Call *69 is not a sequel. It's a revised, or as I like to say, a Remix edition of the first book. But it's better and tells more of a story about love, and young adults.

For those who have read the first Booty Call edition, and are familiar with the story, take note that Spanky was taken out and replaced with Jakim. And with Jakim, the drama gets a whole lot real, and the sex is even crazier. Now Shana's story is the same somewhat, but with a few bonus scenes that will have you like Whoa!

But it's a great story still, like the first one, but I spiced it up even more, because I believe in perfection, and I give my readers and fans nothing less.

And guess what, for those who remember the first edition. In this new edition I actually tell who's the father of Shana's baby is, and there's also a new shocking ending to this book.

So please read and enjoy, and to note...if you love this book, look out for Nasty Girls coming soon in the spring, because in that book I continue on with Shana's cousin Jade, and even Shana herself. Thanks.

SHANA 1

Damn, I wish he would hurry up and be done wit' it down there already. I should've never agreed to let this niggah eat my pussy. He's wack! Done talked all that shit in the club last night. He got this, he got that, he can do this. I was feeling him for a minute, but now I'm at the point where I need to get the fuck outta here and go home. There ain't nothin' worse than a niggah that lies on himself, especially when it comes to his dick game. And if he got a small dick, he better know how to eat some pussy.

His first fuck-up was lying about his talents in the bedroom. He doesn't have any, and probably never will. His second fuck-up was lying about his penis size. His dick is small and all shriveled up. He's hung like a light switch—three fuckin' inches, I swear. On top of that, he's weak. He couldn't keep his game strong for twenty-four hours. He ain't no real playa; even his boys be dissin' him. Now I'm starting to wonder if he really works for Def Jam; he couldn't even afford to fill his tank up at the gas station. He put in ten dollars worth of gas for an SUV—and a Lincoln Navigator at that. It probably ain't even his. His wack ass probably rented or borrowed it from one of his friends.

I should smack myself for falling for this stupid muthafucka last night. And right now I'm doing him a favor, being that he couldn't even afford a hotel. Shit, he got me downstairs in his man's basement apartment—talkin' 'bout he don't like hotels; they ain't his thing. If the niggah was really a baller and wanted some pussy, then he would've put money up for a hotel and not have me chilling in his man's basement. When I asked to go back to his crib, he denied. He said it's under renovation. He probably still lives at home with his mama.

I wonder why he keeps stopping and looking up at me? Now I'm starting to think he's scared of the pussy, with his goofy fuckin' smile. He is one huge fuckin' turn-off.

I lay my head back down on the bed and decide to give him a few more minutes. After that I'm leaving. I know he's gonna want to fuck, but it ain't happening—not tonight and definitely not with him. I must have been tipsy to leave the club wit' this niggah.

He's finally stopped. I rest myself on my elbows and look down at him. This clown-ass niggah already has his jeans off and a condom in his hand. I quickly get up and pull my dress down. He looks baffled when he sees me reaching for my stuff.

"What...we're not gonna do this?" he asks.

"No, we're not gonna do this," I sarcastically reply.

"I'm sayin'...I done went down on you and shit...."

"And...what? You were expecting some pussy just because you put your tongue between my legs?"

"Yeah, I mean, you got yours; can a brotha get his? I thought you were feeling me?"

"Please, niggah, I didn't get mine; you're wack! You can't even eat my pussy right, so what makes you think you can fuck me right?"

Now he looks really hostile. The condom is crushed between his fist and he's staring hard at me. But I wish he would try to come over here and assault me; my older cousins taught me how to box and handle anybody who might try to force himself on me. I'll fuck this fool up, like I'm Ike and he's Tina. But he does nothing but cuss.

"That's fucked up. Then leave, you stupid bitch. Your pussy was stink anyway!"

"Yeah, well, you must've liked it, because it's all over your fuckin' face...and you were enjoying this stink pussy for a few minutes there, right?" I say with a smirk. "Don't hate on my shit just 'cause you ain't stickin' it. And many niggahs done already appreciated it."

I collect my things and leave. I'll take a cab back home; this trip wasn't worth my time.

My name is Shana, and I'm tired of brothas who claim to be all that but turn out to be totally wack. People say I'm too promiscuous, conceited and sometimes too rude. But I keep it real and like to be straight up with brothas and sistas. If I think you're ugly, then I'm gonna tell you to your face—not behind your back. And if you're cute, that's what's up; I'm definitely gonna let you know. I don't keep secrets, and I'm honest with myself and others. I know what I want, and that's a sexy, wealthy, well endowed, successful black man. Sometimes I slip into other races, but it's all good.

I like to have fun and enjoy life. I'm only nineteen, and I live like a nineteen-year-old partying, meeting guys, admiring the cute ones and dissin' the ugly ones, having sex, roaming the streets and being cool. I've already graduated high school, and I'm in no rush to go to college. Whatever I own or have, I get it from guys who willingly buy it for me. They offer, I accept. I'm not going to turn nothing down; everything I get goes to good use.

I live with my mother and aunt, who are just as promiscuous and conceited as me; that's where I get it from. My mother's only thirty-five and my aunt is only twenty- eight. They're still young and doing their thing. We all go clubbing and hang out sometimes. Most of the men think we're all the same age, but when I tell 'em that one of them is my moms and the other one is my aunt, they freak out. "For real?" they always ask.

I don't have any sisters or brothers, but I have a shitload of cousins. My grandmother gave birth to seven children. My Aunt Tina is the youngest. She's the one who lives with us. The oldest is my Uncle Tommy, who's forty-nine. He lives out in Seattle, Washington. I haven't seen him in years. I get along with my family overall, even though we often argue and fight and want to sometimes kill each other, but that's a regular black family for you. And we all grew up in the projects.

My mother always told me that I was born to be a model. I don't argue; I get compliments wherever I go. I got guys wanting to take me away on vacation–Jamaica, Bermuda, Barbados, you name it–all expenses paid. But so far, I've always turned 'em down. I really don't know why. Maybe it's the type of men who ask me. I'm not really feeling them like that. And you know if they're paying to take you to some tropical island, they're going to want some pussy in return. I'm not at all for fucking a niggah just because he paid for my plane ride so I can lie on a beach in the sun. Don't get me wrong, I do like to fuck. But I just don't give my pussy up to any niggah with fat pockets and a cute face. I can be a bitch, but I'm no ho or slut—don't get it twisted!

I arrive home and quickly jump in the shower, pissed the fuck off. That niggah wasn't worth my precious time. My friends tell me that I'm very picky, but I have the right to be. I feel that my body is my temple and my time is precious, so a brotha must be about something. He must be honest, funny and smart. And also, one of the most important things of all, he must look good. I want my kids to be cute, so you know the niggah I'm with gotta be attractive. They say it's what's inside that matters. Bullshit! I know I don't want to be waking up every morning looking over at some butt ugly man for the rest of my life, and worrying about what my kids are going to look like when I give birth. Looks have everything to do with a relationship. The first thing that attracts you to someone is their appearance and the way they dress and talk. Then you get to know the personality and attitude, see what they're about.

My mother, Denise, knocks on my door and then walks into my room to tell me that Jakim is on the phone. I look at the time. It's eight o' clock in the morning.

"What he want?" I ask.

"He wants to talk to you."

Jakim's my ex-boyfriend. We broke up a month ago. After being together like Barbie and Ken for two years, he started to act like a jerk. I guess he thought he was a *mack* or something, 'cause a few bitches wanted to give him some ass. What really made me mad was that he was paying more attention to them than me. I'm sorry, but I'm not the type of girl to play second to any bitch; if I can't be first, then I won't be anything. Now he's calling, trying to seduce and romance me over the phone. Just a week after we broke up, four of his friends tried to talk to me. But of the four, I'm only feeling one of them—Tyrone; he's definitely a cutie, and he drives a BMW.

"Shana, did I wake you?"

"No. I was gonna call you," I say being sarcastic.

"You were?" he asks.

"No, stupid. You woke my ass up. What do you want?"

"I wanna talk to you."

"Jakim, it's eight in the morning. I ain't get in the house till five."

"Where were you?" he asks.

"What? That's none of your business; we're no longer together. Remember, you wanted to fuck with them other bitches around the way...."

"But I'm sayin', though..."

"You're saying what, Jakim? Just do you and I'll do me. Look, I'm going back to sleep." I hang up the phone. A few seconds later the phone rings again. "I'm not here!" I shout out. I know it's Jakim calling back. He doesn't like to be hung up on—not that I care. As far as I'm concerned, he can kiss my ass.

I don't get out of bed till one in the afternoon. Besides Jakim calling me so fuckin' early in the morning, I had a good sleep.

Like the other women in this house, I get money from men, so I don't stress employment. You'd be surprised how much cash brothers like Jakim, Tyrone and a few others will hand over when they think they gonna get some ass.

My mom's on public assistance and sometimes works different

jobs here and there. But like me, she gets men to support her wants and needs. They swarm around her, just wanting to taste a piece of the action. My mom has long, gorgeous, silky black hair that hangs down her back—as mine does—and it's not a weave either. She's red-boned, pretty and sporting the hell out of a terrific, full-figured body. The only difference between me and my moms is that I'm taller, slimmer and have light brown eyes. My Aunt Tina's a fuckin' gold digger. I be hatin' 'cause she be doin' her thang out there.

I walk into the living room and see Danny on the couch watching TV. He's my mama's man, five years younger than she is and got it going on. He has neat, well kempt, long dreads, muscular arms and a strong-looking chest—something a female can definitely work with. He's tall, handsome and has a nicely trimmed beard. He goes to the barber to get his shit shaped up like once a week. He also got money! He drives around in a green Range Rover. They say he's a big-time drug dealer, but he owns his own barbershop and a nice little bar on Merrick Boulevard. I be envying my mother sometimes; she got the kind of man I dream about every night. I know he be doing her right in the bedroom, too; I be hearing her through the walls. Shit, Danny makes my pussy wet every time I see him. But I keep my affection and hormones to myself. I mean, he is my mother's man.

I walk past him as he sits there flipping through the channels with the remote. My robe covers me, but I'm wearing nothing underneath. A part of me wants to jump on this fine man's lap and fuck the shit out of him. But I just smile and say, "Good morning."

"What up, Shana?" he replies smiling back at me.

He watches me as I walk toward the kitchen, where my mom is cooking up a late breakfast—scrambled eggs and sausages. I go to the fridge and grab a pitcher of orange juice. I then pour myself a cup.

"Late night last night?" my mother asks.

"My night sucked," I tell her, leaning against the sink drinking my orange juice.

She's in her robe, too. I know she just finished getting her groove on with Danny. "So, Aunt Tina left already?" I ask.

"No, that bitch got a date with Michael tonight."

"Michael? What the hell she doin' goin' out with that faggot? What happened to T.J?"

"He got locked up last week."

"Oh! I know she's mad."

My mother nods her head in agreement. "So what's up with you and Jakim? Y'all getting back together again or what?" she asks.

"No. He had his shot, and he fucked up a good thing. Shit, I'm over that muthafucka now." Yeah, I curse in front of my mother.

"You know, y'all do look good together," she says.

"We used to, but now I've moved on." My mother doesn't say another word to me. She fixes Danny's plate and serves it to him as he continues watching television. She then snuggles up to her man as he eats his breakfast. That dick must have been real good to her earlier. I grab the two pieces of sausage left on the stove and head back to my room.

I sit in my room and contemplate on where to go or who to call. I'm not about to stay in the house today. I turn on my stereo and listen to some Mary J. Blige. Soon after, the phone rings and my mother picks up and shouts that it's for me. I pick up. It's Sasha.

"What's up, bitch?!" she hollers.

"Nothin'. What's up with you?"

"Yo, Shana, you know there's a party tonight over at that new club on Merrick, right?"

"Word? Who's poppin' there tonight?"

"Everybody, you ain't heard? There's supposed to be mad cuties rolling through," Sasha says excitedly. "So you rolling or what?"

"Yeah, I'm rolling. Come pick me up now, though. I ain't got shit to do for the rest of the day."

"Aiight, then. I'll be through there in a half. Be ready, bitch."

"Bitch, just hurry your ass up...Danny's here," I blurt out. She has a crush on him, too.

"Word, what his fine ass up to?"

"You know, chilling with my mom."

"Damn, your mom is a lucky bitch," Sasha says. "Look, I gotta go. See you soon."

I hang up and rush over to my closet to throw on something to wear. I know there's no reason to rush; Sasha ain't gon' be here in no half hour. Shit, I'll be lucky if she shows in an hour. I jump into the shower and fantasize about having Danny in here with me. I wonder how big his dick is and what he could probably do with it. I get so carried away dreaming about him that I slip my hand inside my pussy and begin to play with myself. Once I get good and started, there's no reason for me to stop. After my shower and a good nut, I walk to my room and leave my door ajar, just in case Danny walks by. Oh, well, that idea's a bust; he's with my mother in her bedroom.

I throw on my tight-fitting, blue Guess jeans, my gray Guess sweater and a gray baseball cap—just something casual for the day. All I'm going to do is hang out with my girls.

It's going on three, and this bitch, Sasha, still hasn't come around. She got me sittin' around watching afternoon talk shows. My mother is still in the bedroom with Danny, which is making me even more impatient. *Shit, I wish this bitch would hurry up,* I say to myself. Soon after, the doorbell rings. I jump off the couch and go answer the door. To my surprise, it's not Sasha. Jakim decided to stop by—unannounced.

"What's up, Shana?" he says standing there smiling.

"What the fuck do you want, Jakim?"

"What, I can't stop by no more?"

"No, you can't just be stopping by. Why are you here?"

"I just came to see how you were doing," he says.

"Niggah, I'm doing fine without you. I know what you want, and it ain't happening. Go get your dick wet with one of your trifling hoes down the street," I angrily state.

"Shana, it ain't even like that...."

"Niggah, didn't I hang up on you just this morning?! Didn't you get the fucking hint? Bye!" I shout. I try to slam the door in his stupid-looking face, but he blocks it with his foot.

"C'mon, Shana, I've been thinking about you. I've missed you, baby," he says with his foot still jammed in between the door.

"Move your foot, Jakim!" He's still standing there, pleading. *Damn, is my pussy that good to niggahs?* I can't really get that mad with him, because I know I still love him. He's my heart, but he needs to know that I should come first in his life. He thought we were going to break up and he'd be able to fuck other bitches. Then when he got done, he'd come running back to me, begging for forgiveness. No! It doesn't work that way. I got too much respect for myself. I'm not one of these stupid bitches in the street he can game and have his way with. After being together for two years, he should've known better. He should've known how I get down. But I guess he wasn't taking notes.

"Jakim, I ain't playing with you. Please move your fucking foot!" I continue to shout.

"What's going on out here?" my mother asks, coming out of her bedroom tying her robe together.

"Fucking Jakim won't leave the door!" I scream.

"Jakim, respect my daughter's wishes and leave here," my mother calmly tells him.

"But I just want to talk to her, Ms. Banks," Jakim says.

"It's obvious that she doesn't want to talk to you right now, so do yourself a favor and come back and speak to her another day. Don't get her more upset than she already is," she tells him.

Jakim backs off, removing his foot from the door. He apologizes to my mother for the noise and disturbance he's caused. He then stares at me and leaves. I stand in the doorway and watch him drive off in his black Nissan Maxima before closing the door. I turn around and see my mother standing there watching me, and watching Jakim leave.

"You still love him," she says. "I can see it in your eyes."

"Yeah, right," I try to deny.

"It's okay, Shana. We all go through the same problems with men. It's just knowing when and how to deal with them," she advises before going back to her bedroom to her own damn man.

My mother sees right through me most times. She knows that I'm still in love with Jakim, and she knows how stubborn I can be. But he fucked up and needs to be taught a lesson.

Just as I'm about to give up on that bitch, Sasha, showing up, the doorbell rings again. I go open the door, and there's Sasha standing in the doorway smiling.

"Bitch, you know what time it is?!" I shout.

"Yeah, and your day ain't wasted," she quickly responds.

"Fuck you!"

"Yeah, I love you, too. C'mon, let's go." She grabs me by my shirt and pulls me out the door.

As we're driving, listening to music and staring at cuties, Sasha says, "I saw Jakim turn off your block. What's the deal wit dat shit? I thought y'all broke up."

"Yeah, we did. But you know, he's still sweatin' a sista."

"Word? I saw him with that bitch, Theresa, the other day," she says, sharing unimportant news with me. "He was all hugged up with her in the park and shit."

"Well, thank you for that useful bit of information," I unpleasantly say to her. She could have kept that kind of news to herself.

We pull up to Mickey D's, because I haven't had anything to eat since those two sausages I had for breakfast. Sasha wants to pull through the drive-thru, but I prefer to go inside; the drive-thru always fucks up my order. I persuade her to park and eat inside; we're in no rush to go anywhere. As soon as we enter the restaurant, three niggahs start clocking me. I just turn my head and ignore 'em. Only one of 'em is cute, but his shoes are jacked up. Sasha pays them no attention either. She just stands on line with me and looks up at the menu. I turn around to see if they're still gawking, and yes, all three of them still are. I just sigh and continue to stand on line. As we approach the counter, I can feel the bitches who work here hating already, some of them staring and screwing up their faces at us. I place my order with the cashier, who has a bit of an acne problem on her face.

"Yo, do they still got that game where you connect the dots?" Sasha says loudly enough for everyone to hear.

"You're wrong, bitch," I say laughing. The cashier looks up at us in disgust and continues to take our orders. She looks like she doesn't want to be here. Me, personally, I could never take a job at McDonald's and get paid minimum wage.

"I don't wanna see any foreign skin floating in my Pepsi," Sasha goes on, causing me to laugh again. We're so wrong, not much caring that we're probably hurting her feelings. But she never says anything back to us; she just keeps on being polite and filling our orders. A few people on line with us think we're funny, while others look on with disapproval and shame.

We receive our food and go and look for a table. "Yo, shorty, let me holla," I hear someone whisper. I know which one of the three guys is trying to call me out, but I don't answer. I just sit down at a table and look the other way.

"Yo, Shana, look at them three sorry bums over there clocking us."

"Yeah, I already saw 'em." We continue to eat, laugh and make fun of the three guys who've finished their meals a while ago but remain at their table, probably trying to cough up enough courage to approach us.

"It's a damn shame how some men can be so soft when they see pussy. A scared man can never get none," I say.

Sasha is dying laughing, almost choking on her drink. She gobbles down her last bit of fries and we're ready to leave. We get up and head out the door, still ignoring the three guys. They follow us out into the parking lot, and one of them finally gets the courage to shout out, "Yo, shorty, come here. Can I chat with you for a minute?" And it's not the cute one. It's the black, monkey-lookin' muthafucka!

I just keep walking to the car. He should've been figured it out, but he keeps coming toward us, thinking he's going to get some play. As I'm about to get in the car, he grabs a hold of the passenger door, preventing me from closing it.

"Excuse me!" I yell.

"I'm sayin, though, a brotha can't get no love from y'all?" he asks.

Seeing him up close is even worse. His lips are dry and cracked. His skin is so black it looks purple. His clothes are wack and dirty, and his hair is nappy. Shit, I could go on with so many things that are wrong with him. "*Ee-ill*, niggah," I say looking up at him in disgust. "Did I look like I was interested?"

"Blackie, please don't touch my car," Sasha adds. He looks over at her for a second and then focuses his attention back on me. I don't even want him near me, and he has the nerve to be trying to talk to me as his two friends stand by and watch.

"I'm sayin' though, you look too good, boo. I can't get your number and call you sometime?"

"Hell, no, muthafucka. Please get away from me," I say.

"Oh, it's like that, boo?"

"Yeah, it's like that, ugly—leave," Sasha chimes in.

His two boys laugh, seeing him get dissed. I guess he was trying to impress them or something. He tries to play it off. "Fuck y'all bitches!" he says.

"You wish you could!" I reply.

I know he feels stupid. We drive off laughing. *Ee-ill*... me and him—

never in this fuckin' lifetime. "Next time, we're going though the drive-thru," Sasha says glancing over at me. I can't argue.

We shop for the rest of the day on Jamaica Avenue. I buy a few outfits, including something to wear for tonight. Sasha buys a pair of fly, three-hundred-dollar, Donna Karan shoes, and they break her pockets. It's going on seven, and it's time to leave and get ready for the party Sasha was talking about. The only reason I'm really going is to get my mind off of Jakim. I'm not stressing him like that, but I still have feelings for the man. Sasha drops me off at my front door and promises to pick me up around nine, nine-thirty.

I don't rush to get dressed. I talk to a few people on the phone, take a shower and do my nails. I'm home alone, so I walk around the house butt naked. It feels good to just let my body breathe every once in a while. I stop and look at myself in the hallway mirror. "Damn, bitch, you got the perfect body," I say, posing and admiring every aspect of my figure. Noticing the time, I run to my room to get dressed. I already know what outfit to sport tonight—my black leather mini skirt, my slate blue, stretch silk shirt and my open toe heels. I let my hair fall down past my shoulders and comb it out briskly. I put on just the right make-up and spray on some Michael Kors fragrance.

It's twenty past nine when Sasha comes to pick me up. Latish and Naja are in the car with her. Naja's already riding shotgun, so I climb into the backseat and greet everybody. I've only known Latish for two years, but Naja and I go back to the sixth grade. She's one of my closest friends. Latish and I had our little feuds back in the day, because she always tried to talk to Jakim when the bitch knew he was my man. She said they just talked, and that it wasn't intimate. But deep down I know she fucked him; they just aren't telling. I've kept it cool with her so far, and I try not to have any beef wit' her.

We arrive to the club at a little past ten. There's already thirty to forty people lined up outside. Sasha parks the car two blocks down, around the corner from the club. We all step out of the car and straighten out our clothes, make-up and hair. I know I'm looking good, so I don't stress too much.

"Fuck this!" Sasha blurts out.

"What's wrong, girl?" I ask.

"This fucking line, that what's wrong." She steps out of her place in line and heads for the front entrance. "I'll be right back."

About ten minutes later, Sasha makes her way back to us. "C'mon, y'all, we're getting in," she says.

We all look at each other, thinking, *what is this bitch talking about?* But we follow her to the front of the club anyway, causing many who are still standing in line to hate and begin to bitch and moan. *I hope this bitch don't embarrass us—we get to the entrance and get sent back to the end of the line—not tonight in front of all of these people.* We get to the entrance and to my surprise, we're easily escorted in by a 6'2", dark and muscular man. We pay the ten-dollar admission and strut our way into the party. I look at Sasha in amazement. "What did you do? Who hooked you up?" I ask.

"I gave the main bouncer my phone number and promised to suck his dick before I leave tonight," she says smiling at me.

"You serious?"

"Hells yeah. We got in, didn't we?" I have no other words for her. She's definitely bugging the fuck out. I'd rather have waited on line for two hours. But it's all good. We step into the dimly lit club. The music, the crowd and the scenery is bumping. The deejay has everybody hyped. He plays that new jam by Ja Rule and Ashanti. I glance around the place, checking out the cuties. And I look around for a familiar face, but I don't see one.

"I'll be back," Latish says. She goes straight to the bar. It figures. She always has to get her drink on before she can get her party on.

I'm standing alone, and this chubby niggah walks by and stares me down from head to toe. *I hope he doesn't come my way.* The only thing he has going for him is the piece around his neck. It's kind of fly, and I know it's real—Cuban links with the phat diamond cross. His stomach sticks out too much, though. But he only checks me for a moment from the corner of his eye and walks away. Thank God.

After about an hour, the place is packed tight like sardines. Drinks are being spilled on people bumping into one another, and a fight breaks out between two guys on account of this. A few punches are thrown and they're both put out of the club.

I've been dancing with this cutie for the past half hour. He gets love, with his hazel eyes and fade. He smells good, too. Too bad I can't say the same thing for the majority of the niggahs up in here; muthafuckas don't believe in cologne. But my newfound cutie is cool. He buys me two drinks at the bar and asks for my number afterward, but I don't give it to him. I tell him I already have a man. He doesn't take it to heart. He still chills with me for a while.

Latish is now a little tipsy. She's on her sixth drink, and she's with some chocolate, fine-looking brotha by the bar. Sasha's doing it up on the dance floor, grinding and hugging up on a few men. Naja chills with me at the bar.

I need a little break; with each passing minute that goes by, a different guy grabs me, touches me or wants to dance or talk. I tell Naja that I'm going to the bathroom, and she comes along with me. I barely make it there when I feel someone grab at my arm. Now totally fed up, I angrily turn around, only to see Tyrone, Jakim's best friend. He is a cutie.

"What up, baby girl?" he says smiling and gently takes my hand.

"Oh, what's up, Tyrone? I ain't know you was up in here," I say to him. I can't help but show my excitement. It's all over my face.

He's chilling with three of his friends, all of 'em looking thugged out, wearing hoodies, jewelry, Timberlands and attitudes. He continues smiling and gives me a hug. "Damn, you look good, Shana," he says gazing at my outfit.

"You're not looking bad yourself," I reply. He's wearing a blue and gray Sean John sweatshirt, blue denim Rocawear jeans and black Timbs. His braids are freshly done and his diamond earring sparkles brightly. *Damn, he is too fine!*

"Can I get this dance with you?" he asks.

"Sure," I say, forgetting about the bathroom and forgetting about my girl, Naja.

We stroll over to the dance floor. It seems as though room is being made especially for us as we pass through the tight crowd. He grabs me and grinds his pelvis against mine. His moves on the dance floor are so smooth and coordinated, like he practices them every day. He knows how to move his feet, hips and shoulders. He has so much rhythm and energy that it's hard for me to keep up with him. I notice the other ladies on the floor checking him out, too. They're looking mighty interested as he grinds up on me. I'm getting wet and aroused and I'm starting to feel guilty.

We eventually stop dancing, and he asks me if I want a drink. I say yes, and he escorts me over to the bar. We talk and laugh until Sasha interrupts us. She says hi to Tyrone and gives me this weird look.

She then pulls me a few feet away. "You know you wrong; that's your ex's best friend," she says.

"So!" I reply.

"What do you mean *so*? Jakim will kill you if he finds out you're flirting and playing touchy-feely with his boy."

"Did you forget that we're no longer together, that I can do whatever the fuck I want?! Besides, I'm just trying to get my itch scratched tonight, and he seems like the right one to do the scratchin'."

"You are so wrong, Shana," Sasha says, finally leaving me to my business. She doesn't understand. Shit, the last time I had sex was two weeks before Jakim and I broke up. That was a while ago. Tyrone will understand; it'll be just sex. He'll get what he wants, and I'll get what I want. I know he'll do me right tonight; I've heard stories about him from my girls.

I go back to the bar and tell Tyrone that I want to leave with him tonight. He doesn't even ask why. He gives his boys dap and leaves with me under his arm. Sasha glares at me as we walk past her, but I don't give a fuck what she thinks. That bitch is no angel; she does her dirt, too.

A slow jam mix CD plays in Tyrone's BMW, and his hand is deep between my thighs. He's fingering my pussy, and it feels so good. I spread my legs apart even more so he can get a better feel. "You're bugging, but I'm feeling you, boo," he says smiling.

We're heading to his crib for the night—not his mama's, but *his* shit, which he shares with his roommate in Rochdale Village. I've been there once with Jakim. It's real cool. It's a two-bedroom, with the phat entertainment center. We stop at a red light and begin to kiss, tonguing each other down passionately. The light turns green and we pull off. I'm so horny, and my panties are so wet that I end up pulling them off and throwing them in the back seat. I think I'll leave them there.

We're at his crib fifteen minutes later. His roommate is still at the party, and he's not coming home any time soon. We begin to do our thing. He pulls up my leather mini skirt and lays me down on the carpet. He begins eating me out. He spreads my legs wide apart and sticks his tongue deep inside me. I moan with pleasure. He lifts his head up for air after several minutes. I'm done with the oral action anyway; it's time for us to move on to the next stage. I want to fuck him. I get naked, and he gets to his feet and does the same. He has eight inches to play with, a chest like Tyson, the model, and a washboard stomach. I push him down to the floor, mount him and start riding that dick. I'm definitely feeling him up inside me; he's so big and hard. It feels as though his cock is reaching into my stomach. He palms my ass with a tight grip, and he thrusts himself into me harder and harder, absorbing my juices and fulfilling my needs. He then turns me over to lie down on my stomach. He rams his rod into me from the back. I want to bite down on my tongue; he's banging me so fast and so hard, and it feels so good. I claw the carpet and begin to pant. He speaks not one word as he fucks me vigorously. Position after position, the dick is feeling too good; it puts me in tears. This muthafucka, Tyrone, has strength, stamina and endurance. Thank God for him.

We feel no regret after we're done. I needed exactly what he just gave me. My pussy has definitely been scratched. I get up and begin to get dressed. I zip up my skirt as he buckles his jeans, but we don't leave right away; Tyrone has other treats in store. He goes to his bedroom and comes back out with a phat blunt—some bomb Haze. We smoke and talk as we continue to get high and fondle each other. I am definitely feeling this niggah's groove.

Tyrone drops me off at my front door a few hours later. He kisses me goodnight. "Whenever you need that favor again, you know who to call," he says.

I nod my head, get out of the car and walk to my front door. I turn around and watch him drive off the block when I finally begin to feel guilty. *Damn, Jakim would trip right now if he knew his man kissed me goodnight and dropped me off at my door.* My eyes dart about nervously, looking to see if his car is parked anywhere on the block. Luckily for me, it's not. I'm in the clear—not that it really makes a difference; *we're not together anymore*, I try to convince myself.

I go inside and see my aunt all over some man on the living room couch. His pants are down, and her blouse is fully open. She smiles at me and asks if I had a good night. I smile back and tell her that my night was too good to me. She feels where I'm coming from and continues doing her thing with her male company. The one thing about us females in this house is that we aren't humble or shy when it comes to getting our freak on in front of each other. I remember the time I came home early from school and caught my moms ass naked on the floor, with some red-bone niggah in between her knees. It didn't take a miracle to know or see what was going on. She looked up at me, grinned, asked why was I home from school so early and then went right back on with her business—not giving a fuck that I caught or interrupted them both. Shit, there were a few times when my mother caught me and Jakim doing our thing. She would always ask if I was using protection. That's the only thing she was concerned about.

I get ready for bed, but I can't stop thinking about Tyrone and it's bugging me. I don't know what it is—maybe just the good dick and get-high afterward...or maybe I'm catching feelings for the man. Shit, I hope not; that would cause problems. Yet and still, no matter how hard I try to stop thinking about him, he keeps creeping back into my head. I throw the sheets over myself and try to get a good night's rest—without Jakim, Danny or Tyrone in my thoughts.

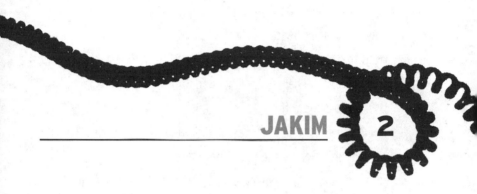

JAKIM 2

"**Yo, Ja,** you shoulda came through last night," Evay tells me. "There were mad bitches at that club."

"Word?" I respond nonchalantly. I'm hearing Evay talk, but I'm really not listening. My mind is preoccupied with something else.

"Yeah, Jakim...it was me, Tyrone, Lovell and Rocky. I bagged like two numbers last night."

We're chilling on the corner of Hollis Avenue and 200th Street, gulping down forties and passing the evening away by getting drunk and watching the ladies stroll by. I'm leaned up against my Maxima with a forty clutched in my hand. Evay continues to talk, and he informs me about his dynamic night at this new club on Merrick Boulevard.

"Yo, I'm gonna try and fuck this bitch I met last night by next week, son—watch, Ja."

I take another swig from the forty and pass it to Evay. He downs a mouthful. Evay's a hefty fuck and not too easy on the eyes, but he's mad cool. He talks a lot, but that's Evay, always in your ear about this and that, and sometimes even other people's business. He doesn't mean any harm, though. He stays trying to be a playa or a pimp, but most times with no success. Some girls have given him a little play, but Evay gets as much action as the Knicks have championship rings.

"Ay, yo, Shana was there, too."

Now that catches my attention. "What? She was?" I ask.

"Yeah, Ja—and she was lookin' good, too."

"Who she came with?"

"She came wit' her girls—Sasha, Naja and that ho, Latish. Damn, I wanna fuck dat bitch. Yo, Ja, she got a man?"

I ignore his lustful inquiry about Latish and ask more questions about Shana. "Yo, did she dance wit' anyone?"

"She kept mostly to herself, but she did dance with Tyrone."

"Oh, word?"

I can't help but get a bit jealous, thinking about Shana going out and grinding on the next niggah. And even worse, taking it a step further and *fuckin'* da next niggah. I still have strong feelings for her, but she's acting like a bitch about us getting back together again.

"Evay, who she leave with?" I ask.

Evay is quiet now. He stares off in the distance, and I know it's bad whenever the niggah hesitates to give me an answer; so I answer for him: "She left wit' some other niggah last night, right?"

"Nah, man—she was just doin' her," he explains. But I know Evay's hiding something from me. He passes the forty back to me, and I quickly down it until it's empty.

I'm beginning to feel even more jealous, entertaining thoughts about Shana fuckin' some other niggah last night. I was the only man in her life for more than two years. Shana fuckin' other niggahs is a hard possibility to swallow. She's still my prize, and that pussy is so hard to give up. I try to contain my emotions in front of Evay, but inside I'm truly hurting from our break-up.

"Ja, you okay?" Evay asks.

"Yeah, I'm aiight," I lie, becoming aloof as I stare off into space thinking about Shana.

"Yo, don't stress dat shit, Ja. I'm sure Shana ain't fuckin' other niggahs."

"Niggah, how you know?" I shout. "You wit' her twenty-four seven?"

"No, but—"

"Whatever, man! Fuck her!" I continue to shout, becoming frustrated by the thought of her fuckin' the next niggah. Evay looks like I've hurt his feelings. He stands there quietly, at a loss for words.

"Yo, I ain't mean to scream on you, Evay...my bad 'bout dat."

"It ain't nothin', Ja. I'm a big boy; I can handle it."

I get up off my car and hurl the forty, smashing it against a brick wall.

"You sure you're aiight?"

I nod my head. "I'm out, son."

"Yo, I'm gonna meet Tyrone and da fellows later on Jamaica Ave. You comin' through?" Evay asks.

"I'm gonna think about it," I say jumping into my car. I sit in the driver's seat for a few minutes, contemplating whether or not to give Shana a call. My heart is telling me to call her, but my ego is saying, fuck dat bitch! I listen to my ego and decide to make other moves right now. I pick up my phone and dial a quick booty call. I know she's guaranteed ass for the day; every time I call, she never tells me no. I'm horny, and fuckin' with her would help me take my mind off of Shana for a minute.

I speed dial her number and she picks up after the second ring. "Hello?"

"Hey, what's up, love?"

"Hey, you, what's going on? I ain't heard from you in a few days. You okay?" she asks with concern.

"Yeah, I'm good. So what's going on wit' you?"

"Nothin'. You comin' through?"

I smile knowingly. "Dat's why I called."

"I hear dat, baby. I miss you."

"So what you got for me?"

"Same thing I had for you last time."

"Oh, word?" My smile grows bigger. The last time we hooked up, she gave me head for an hour. And her pussy is good. "Aiight, I'll be at your place in fifteen minutes. You cool wit' dat?"

"Yeah, just come through. You know you miss it."

I laugh, hang up and start my engine. I keep telling myself that I'm not gonna stress Shana as I drive to my booty call's destination. I have a pack of Trojans in the glove compartment and a hard-on as I think about the pussy I'm about to get into.

I drive down Farmers Boulevard doing fifty miles per hour. So far I'm lucky that I'm not getting pulled over by 5-0. I make a right on Linden Boulevard and another right a few blocks down on 179th Street. She lives in a basement apartment of a two-story brick home in a prestigious area. I pull into a parking space out front and quickly exit my ride. I strut to the side entrance of her basement apartment. I ring her bell twice and stand off to the side, waiting for her to come to the door.

She appears almost instantly, opening the screen door with a Colgate smile. "Hey, baby." She throws her petite arms around my neck and embraces me. She then gives me a quick kiss on the lips. I have to step back and admire her rawness; there's no shame in her game—coming to the door in a pair of lacy, boy-shorts and a T-shirt so scanty that it barely covers her tits. "You like?" she asks throwing herself into a quick pose for me to admire.

"Yeah, I love how you get down," I reply.

"You gonna stand out here and drool, or come inside and handle your business?"

"What you think?" She playfully pulls me by my shirt into the doorway and drags my ass down the steps to her place.

Latish is a freak on a level that most niggahs can't handle. Like I said before, she never says no to the dick. Even on her period, she wants to fuck a niggah, but running red lights ain't my thing. She's got every sex toy imaginable locked away in her bedroom closet. I mean, she even has a swing that hangs down from the ceiling; you strap a bitch in and fuck her as the two of you just swing away...it's crazy. We tried it once and I have to admit, it was definitely an experience I'll never forget.

Latish and I started fucking a few days after Shana and I broke up. But to be honest, we've had a few affairs even when Shana and I were together. Of course she knew about Shana at the time, but she didn't care; the dick was too good to her and she wasn't trying to give it up, despite her friendship with my ex-girlfriend.

I hear a song by Jagged Edge. The lyrics of *Promise* blast from the six speakers situated throughout the room. I stand in the center of her liv-ing room as she slowly begins unbuttoning my shirt and saturates my neck with slow, pleasing kisses. She pulls my collared shirt down around my shoulder blades, and her lips and tongue go to work on my nipples. I let out a slight moan and grab a handful of her beautiful silky hair.

Latish's basement apartment is lavishly decorated in imported leather furniture and African décor. She definitely has taste. Her dark-skinned complexion, well-toned body and full, glossy lips give her the appearance of an African beauty.

Latish slowly removes my shirt and continues to kiss my body pas-sionately. She gradually makes her way down to my crotch area, and she gets down on her knees and begins undoing the zipper to my jeans. I watch her reach into my pants and pull out my dick.

"Ooh, baby, dat's what I'm talkin' about," she purrs while smiling up at me. She gently strokes my hard-on, teasing me.

She kisses around the tip of my dick, and then she slowly places it on her tongue. I let out a slight moan.

"Stop teasing me and suck my dick already," I say impatiently.

Latish continues to smile, gripping my erection in her hand. The bitch can be such a tease with the dick until it gets to a point where you become annoyed. But once she puts your dick in her mouth, it's a wrap. She can suck a dick so long and strong that she can make a niggah's forehead cave in.

"I thought you liked being teased, baby," she says stroking my shaft tenderly in her soft grip.

"I do, but damn, you know how you do, baby." She lets out a slight laugh. And then she leans forward and devours my dick, causing me to gasp and clench her shoulders. I look down at the top of her head and watch her bob back and forth, her strong jaw going to work on my shit.

"Aaaaaahhh...damn...oooh, Latish...shit," I cry out. My jeans are down around my ankles as I stand in the center of her living room, getting my blowjob on. Not once does Shana come to mind. "Yo, I need to sit down," I tell her, feeling my knees buckling.

I carefully back-step toward the couch, my jeans still around my ankles with Latish in tow—still on her knees and still holding my dick in her hand. I plop down on her couch and step out of my pants. Latish positions herself on her soft, leather couch and starts kissing my nipples. She slowly slides her way down to my stomach, back toward my shaft again. I grunt and throw my head back as I grip a handful of her smooth, black hair. Her exceptional blowjob goes on for at least twenty minutes, and I have to fight to keep from cumming in her mouth like I did the past few times. But Latish loves it when a niggah comes in her mouth; she becomes more aggressive, a fuckin' freak.

Shortly after my blowjob, Latish stands up and comes out of her boy-shorts, but she keeps on her scanty T-shirt. Her pubic hair is cut very low and trimmed nicely. And her apple bottom ass makes a niggah want to fuck her in the butt—which, mind you, I've done many times before.

She walks back over to me, leans forward and starts to tongue kiss me wildly, while simultaneously jerking me off. Our lust for one another is intense. I pant loudly, feeling the need to explode inside her. "You ready for this pussy?" she whispers in my ear before nibbling at the lobe.

"I wanna fuck you!" I say with intensity.

"Take it, Jakim!" She presses her body against mine and starts to mount me.

"Shit!" I shout.

"What's wrong, baby?"

"I forgot da condoms in the car."

"Oh, word? Don't worry about dat, baby. I wanna feel dat dick raw in me anyway."

"Yeah, but—"

"C'mon, baby, touch me. Feel how wet I am for you," she says, taking my hand and placing it between her bare thighs. I feel her sweet juices flowing onto my hand. She's definitely wet. I stick my index finger deep into her pulsating pussy. I begin finger-popping her gently, and she begins to moan. This action goes on for about a minute until I can't take it anymore. I remove my finger from inside her and grip my hard dick in my hand. Latish slowly moves her lower half onto my erection, straddling me on the couch. H-Town's *Knockin' Da Boots* plays faintly in the background. I grip her hips as she rocks back and forth against my lap. She throws her arms around me and cries out in ecstasy.

Sweat profusely escapes from our pores as we touch, rub, grind and fuck the shit out of each other. We assume position after position, from missionary to straight up doggystyle until we just can't fuck anymore. We lay motionless on her living room floor. My body feels numb and exhausted. But this was worth it. I've definitely released some stress with Latish tonight. I breathe heavily and stare up at the ceiling, lying nude with her next to me. "You okay, baby?" she asks, her hand gently moving up and down my chest, tickling me a little.

"Yeah, I'm good," I reply. We continue to lie around her apartment until she gets up to use the bathroom. I watch that ass jiggle as she sashays down the hallway. I'm feeling a little excitement down below again. But enough is enough; she's about to kill a niggah with all the fuckin' we're doing.

I look at the time. It's twenty minutes past nine, time for me to go. I get up off the floor and pick up my clothing, which is scattered all around the room. I start to get dressed. Latish, still naked, comes out of the bathroom. "You leaving me already?"

"Yeah, I got things to do," I say.

"I want you to spend the night with me."

"Next time, love."

She sucks her teeth, plops her naked ass on the couch and crosses her legs. "You seen the remote?"

"Nah. You ain't gonna get dressed?"

"For what? It's my crib Niggah, I walk around naked all day," she informs me. I shrug my shoulders and throw on my Timberlands. After putting on my last piece of clothing, I glance over at Latish. She's still lounging naked on her couch, now channel-surfing with the remote.

"Yo, I'm out," I tell her.

"When I'm gonna see you again?" she asks.

"Whenever—you got my number." She sucks her teeth again and follows me to the door. "You ain't gonna throw a robe on at least?" I add.

"For what, Jakim? My body is my treasure. I go outside like this all the time. And most of my neighbors are niggahs; they ain't complaining."

I laugh. "You be buggin."

"Whatever, niggah. I wanna see you again."

We stand outside in her doorway under a canopy of stars, with Latish still in her birthday suit. She throws her arms around me and gives me a passionate kiss. I grip her firm apple bottom and squeeze it like I'm squeezing the juice from a piece of fruit. It's hard to let her go; being up against her makes me want to set it off again, but it's getting late and I have to go. I strut back to my car a very happy and sexually satisfied man.

I get in my car, turn the ignition and let my Maxima idle in front of Latish's crib for a few moments. It's funny; no sooner than Latish is out of my sight, thoughts of Shana creep back into my mind. After all of that freaky, bumping and grinding, hot, sweaty sex with Latish, I want to give Shana a call. I know I have to beat the infatuation I have for my ex-girlfriend, but it's hard. I want to give her a booty call, too, but I know it's not happening any time soon. I want to win back her love and affection, but she's being stubborn and putting a brick wall between us.

I pull off and decide not to call Shana. I'll call Tyrone or Evay instead and see what's up for tonight; when I'm alone, my failed relationship with Shana be fuckin' wit' me. But when I'm amongst company, I'm good.

During my drive home, I break down and call Shana anyway. Her aunt picks up.

"Hello, is Shana there?"

"No, sweetie, she's not," her aunt replies. "Who's calling?"

"It's Jakim."

"Hey, hon, I haven't seen you around in a while. You okay, baby?"

"Yeah, I'm good. Can you tell Shana that I called?"

"No problem, sweetie."

Now, I should just hang up and let it be, but my curiosity gets the best of me and I ask, "By the way, do you know where she might have gone?"

"She went out on a date wit' some niggah."

I'm speechless. The only thing I can say is, "Oh, aiight...just tell her I called." I hang up, feeling my heart in my stomach as envy and resentment spread throughout my body. *Why did I ask, when I didn't want to know the answer?* I say to myself.

Now frustrated, I decide not to hang out with Tyrone and Evay. I do a quick U-turn and make a beeline back to Latish's place. *Fuck it. Shana wanna be out all night, fuckin' this niggah and that niggah, then I'm gonna be doing me with no regrets.* I keep telling the bitch I've changed, but she's not trying to hear what I have to say. I know I fucked up when I cheated on her. But she can't let bygones be bygones, and now she's on some ho shit— I assume. I want her to give us a second chance, but the dumb bitch won't let my mistake be water under the bridge.

3 SHANA

I lay naked on Tyrone's bed as he gets dressed. He's letting me stay the night in his apartment. It's two o' clock in the morning, and he just got a page from one of his workers. Now he's heading out the door to take care of some business. This is the sixth time we've been together intimately. The dick is just too irresistible and too fucking good for me to say no to. For hours we were going at it non-stop, until he received that page. It's business first, then sex. I'm catching feelings for him, and I know he feels the same way about me. I sometimes think about Jakim and what we had. I still love him, which is why being with Tyrone is so hard for me.

I know Tyrone is feeling guilty, too. He keeps telling me to tell Jakim about us. "Y'all not together, so tell him what the deal is between us," he's constantly saying. But I refuse, thinking that maybe one day Jakim and I can rekindle our relationship. I know someday we could probably get married and have kids. He just might be the marrying type.

Tyrone is a straight-up street thug, a roughneck brother who did a few years on Riker's Island for a gun charge, drugs and assault. Yet and still, there's something about him that just drives me crazy.

I watch Tyrone walk out the door. He leaves me a hundred dollars and tells me to order something if I get hungry. I go in the bathroom and throw on a robe. I return to the bedroom, flip on the television and relax. I'm kind of upset that he didn't complete his business with me, but I blow it off; I know he's coming back soon to finish fucking me. When he doesn't, I drift off to sleep, horny and frustrated.

I return home the next afternoon to find Jakim parked in front of my crib, awaiting my arrival. It's a good thing I took the bus home.

"Shana, what up?" he hollers through the car window.

"Nothing. What up with you?"

"I'm sayin', though, I came through twice last night looking for you and you weren't even home. You fucking some other niggah?"

"That's none of your fucking business. I'm gonna fuck who I wanna fuck. I ain't your property! I don't see your name anywhere on me!" I yell.

"Why you always gotta catch an attitude with me when I ask you a question?"

"Because you be asking stupid questions."

He just stares at me. I don't want to argue with him today. I start to wonder if he waited out here for me all night. He's either really stupid or he's really in love with me.

"Let me take you out to get something to eat," he says.

"I already ate."

"So, let's go for a ride."

"I'm too tired."

"Damn, so what the fuck do you wanna do?"

"Right now? Get the fuck away from you," I rudely respond. I walk away from him, storm into the house and slam the door behind me. Seeing him right now is not an option for me. I peep out the window. He's still standing there, sulking and looking miserable. I remember back in the day when we were together, if I would have played him like this, he would've cursed me out and tried to slap the shit out of me; it would have been seen as totally disrespecting him. Now he's acting like a straight-up pussy. Damn, is his heart really that broken from our break-up? He's the one who felt we should be separated for a while because he wanted to fuck with other bitches.

My moms comes into the living room. "Jakim came by for you last night," she says.

"I know."

She sees me staring at him through the window. She gives me an unpleasant look and goes back to her business. Then my Aunt Tina comes out in her robe. "Jakim came looking for you last night."

"I know!" I spit.

"Well, damn...you need to give the niggah some pussy. You can't be letting your man starve out there. He'll go eat somewhere else," she warns.

"He's not my man; he's my ex—get it straight!"

"*You* get it straight, bitch! You keep teasing his head like that and he'll bite you and go find comfort somewhere else," she continues.

What the fuck does she know? Aunt Tina can't hold down a man her damn self. And she can't keep her legs closed long enough to be in my business. She got dumped three times this year.

I walk to my room, peel off my clothing and then go and take a long, hot shower. Tyrone calls me before nightfall. He wants to see me.

Damn, I just came from his crib. He apologizes for skipping out on me earlier. He says he had to take care of some business. I tell him that I'll see him tomorrow. I'm tired and not leaving this house any time soon. I need some rest. He's pretty upset. He wants to finish what we started earlier. It's tempting, but I tell him no and that's that.

Sasha gives me a call around ten. She tells me that she just found out about a party tonight, and she wants me to come along so she won't have to roll alone with Cell and his friend. I tell her no. I don't go out with muthafuckas I've never seen or met before. Next thing you know, you're going out with a big, black, nasty, toothless muthafucka who thinks he's all that and wants to stay trying to get up in your drawers. She begs and pleads, and says that his friend is real cute. But if a bitch is that desperate, she'll say anything about the next guy just to have you tagging along.

Cell is the same bouncer who helped us get in the club a few weeks back after Sasha offered him that favor later on. And she did grant it, she tells me. They went out to his truck in the parking lot, and she sucked him off real good. She said for a big dude, his dick didn't match the rest of his body. He was feeling her so much afterwards, that he passed her his home and cell-phone numbers and begged her to call. She gave him her number as well, and she actually did call him.

"Why?" I ask.

"That niggah might have a small dick, but his tongue is wicked!" That's her. I personally like for a man to come with the full package.

After listening to her beg, plead and say that she'll owe me, I give in. She says she'll be at my crib in an hour. She's lucky she's my girl.

I go over to my closet and look for something to wear–a closet full of clothes, and I can't decide what to put on tonight. I throw on my animal print mini skirt, black stockings, a black, low-cut, keyhole-neck top with flare sleeves and my ankle strapped black pumps. As usual, I'm careful to apply just the right make-up and the right amount of perfume; you never know whether or not you'll meet a cutie at the club. I look at myself in the mirror. I'm looking too fine.

About an hour later, I hear a horn blowing outside. It has to be Sasha. I walk to the door, open it and see her standing outside. A white Escalade is parked in front of my house. I see two silhouettes in the truck. "You ready?" she asks.

"I see you came early this time," I say looking at her outfit. She's wearing a very tight, blue, strapless stretch Ottoman dress and blue pumps.

I pull her into the house, and the first thing I say is, "Got-damn, girl. Where did you get that stink, tight, hoochie mama dress? You look like a fucking tramp."

"Yeah, but Cell thinks it's cool. G-i-r-r-l, he got money. He took me out to his crib in Long Island. That muthafucka got a four-bedroom house with a swimming pool in the back."

"You fucked him already, didn't you?"

"Yeah, he got a little piece of it."

"Damn...."

Before I'm able to say anything else, she hits me with, "You can't say shit, Shana. I'm not the one fucking my ex's best friend. You wrong, bitch!"

"I'm wrong? I'm looking out for *you* tonight. Don't forget that," I add. "I don't know why...."

"His friend was asking about you. He wants to meet you and shit."

"What? I don't even know his friend...Sasha you run your mouth too fucking much," I tell her.

"I ain't said shit about you to him; Cell was bragging his mouth off about you. Then he put me on the spot, asking me to hook his friend up with you."

"Is he cute?" I ask with much concern.

"He's cool," she says, sounding not so assuring.

"Ill! I got a fucking pit bull waiting for me outside, right?"

"No! Go chat with him...homeboy pushin' a Lexus," she adds.

I want to turn away from this so-called, double-blind date Sasha's planned. I know he's ugly just from the tone of her voice when she described him to me; she didn't sound so excited about the guy. But I'm a woman of my word, and I promised to come with her.

We walk out together toward the truck. I desperately try to see inside the window, to get a better glance at my doomed blind date. "Promise to be nice to him, Shana," Sasha pleads. But that's a promise I know I can't keep; if he doesn't attract me, why be nice? I believe in getting shit out the way fast, let a brotha know the situation between him and me: *I'm not interested!* Plain and simple.

As we get closer to the truck, Cell steps out from the driver's side and walks up to the both of us. *Ee-ill*...he looks different from the other night. I didn't realize that he was so ugly up close in good light. His face looks fat and swollen, and his lips protrude more than I thought they did—especially the bottom one. He has a weak fade and his gear is totally off balance; he's wearing black slacks, alligator shoes and a tight, bright yellow, muscle shirt. Muscle shirts are not sexy!

His arms are large, but so is his gut. And to think, Sasha actually gave him some head and fucked him. "How you doing?" he asks. His voice is loud and raspy, and he sounds retarded. He stares at me, making me feel uncomfortable.

A few seconds later, his friend steps out from the back seat of the truck. He looks even worse. His eyes are big like a fucking bug's, and he has an unattractive, scruffy goatee. His lips are chapped and his hair is braided in tiny twists, which make his head look deformed and weird. He has a shiny, gold tooth in the right corner of his mouth and a thick, gold rope chain hangs from around his neck. They're so played out. He also has the nerve to be wearing a bright orange shirt with the collar flipped up, like he's Elvis, and a pair of cream-colored khaki pants. I want to throw up!

He introduces himself as Jimmy, and he extends his hand. I stand there and just look at him. I'm not shaking his hand. I don't want to touch him. I look over at Sasha. She knows the deal. I want to strangle her for hooking me up with some horrendous looking shit like him. I don't want to be seen anywhere in public with him.

"What the fuck is that?" I whisper in her ear after pulling her to the side.

"Jimmy..."

"I'm not going out. Shit, I don't even wanna be seen with him. That niggah is so ugly I'm about to throw up," I warn.

"C'mon, Shana, just chill. You ain't gotta fuck him; just keep him company. He's a nice guy."

Now, she knows better. As much as we be hanging out together and dissing ugly muthafuckas like him...is her mind warped? Cell and his friend look like something out of Swamp Thing.

She pleads and begs, but I refuse to give in. Fuck a promise. He makes me shiver every time I turn around and look at him...he's just so ugly.

Cell and Jimmy stand next to the truck, talking and waiting. Sasha goes as far as offering me fifty dollars. Then she offers me a hundred. I agree to the hundred, and she slips it to me on the low. I take a deep breath, exhale and walk back over to the truck.

"Y'all ready?" Cell asks.

"Yeah, we're cool," Sasha says.

Jimmy—Mr. Too Ugly—tries to be a gentleman and opens the passenger door for me. I give him a nasty look and let myself in through the other door. Cell looks back at me and then over at Sasha. Jimmy enters the truck last and manages to smile at me. I sit as close to the door as I can.

Cell suggests that we go out to this nightclub in Brooklyn called The Jackpot. It's becoming one of the more popular night spots. He has friends there that will let us all in for free—no long lines, no waiting. I out right refuse to go; the Jackpot is a well-known spot. Everybody goes there, and I do mean everybody. Unfortunately, my refusal is overruled by a three-to-one vote.

Mr. Too Ugly is trying to make conversation. He keeps glancing over at me and smiling. "You go to school?" he asks. His voice and speech are so ugly. I ignore him and just stare out the window. Sasha looks back at me, and I give her a counterfeit smile, while thinking, y*eah bitch, you're gonna get yours.* "You got a man?" Mr. Too Ugly is still smiling and trying to be friendly. I go on ignoring him, asking Cell to turn up the radio a little. As I continue staring out the window, I can feel his eyes trying to undress me. It gives me goose bumps, just thinking about him seeing me naked. "You're so beautiful."

I don't respond. He tries to put his hand on my knee. I turn and glare at him like he's crazy, and I quickly smack it away. "Don't touch me," I say in a harsh tone.

Sasha and Cell are chillin' up front, while I'm in the back seat trying to tame a wild animal.

"You don't speak?" he asks.

"Only if interested," I spit back.

I've already said six words too many to him. *Why me?* Mr. Too Ugly starts making conversation with his boy up front. I guess he's beginning to get the picture. I cross my legs and try to isolate myself from everyone in the truck as much as I can. *As soon as we get to the club, I'm ditching Sasha, Cell and The Creature From the Black Lagoon.*

We pull up in front of the club. There are so many people outside it looks like the Grammys. I'm so embarrassed. I can't be seen with him—not in *this* fucking lifetime. Cell parks the car and everyone gets out except me.

"C'mon, Shana," Sasha says.

Cell and Jimmy look at me, and I catch a serious attitude.

"What's up with your girl?" Cell asks Sasha.

"Shana, what's the matter? You coming or what?"

"What the fuck do you mean, *what's the matter?* You know what the deal is, bitch," I protest.

Sasha's face tightens and her eyes become slits. Cell and Jimmy look at each other and then glance back at me. "I think y'all two ladies need to sort this out in private. Jimmy and I will be standing at the corner," Cell says. They walk slowly toward the corner, and Sasha's focus is now totally on me.

"Get the fuck out the car, bitch!" she snaps.

"I know you not about to trip!" I bark.

"No, I'm not gonna trip, but why the fuck you gotta be embarrassing me like this? All I'm asking is for you to just keep him company. You act like I want you to give him the world, bitch. You can keep your stingy pussy to yourself."

I don't say anything back to Sasha; I just stare at her and slowly step out of the truck. She looks at me and walks away. I follow her. Cell and Jimmy are at the corner waiting for us. When we get to the corner, Sasha walks off with Cell and Jimmy remains standing there. He's still smiling, and it's getting on my damn nerves. I want to smack that fucking disgusting grin off his face. I guess he's expecting to walk side-by-side with me into the club. But I just hurry by him and catch up with Cell and Sasha. We get in with no problem. I turn slightly around, and there's Mr. Too Ugly, already breathing down the back of my neck. I move away.

The Jackpot is jam-packed. And of course, the deejay just so happens to be playing *It's A Groove Thang* by Zhane. This was my jam back in the day. I start dancing and grooving, and then I feel this figure pushing up behind me, grinding against me. I turn around, and I see Mr. Too Ugly again. I quickly stop dancing and walk away; he done fucked up my flow now. He follows me and asks, "Can I buy you a drink?"

"No!" I shout. I continue to try my best to get the fuck away from him. I can't be seen with him up in here; there are too many cuties around. He tries to follow me, but I evade him by sneaking into the women's bathroom. I'm getting frustrated. I can't get my party on with this ugly muthafucka following me around all night. And shit, no matter how nasty and rude I am to him, he still doesn't get the picture. Maybe he really is slow or retarded.

I lay low in the bathroom for about five minutes before heading back out to the party. I'm just not feeling it anymore. I know that once that ugly muthafucka sees me, he's going to start hounding me again. And if he does, I've decided that I'm gonna curse him out so dirty and nasty and embarrass him in front of everyone in the club. I bet he'll finally get the hint then. He doesn't know who he's fucking with...but the club is so crowded I might not run into him again.

I go to the bar and order myself a drink. Maybe I should've let him buy me one; at least he would have been good for something. But it wouldn't have been worth it; he would have probably thought that I was starting to like him.

The deejay is definitely doing his thing—one nice jam after another. Right now he's playing *Cream* by Wu Tang Clan. Them my niggahs right there. The cutest and illest one—to me—is my niggah, Method Man.

I feel somebody's hand grab my arm from behind. I think it's Mr. Too Ugly, so I turn around and prepare to smack him, but I see a light-skinned cutie with baby brown eyes and braids instead.

"How you doing, love?" he asks.

"Fine." He's more flamboyant than rough, but he's still cute. We make our way to the dance floor, where he pulls me in front of him and starts grinding up on me. I can feel his dick getting hard in his slacks. It's poking me repeatedly in the butt, and it's starting to get annoying. I continue to dance with him, but when he squats down and tries to feel my crotch through my skirt, I proceed to put him in check. I grab his nuts tightly and make a fist, squeezing the living shit out of them.

"Niggah, don't you ever disrespect my wonderful body like that ever again! You don't fucking know me to be trying to feel me up. I should rip your fucking balls off right now!"

A few people are laughing and pointing, and others just watch.

Homeboy's eyes start to tear up as I continue to squeeze his nuts. I finally let them go and he falls to his knees, clutching his hands between his legs. Every male in the club gets the message: I'm nothing to play with.

I return to the bar and order a Long Island Ice Tea. A few men gape at me as I sip my drink. I know they want to approach me, but after that little incident on the dance floor, they're probably feeling hesitant. It's cool. I'm not in the mood for any more negative male attention anyway; after dealing with Mr. Too Ugly and Mr. Touchy Feely, my need for male company has disappeared.

I continue to drink and chill at the bar. I see Sasha with Cell on the dance floor. She's feeling all over him. There's no shame in her game. The bartender's smiling at me as he serves me my fourth free drink. Still, I'm not interested; he's too beefy for me. I like a brotha who's slim and cut up with a nice, long dick, smooth skin, good hair and a nice butt. He also has to have a good job—or at least some kind of income and a little integrity to go with it. The man has got to respect himself, and he definitely has to respect me. He must know that I'm not a sex toy, somewhere to stick his dick. If a good man treats me with respect and dignity, then I'll treat him like he's my world. I'll do anything in my power to satisfy him and take care of him, as long as he is willing to do the same for me. My pussy would always be open and willing to receive him.

I look at the time. It's a quarter to eleven and I'm getting restless and bored, even though I'm still receiving free drinks. The club is getting overcrowded, and the cuties are becoming less interesting to me. I don't want to be touched or approached by anyone. I'm feeling a little tipsy, and I'm not in the mood for stupidity. The deejay throws on *Doo Doo Brown* by Luke, a former 2 Live Crew member, and the whole club goes crazy.

Everyone starts rubbing and grinding on each other. There's sweating and bumping, and girls are hiking up their skirts. I can't front; every time I hear this jam, I want to get my grind on and feel up on a niggah, too—especially a really cute one.

Some niggah abruptly grabs me by the arm, indicating for me to follow him into the crowd. I tell him no; you just don't be pulling on me like I'm some fuckin' rope. I give him a nasty glare. He gets the hint. Now I'm feeling another niggah close up behind me, pushing his pelvis into me. Damn, his dick is already hard. I turn around. It's Mr. Too Ugly! *Oh, my god! No, he didn't*. I'm so angry that I shove his ugly ass, pushing him into another girl, who falls into some guy. Mr. Too Ugly looks embarrassed, but I really don't give a fuck at all how he feels at this point. You just don't be pushing your nasty self up against me like that. He's brazen; I give him that.

Bitches start to stare. I stare back. I'll scratch out every last one of these bitch's eyes up in this club. I make my way back to the ladies bathroom. Sasha comes in behind me, pulling down her stink hoochie dress.

"What's the matter, Shana?" she asks me, like she doesn't already know.

"Nothing!" I tell her while fixing my hair. I have no words for her for the rest of the night.

Other bitches start coming into the bathroom, whispering amongst each other and staring hard at me. I know they're saying dirty things. "If y'all bitches got anything nasty to say about me, come say it to my fucking face! I'll bring it to any one of y'all fake bitches up in here!" I shout.

They all just look, but none of them has the courage to say anything. I throw up my middle finger and go on with my business. Sasha scowls at me and gives me attitude. She walks out to go back and tend to her dilly ass man. If she wants to act up, she can get it, too.

After checking myself in the mirror, I leave the bathroom. My temper and attitude is on high volume. I look hard at every niggah and bitch who pass my way. It's definitely time for me to leave, but Cell is my only ride. And I'm not trying to hitchhike with some perverted, no-pussy- gettin' niggah, who thinks just because I'm riding in his car he has the right to put his hands all over me.

I approach Sasha at around two a.m. She's dancing and hugging up on Cell, and I pull her to the side, away from him. "I'm ready to go," I tell her.

"Don't be pulling on me," she spits. We've both gotten on each other's nerves tonight. I can see in her face that she wants to fuck me up for having been such a bitch. But she knows better. "I'll see if Cell's ready, bitch!" she says harshly. *Fuck her, too.*

Mr. Too Ugly appears. He's so embarrassed that he can't even look at me. I laugh and walk away from him. I go back to the bar, and the bartender slips me another free drink, but this time he also gives me his number written on a napkin. I give him a little smile, and then I crumble it up and drop it to the floor when he turns away.

We finally prepare to leave the club at two-thirty. On the way out, Cell stops and gives everyone he knows dap and chats for a few seconds here and there. He must think he's the fucking man because he was able to get us in here for free. I have to laugh. We all pile in his truck and leave. Mr. Too Ugly finally got the hint; he doesn't say a word to me. He doesn't even look at me. Unable to take it anymore, I look over at him and ask, "Why are you so ugly?" He still doesn't give me eye contact. Sasha knows she wants to laugh, but she never looks back at me.

"Yo, why you trying to play my man out like that?" Cell asks defending his friend.

"Ain't nobody trying to play your man out. He played himself out thinking he could get with me," I reply. It's on now. I'm about to rank on the both of them. They ruined my night, so now I'm about to ruin theirs. "Look at your man. He would never see my pussy, no matter how hard he tried," I say laughing.

"You think you're all that! You ain't nothing but a stuck-up, stink-ass bitch!" Cell says.

"Niggah, don't get jealous because you're not sniffing it, too. I don't even know why Sasha is with your ugly ass."

"Shana, chill," Sasha pleads.

"Bitch, *you* need to chill—or wake up! I've seen you date much better looking guys than him. That niggah look like a fucking spider monkey! He tryin' to be sexy in that tight, banana-looking muscle shirt. How you gonna wear a muscle shirt with a gut big as yours?" I say to Cell.

"Fuck you, bitch!" he shouts.

"Yeah, you wish...don't get mad when you know I speak the truth."

Cell quickly makes a short stop at the light; he almost ran it arguing with me. I jerk forward. So does everyone else in the truck. Mr. Too Ugly just sits there in silence. Shit, not only is he ugly, but he lets me dis him in front of his man. If you're gonna be ugly, at least have heart, be a man and stand up for yourself. I knew he was pussy.

"Yo, Sasha, I'm about to throw that fake bitch out of my car," Cell warns.

"*Fake bitch*! Niggah, you need not talk, with your tight little dick," I say, throwing up my small pinky and wiggling it high for him to see.

"What?" he says stunned.

"All that gut and a penis lost somewhere under it," I add to the insult.

"Fuck y'all bitches!" he says looking directly at Sasha.

I look over at Mr. Too Ugly and see him crying and staring out the window. *This niggah is pitiful.*

"Take me home, you fat, small-dick, no-pussy-gettin', stink-ass nig-gah!" I say to him. Sasha tries to put her two cents in, but Cell curses her out. That leads to an argument. Jimmy remains quiet in the corner.

The ride home is full of insults. Sasha and I are arguing with each other, too, now. The shit gets so crazy, and this punk niggah kicks me out of his truck and tells my ass to walk home. Sasha doesn't even stand up for a sista; she continues to sit there in the front seat and lets the niggah put me out of his truck. But I don't stress it. Fuck that bitch!

Two days later, Sasha and I have it out in front of my crib. She comes banging on my door in the early afternoon talking nonsense. She has the nerve to say I disrespected her. *I disrespected her?* I'm pissed. She's the one who disrespected me. And she knows my standards. She knows the type of guys I prefer and fuck, so how the fuck *she* gonna get mad after hooking me up with some wildebeest? Every day we make fun of niggahs like Jimmy, trashing 'em and dissin' 'em...and she had the nerve to bring one to my front door, talkin' 'bout he's cool. Then she says I embarrassed her in front of Cell. Bitch! Who is Cell supposed to be first of all? He's nobody—just some fool whose dick she sucked to get into a club.

Next thing I know, she's up on me screaming and yelling, arms flailing like she wants to take a swing at me. Then I get up in her face, and that sets the beef off right there. I punch the bitch in her face and grip her firmly by her hair as we wrestle each other to the ground. I continue punching her in the face, and then we scratch and tear at each other. It seems like the whole neighborhood has come out, crowding around us to watch. "Yo, ain't they best friends?" I hear someone in the crowd ask.

I'm wearing a pair of Sean John jeans and a blue Gap T-shirt. My Nikes are laced up tight, and my hair is swept up in a ponytail; so it's hard for her to get at it. But her hair is loose, hanging down past her shoulders. I yank it, snapping the bitch's neck back. Her nose starts to bleed, and I pin her to the ground and hit her some more.

"Stupid bitch!" I scream out. Sasha's smaller, and I'm stronger, wilder and faster than she is. Nobody attempts to break up the fight until blood is drawn; somebody comes up and grabs me from behind, pulling me off of Sasha. A few niggahs cop a feel on me as we're broken apart, but I think nothing of it. Now a few people are holding each of us as we threaten and curse at one other.

"You gonna get yours, bitch!" Sasha repeatedly shouts.

"Fuck you!" I reply.

"Get the fuck off me!" she yells. "I'm gonna kill that stupid bitch!" People continue to hold us back, keeping us from tearing into one another. I struggle fiercely, trying to free myself.

"Take her home!" I hear a woman shout. I see a man carrying her off my lawn and into the streets. He drags her down my block as she continues to curse and holler at me. Her car is still parked in front of my house. I hope she leaves it there; I guarantee that her shit will be demolished by tomorrow morning. But, oh well...someone got a hold of her keys and they drive her car down the block to where she's being dragged away to.

"Stupid bitch!" I scream out one last time before going into my house mad and heated, slamming my door shut.

I look in the mirror and notice that the bitch scratched me over my right eye. Then I look out my window and see a crowd still standing out front, excited over what just happened. Some are even playing out how it all went down. I close my blinds and go to my room. *Damn, she was my homegirl, one of my best fr*iends. Now we're against each other over some silliness.

Nighttime comes, and I cry myself to sleep.

4 SHANA

It's been a week since my fight with Sasha. The day after it happened, everyone around the way knew about it. Word spreads around quickly in the hood.

Jakim came by the very next day after it went down. He asked if I was all right, like I was the one who got fucked up. I didn't flip on him for once, and it was kinda cool to see him. Ten minutes after Jakim stopped by, Tyrone drove up. My heart skipped a beat when I saw his black BMW pull up with Jakim sitting outside on my front porch. I know they're boys, but how would Jakim have reacted if he knew his man was coming to check me? I just sat there next to him as Tyrone came walking up. This is how it all went down:

"What up, Ty?" Jakim said. He got up and gave his man dap and a hoodly hug. I smiled and stared up at Tyrone. I played it cool. I knew he would.

Tyrone and Jakim began to talk. Then Tyrone asked me what hap-

pened with me and Shana. I explained. He laughed. "Yo, Shana, you be trippin'," he said. I just sat there staring at the two of 'em; they both were looking good. Jakim, he's my sweetheart, but Tyrone is my freak thing. He can
put a hurting on some pussy, I thought to myself. I couldn't help but clock
him even more.

Tyrone had a bag of weed on him and we went through that in no
time. We sat around just smoking and talking for the next hour or so. My
uncomfortable feeling was relieved when I started getting high; I forgot
about my worries and chilled out. Jakim tried to push up on me with Tyrone
still present. "You know I still love you," he said.

Tyrone gave me a look. It was sort of unpleasant, but he didn't say
anything since he already knew the situation between Jakim and I. He
appeared to relax a little and continued to smoke. It started getting late
and Tyrone decided to leave, but I knew he wanted to say a quick little
something to me before he left; I could tell by the look in his eyes. But I did-
n't want to have a private conversation with Jakim still around. He's not
stupid, I thought to myself.

"Yo, Ty, jet me to my crib real quick so I can pick up my whip,"
Jakim said. His man dropped him off earlier. His Maxima was parked at his
father's house.

"C'mon, niggah, I should charge you for gas," Tyrone joked. They
both walked toward his car. I followed behind them. As Jakim went around
to the passenger side, Tyrone gave me a look. He quickly whispered in my
ear while Jakim was getting in the car. "I'll be back around tonight. Be
here." He was smooth with his.

Tyrone then got in his car and drove off. I stood outside for a
moment, collecting my thoughts, until the cool October wind picked up

heavily, causing me to run back into the house.

My mother came home later that evening with Danny. They had just come from Kentucky Fried Chicken. She was staying over at his house when I had that fight with Sasha. I swiped a leg, two thighs and a couple of biscuits, and ran my ass to my room. Naja gave me a call. She wanted to know the deal between me and Sasha. Latish called, too, wanting to know the same.

Tyrone, just as he promised, came back around eleven that night. I brought him into my room where we talked for an hour, then fucked our brains out. He wanted to know if it was really over between Jakim and me. I told him yes, but that he still had feelings for me.

And that's how that went down. Tyrone's feelings for me have grown even more now. But he knows what it is between us—just sex. We even had a quick talk about it. We agreed that if our feelings got involved, it would fuck up everything. Tyrone continues to see other people. I do the same, but when we're together, we both get what we want.

There's a rumor spreading around the neighborhood that Sasha and a few of her girls are planning to retaliate and jump on me. But that's a rumor I heard a week ago, and there still hasn't been any action. And I haven't seen her since our little incident, so I'm not sweating it. I'm just going on with my life.

My girls, Naja and Latish, are planning on going out to Manhattan to check out Club New York. I decide to roll out there with them and get my party on, too. My plans change when Jakim pulls up. He insists that I go out with him tonight. He says he wants to talk to me about something serious. I tell him yeah; I'm really in no mood to travel out to Manhattan anyway.

I remember how sweet he can be when he opens the passenger

door of his car for me and carefully lets me in, shutting the door behind me. I inform him that this isn't a date; we're just hanging out together. It doesn't mean that we're getting back together. He agrees.

We stop at a Burger King and then he drives out to Coney Island in Brooklyn, where everything is closed down for the winter. He parks the car, and we get out to walk across the boardwalk.

We discuss old times, and I gaze out at the ocean, arms folded across my chest. I try to keep warm as Jakim makes conversation with me. "I'm surprised you're not cursing me out," he says.

"No reason to right now."

"You always had a wicked tongue."

"That's because I keeps it real. You should've known better—my man or not. You played yourself when you hurt my feelings, Jakim."

"But I didn't play *you* out."

"Two years together and you want to fuck that stink ho down the block from me."

"Well, I was wrong about that, Shana. You know how we men get; sometimes we think more with our dicks than with our hearts. I know I fucked up with you."

"Yes, you did."

He stops walking. "But me and you, we're cool, right?" he asks.

"Yeah, we're still cool," I say smiling.

"That's all I need to hear," he replies.

We continue to walk further down the boardwalk. He does most of the talking while I mainly just listen. I gaze out at the ocean again and see the moonlight gleaming over it. I start to reminisce on the days when he and I would do this frequently. Jakim was always so romantic and smooth.

He knew all the hot spots to take a girl to. He knew the right words to say. If we got into an argument, then the very next day he would show up at my door with flowers and candy like it was Valentine's Day. I would forgive him and we would have make-up sex. If he was running the streets with Tyrone and the rest of his boys, he would always take time out to give me a call. And the thing I liked the most about him was that he never showed off in front of his boys while I was with him; he would always show me affection right in front of them.

They would watch us and hate. They would say he was pussy whipped. But he didn't care. He even told me "I love you" in front of his friends a few times. Sometimes I wonder whether it was even necessary to break up, but like he said himself, men think with their dicks more than with their hearts. I still think that's just an excuse.

Jakim takes my hand into his and holds it gently. I don't resist. It feels like we're a couple again. I quickly get rid of the feeling and get back to reality. He cheated on me. He hurt me, and now we're separated. I still need time away from him.

We stay out on the boardwalk for another fifteen minutes before going back to his car. I know Jakim wants this night to turn out to be something more. It's obvious to me that he wants to be out here as lovers instead of just friends.

"You ever think about us?" he asks after we get back in his car.

"Yeah, sometimes."

"I miss you, Shana." I remain quiet and look out the passenger window as we head east on the Belt Parkway

Jakim continues. "Do you ever see us getting back together?" Still, I have no words. I have mixed feelings about the situation. I still love him, but us getting back together again is not an option. I'm still having my fun being young and living my life. I finally speak and explain this to him. He listens and nods his head.

It's a quarter past ten when he finally drops me off at my front door. "Shana, just think about us. I love you," he says as I get out of the car. I look at him for a few seconds and then head toward my crib. He watches me enter the house. I know I'm his one and only true love. Many females have tried to take my place, but they couldn't conquer what he still feels for me. They wanted him so badly, but it wasn't happening with me still around. Even though we're separated, we're still in love with each other. He openly shows his love for me, while I keep my feelings more discreet.

I walk into the living room, flick on the lights and see my mother getting her pussy eaten out by Danny on the living room couch. If any other normal teenage girl had walked in on her mother while she was getting her shit eaten, it would probably freak her out. But as I stated before, I'm used to it. And as usual, my mother doesn't get up and cover herself and Danny doesn't miss a beat.

I can't move. I just stand there watching Danny with his shirt off, going down on my mother. It turns me on. I look at his body. His back is covered with tattoos, and there are jailhouse scars on various other parts of his body. I notice gunshot and stab wounds on both sides of his torso. I remain frozen in the same spot. *Why not me?* I think to myself. He is so fucking fine—too fine for my mother.

"Shana, you gonna stand there and watch us all night?" my mother asks, interrupting my private fantasy of her man.

"No!" I quickly say.

I leave and let them be. I can hear my mother's passionate moans throughout the hallway all the way to my bedroom. I have to shut the door; it's becoming too much for me to bear.

Danny, he could definitely hit this.... I lie down on my bed in a spread eagle position on my back and finger my pussy. I'm horny. I need some dick.

Early the next morning, I go shopping with my Aunt Tina. We hit Jamaica Avenue and Green Acres Mall. I tell her about seeing Danny and my mom getting busy on the couch last night. She laughs. Aunt Tina fantasizes about Danny, too. I mean, what female who knows him doesn't?—with his fine, brown-skinned ass. We laugh and hit up all the stores. It's fun shopping with my Aunt. She has very good taste in clothing. Too bad I can't say the same thing about her choice in men.

As we continue shopping, almost every guy we pass tries to hit on us with the typical male call: "Yo, shorty, let me holla at you," or "I'm sayin', boo, y'all are looking too good. What's y'all name?" I take a few numbers, because I'm not giving out mine.

We get a free cab ride because we flirt with the driver. We always give drivers phony numbers and gas their heads up. Aunt Tina rides up front with some cab drivers, taking it to the next level by giving them a hand massage while they're driving. I always just sit in the back and laugh. She is such a slut.

My day is going great until I run into Sasha. She's with three other girls in a store on Jamaica Avenue. I try not to pay her any attention. My aunt takes notice. She knows what went down between me and Sasha, and she asks me if I want her to help me beat that bitch down. I know she's not kidding. Sasha and the three girls glare at us. I act like I'm browsing through some skirts, paying them no mind at all. Aunt Tina glares back, cursing them under her breath. If anything goes down in this store, I know she has my back. My aunt can throw down better than me.

One of the girls comes toward us. She pretends to be browsing through some stuff as she gets closer to my aunt. I know they're trying to start something with us, so I take off my earrings and discreetly stuff them down into my purse. Sasha keeps her distance while carefully eyeing me. All of a sudden, one of her girls bumps into my aunt. "Watch where the fuck you're going, bitch!" she yells out. That was all she needed to say. My aunt lashes out at her something serious. She pulls her by the hair and knocks her down to the floor. It was so quick and intense that no one saw it coming—not even the girl she's beating down. Sasha and the other two try to come to their friend's aid. That's when I step in and punch one bitch in her jaw. It's fuckin' on! My aunt's holding two of 'em down, while the other two, including Sasha, try to jump on me. I knock Sasha across her head with my purse and then scratch one side of her face somethin' serious. Her friend—some chubby bitch—tries to bum rush me to the ground. She knocks me into a pile of neatly folded clothes. The bitch has the advantage for a quick second, holding me down and hitting me across my face. But that changes when I knock her across the head with a belt buckle. She screams, and I throw her down hard on her fat ass. Then that bitch, Sasha, comes swinging at me. She catches me with a few good hits, sending me stumbling over a rack of clothes. But I yank her by her shirt and toss her hard against the wall, delivering some serious blows to her head. My aunt is more than handling the other two; she's fuckin' them bitches up.

The employees in the store don't know what to do. Some of them just stand out of the way and watch, and others run to get security or the police. A number of customers begin to run out of the store, while a few of them get knocked over. No one attempts to break it up; there is too much confusion.

By now a huge crowd has gathered outside the store, curious to see what all the commotion is about. The fight moves to the street, and I'm battling that same fat bitch that tried to bum rush me earlier. I rip open her shirt, and one of her titties pops out. She doesn't care; enraged, she comes at me in full force and knocks me down to the ground. "Ooooh, that had to hurt!" I hear someone from the crowd yell out.

I'm in pain. She's fat but strong. She grabs a handful of my hair and tries to pull it out. I grab her by her wrist and struggle to get her off of me. Suddenly, I look up and see Sasha standing over me. She has a small razor in her hand...I want to cry; I'm losing, and I can't get up. *Please, God, no! Don't let her cut me,* I pray.

My prayers are answered when about four police officers come and restrain Sasha, throwing her to the ground. Then they pull the fat bitch off of me and restrain her ass, too. Within minutes, eight more officers are on the scene to gain control of the situation. They put Sasha and her crew in handcuffs and start questioning me. My aunt is okay, although she's bleeding from a scratch by her right ear.

The cops are questioning the store manager now, asking what happened and who started it. She points to one of Sasha's friends and explains that she bumped into my aunt and cursed at her. Other witnesses start saying the same thing. I feel relieved. I guess everybody feels it's not fair for four girls to jump on two. When Sasha pulled out that razor, she made it even worse for them.

Sasha and her friends are hauled off to jail, and my aunt and I are asked if we'd like to press charges. The store manager wants to. She says that they ruined her store with their nonsense. My aunt and I refuse to press charges; where we come from, we settle our disputes in the streets.

My hair looks horrendous. My lip is bleeding and my eye is swollen. I am so mad. Whatever friendship Sasha and I had left was dissolved when she pulled out that razor. She's declared war, and there's no way I'm gonna let this shit slide.

Some of my shopping bags got lost—probably stolen—and my new shirt is ruined. Aunt Tina lost her shit, too. She's more upset than I am.

We call ourselves a cab and take our asses home. When my mother hears what's happened, she's ready to go and knock down Sasha's front door and fuck that bitch up. I convince her not to. I stay in the house for the rest of the day. In fact, I stay indoors for the next three days, until my bruises start to heal. Of course Jakim stops by after hearing what happened. He spends a few hours with me, and we talk and laugh. He rags Sasha out and tells me that he never liked the bitch anyway. Tyrone is a no-show. I'm surprised. *Maybe he didn't hear what happened.* I don't stress it.

5 JAKIM

Tyrone lets out a boisterous laugh when I tell him about Shana and Sasha's fight up on Jamaica Avenue. "Yo, why dey fuckin' each other up like dat?" he asks while navigating his BMW through the Queens streets. "Dey used to be girls—best friends and shit."

"Man, listen...you know how grimy Sasha can be," I say. "I *know* it's dat bitches fault. Yo, she tried to cut Shana's face and shit."

"Damn, now dat's fucked up. Yo, I would kill dat bitch if she came at me like that," Tyrone says.

"Word, yo."

"See, dat's why bitches can't stay friends for too long, like niggahs; dey be hatin' on each other too much. As soon as a bitch is out of ear shot, the rest of 'em in the crew start talkin' 'bout her...frontin' ass hoes and shit." Tyrone reaches forward and presses for track five on a Jay-Z CD. *In My Lifetime* blasts from the car speakers as we cruise down Hillside Ave.

I bob my head to the track and think about Shana. That night we spent together at Coney Island plays over and over in my head. It's nights like those that make me miss her even more. I love the way we held hands and strolled under the stars with the calm wind playfully nipping at us.... I peer out the window, gazing at the stores that line Hillside Avenue. Jay-Z's rap continues to blast throughout the car.

"Jay-Z, this my niggah right here!" Tyrone shouts. He starts rapping along with Jay.   I chuckle. When the song ends, Tyrone looks over at me, lowering the volume of the CD player and asks, "What's wrong, playa? You look like you got somethin' heavy on your mind."

"Nah, just chillin'," I reply.

"You sure?"

"Yeah."

"You ain't got no beef wit' no niggah? 'Cause if you do, you know you my niggah, and I'm gonna handle dat for you," he says with confidence.

"Nah, I ain't got no beef," I say smiling.

He focuses his attention back on the road and turns up the CD player again. We fall silent as we continue down Hillside Avenue.

As we head toward the Van Wyck Expressway, Tyrone looks over at me again, and to my surprise he asks, "Yo, Ja, what's up wit' you and Shana?"

"Why you ask dat?" I say.

"Just curious. You lookin' stressed right now, playa," he says. "I know if it ain't beef, then you got a bitch on your mind. Shana's one fine ass honey, and I know you missin' her."

At first I want to confess my true feelings about Shana to Tyrone. I want to tell him that I still have it bad for my ex-girlfriend. It seems like my feelings for her are seeping through my pores, and everybody can see them anyway.

I decide not to talk about it. "Nah, I got dis other bitch I'm fuckin' on my mind right now," I say.

"Oh, word? What she about?"

"Bitch is a freak, son," I tell him, glad about the change in topic.

"My niggah," he says giving me dap. "But yo, I saw Shana up in the club the other night with her homegirls."

"I know. Evay told me already."

"Yo, don't stress her, Ja. You ain't missin' nothin."

"I heard you danced wit' her, too," I blurt out, not really meaning anything by it.

"Yeah, we danced. But you know it was strictly innocent. We cool peoples. You know I ain't gonna disrespect you by fuckin' your ex-girl, Ja. You know I don't get down like dat. Dat ain't even my style."

"Yeah, I know."

Tyrone hits the ramp leading to the Van Wyck. His cell phone goes off as he merges with the traffic. He looks down at the caller ID and smiles.

"Yo, I got dis bitch sweatin' me," he boasts.

"Word, who dat?" I inquire.

"Dis bitch I met in da club a few weeks back. I took her to da crib and dug her fuckin' back out."

I laugh. "Do you, niggah. Dat's all I got to say—do you."

"I'm gonna call her back later, though," Tyrone continues. "But yo, Jakim, what I'm trying to tell you, you're a handsome dude, niggah. You know what I'm sayin? Niggahs like us, we don't come a dime a dozen. You need to do the three fuckin' F's: find 'em, fuck 'em and forget about 'em. Hoes come and go, niggah, and I ain't callin' Shana no ho, but you start forgettin' about a bitch and I guarantee you, she gonna start sweatin' you like you da last dick on earth."

As we travel down the Van Wyck toward the Belt Parkway, Tyrone's phone rings again. He looks down at the number. "What I tell you, niggah? I ain't stressin' to call dis bitch back, and she hounding a niggah—blowin' up a niggah's phone and shit. Yo, a bitch is always gonna call you if you fuckin' her good. And a bitch ain't gonna never forget about a niggah wit' a big dick who's blowing her back out." I laugh.

We continue on the Belt Parkway into Brooklyn. We're in Bed-Stuy fifteen minutes later. Tyrone pulls his BMW to the curb in front of a well-maintained, three story brownstone on Decatur Street, a block from Marcus Garvey Avenue. He picks up his cell phone and makes a call as I scope the neighborhood from the passenger seat. "Come wit' me inside," he says shutting his phone.

I follow him up the steps toward the brownstone. As soon as we reach the top of the steps, a young woman who looks to be in her early twenties opens the door. She moves to the side, allowing us entry into the building. We enter, and she closes the door and proceeds down the hall. As we walk behind her, I can't help but notice how beautiful she is. Her hair is cut short, and she's wearing large, silver hoop earrings. She's brown-skinned, and she has more curves than the letter *S*. She's also wearing a large white T-shirt and tight blue shorts that accentuate her hips and butt. She sashays down the hall, walking barefooted on the parquet floors.

We enter another room that is well furnished, and I notice two more young ladies seated on the couch. One is smoking a cigarette, and the other—a white girl—is reading a magazine in her panties and a scanty, tight shirt. They're both beautiful. The young woman puffing on the cancer stick has flawless brown skin. She's wearing thin, wire-rimmed glasses, and her beautiful, golden-brown, wavy locks fall down to her shoulders. The white girl has brownish blonde hair, baby blue eyes and a pure and innocent, all-American, small-town-girl- from-the-dirty-south look about her.

All of a sudden, I notice twelve kilos of pure cocaine on the glass coffee table. I'm surprised.

"Jakim, this is Mandy," says Tyrone pointing to the girl with the short hair. "This is Sweet," he continues, pointing to the woman with the beautiful locks. "And this is Milk," he says pointing to the wholesome-looking white girl, who smiles up at me and continues to read her magazine.

I smile at all three women and give them a quick head nod. Mandy takes a seat next to Sweet, while Tyrone appears to be more preoccupied with the coke on the table. He picks up two kilos and looks at Mandy, Milk and Sweet. "Y'all bitches ready?" he asks. They all nod.

Sweet takes one last drag from her cancer stick, passes it to Mandy and then gets up and walks over to Tyrone. The ass on Sweet is like *whoa*! I mean, the bitch is wearing sweatpants, and it still protrudes.

Sweet gives Tyrone a quick kiss on the lips and then disappears into a back room. Mandy remains seated on the couch, pulling on the cancer stick as I stand in the middle of the room, clueless to what's going on. I know Tyrone's heavy in the drug game; shit, the niggah was moving ten kilos a week when we were all in high school, sweating the females and trying to look fly. At one time he had me working for him, pushing crack and peddling that shit off to the crackheads. Sometimes he would make me the money man, counting the intake from his lucrative drug business. He was making up to twenty thousand a day at the age of eighteen. After a while I fell off from working with Tyrone and moved on; I didn't have the heart for that type of business like he did; he was born to be a hustler. Me—I was too scared of prison, and I was so in love with Shana that I wouldn't be able to stand being away from her for so long. Tyrone, being my boy, understood my situation and let me be without any beef.

After about ten minutes, Sweet comes out the back room, carrying two unique-looking suits. They're made of soft material—probably cotton—and they have two long straps that clamp around the body.

"Ja, check it out," Tyrone says taking one of the suits from Sweet and tossing it at me. I quickly catch it and take a closer look. The material is soft, as I thought, and it's light in my arms. It looks like a fat suit, the kind they use in Hollywood when a slim actor or actress is playing a fat role, like Eddie Murphy did in *The Nutty Professor*. In this case the suit is white, and I notice that it can make a woman appear to look very pregnant.

I look up and see Tyrone grinning. It finally hits me: the three women in the room are drug mules for him, and he uses them and the suits to move his kilos Upstate and down south undetected. *Damn, that's some clever shit*, I think to myself.

"Yeah, yo, shit is gettin' hot out there, Jakim. Fuckin' cops been on a niggah's ass like a fuckin' magnet over the past two months. They arresting niggahs in my crew like crazy. Cops be knowing about all of my drug runs and where my hidden stash be at. I got a snitch in my crew, Ja, and I'm gonna find out who it is and take care of it. But you see this? Niggahs don't know about this yet," he says referring to the pregnant suits. "This some new shit I've been doing for the past month and a half."

He tells me more about the suits. Each suit is able to hold and conceal four kilos in the stomach area, which is padded with cotton and a special lining to hold each kilo in place as the ladies make moves.

"Yo, y'all bitches start getting ready; it's about dat time," Tyrone says looking at the clock on the wall.

He doesn't have to tell them twice. All three ladies quickly get up, and before I know what's happening, they start to undress in front of me and Tyrone. Tyrone takes two kilos off the glass table and starts carefully inserting his product into the suit. I just watch.

All three ladies have tight and lovely bodies. And Milk, for a white girl, has a nice ass, too. But of course she can't fuck wit' Mandy, and definitely not Sweet. Sweet has an ass that you can sit a cup on.

The more I watch them get undressed, the more excited I become. I want to turn my head, but I can't. I am so mesmerized by their bodies that I want to ask Tyrone for a favor, to take one of his ladies to the back room and handle my business.

Milk and Mandy both smile when they see me gawking at them with lustful eyes. They all begin putting the suits on over their naked skin, crisscrossing the straps against their backs for better support. Then they start to dress. They have each packed exactly four kilos, which are concealed in the special lining of the suits.

It takes about an hour for the ladies to get dressed. Afterward they all pile into the back of Tyrone's BMW. They'll play the roles of pregnant women to a tee, especially Milk, who looks like the unfortunate country girl from the south, who migrated North because of her pregnancy, and was probably an outcast in her hometown.

An hour later, Tyrone pulls his BMW in front of the Port Authority bus station, located on Forty Second Street in Midtown Manhattan. "Aiight, Mandy, you got the first bus out to Albany. It leaves in an hour. You gonna meet up wit' Mike at the bus station on Hamilton and Green. He's your protection. You can't miss him. When you arrive, Mike is gonna take it from there and lead you to my connect. You give him the product, get my money and bring your ass back to the city on the next bus. Your hear me?" Tyrone says. Mandy nods. He then passes her an envelope filled with cash and continues to instruct her about her trip. Mandy listens without saying a word. After everything is understood, she steps out the car dressed in a pair of basic blue jeans, a large white T-shirt and a light denim jacket. Tyrone pops the trunk of his car, and Mandy retrieves a small, slightly tattered suitcase to give off the appearance of a poor, pregnant city girl, traveling out of state. If I didn't know any better, she could have fooled *me*. I mean, she definitely looks the part.

When Mandy disappears into the Port Authority station, Tyrone turns to look back at Sweet and Milk, who sit quietly in the back seat of the car. "Y'all bitches hungry? We got an hour and a half to spare before y'all catch the four o' clock bus."

"Yes, daddy, I'm hungry," Milk says.

"Aiight, we gonna catch a bite over at Applebee's down the block," Tyrone says. We head down the street to the restaurant.

Tyrone pays for everything, and he even tips the waitress a fifty just because he can. It's twenty past three when we all head back to the bus depot. Milk carries a small book bag strapped over her shoulder and sports a blue and white track suit. Sweet is wearing loose fitting sweat pants and a gray hoodie. She's also carrying a brown plastic shopping bag. Just as he did Mandy, Tyrone instructs both girls on what to do. Sweet and Milk prepare to board the same bus to Norfolk, Virginia, where they are to meet up with one of Tyrone's soldiers at the bus depot. Tyrone gives both ladies an envelope filled with cash, and then watches them be on their way to take care of his business.

A half hour later, Tyrone and I walk out of the bus depot. He's in a good mood. His cell phone goes off again. He looks at the number and utters, "Yo, Ja, wait for me at the car. I gotta call this girl back before she has a bitch fit." He tosses me the keys and walks off with his phone pressed to his ear. I go and wait in the car, listening to the radio until he arrives twenty minutes later.

"Let's be out, my niggah!" he says with excitement. "This bitch wanna link up wit' me tonight."

"Damn, niggah, you must be fuckin' da shit out of dat bitch. What's her name?" I ask, curious about who's continuously blowing up his phone.

"Man, I just be fuckin' these bitches; I ain't got time to remember names and shit."

I laugh. "I hear you. Do you, playa. Do you."

"What you gettin' into tonight, playa?" Tyrone asks turning the ignition.

"Don't know. I might give Shana a call and see what she up too," I blurt out with a shrug.

"Damn, niggah, I ain't tryin' to be in your business and all, but you kinda sweatin' dat bitch a little too fuckin' much. I know you got plenty of bitches to call tonight. Don't call dat bitch, Ja. Let her miss you or some-thing. Fo' real, yo."

I hear what Tyrone is saying to me, but my mind is telling me something different. I keep recapping that night we walked and talked on the boardwalk, and I want to spend a night like that with her again.

"Yo, Jakim, you gonna do you tonight and let Shana be for a minute?"

"Yeah, I'm gonna do me, dawg. I hear what you sayin'," I lie, while feeling that this is my business and not his.

"I'm just trying to look out for you, Ja. I hate to see my niggahs sweating one bitch, when there is so much more opportunity out there. You feel me?"

"Yeah, I feel you," I say with a nod.

Tyrone slowly pulls out of the parking garage and merges into the bustling midtown traffic. I recline in my seat and stare out the window, observing the active city life while thinking about my ex. I'm a bit hopeless, I admit. I'm still in love with Shana, and breaking up with her is one thing I truly regret—especially since it's over some bullshit. But I'm not going to stop trying to win back her love and trust for me. I'm missing her.

Fuck what anybody else says to me. I'm going to stop by Shana's crib tonight and see what's up. When I'm around her, it makes me feel good. I just want to talk to her, stare into her beautiful, angelic face and probably reminisce with her about old times.

6 SHANA

Tyrone waits forever to call me back. I swear, if the niggah didn't have a big dick and I wasn't so horny and desperate to see him tonight, I would have told him, "Fuck you!" But the niggah has me hooked on the dick. And he has me open twenty-four-seven like 7-Eleven.

When he finally calls me back, he explains that he couldn't talk because he had Jakim in the car with him. Of course I understand. He's coming to see me around nine tonight, and I'm ready for him.

I lay around my room naked for a good fifteen minutes, fingering my pussy and thinking about Tyrone. I feel like a cat in heat, waiting for him to come through and put that magic stick on me. My pussy just keeps throbbing and throbbing, and I feel that if I don't get any dick soon, I might bust.

As I continue to please myself, the phone rings. I stop for a quick second to pick up the receiver. "Hello?" I answer, thinking it's Tyrone at the other end of the line. I look at the time. It's eight-thirty.

"Shana," I hear a voice that doesn't belong to Tyrone say. It's Jakim.

"Jakim, what do you want? I'm busy at the moment," I tell him, eager to hang up on him and finish satisfying myself.

"I wanna talk to you. I'm parked outside your crib," he says.

"What? You're parked outside of my house—right now?" I inquire. "What's wrong wit' you?"

"I just wanna talk to you."

"Jakim, are you crazy? What if I had someone over?"

"You do?"

"Jakim..." I pause, sighing. Oh-my-God...I get up off my bed and look out of my front window. No doubt, there's Jakim's Maxima parked outside my house. He sounds distressed, and despite our situation I still need to be there for him—even though I have company coming through in a half hour. I don't want him doing anything stupid to himself or anybody else.

I take a deep breath and reluctantly say, "Jakim, give me a minute to get dressed and I'll be outside. Okay?"

"Aiight," he replies.

I go to my closet and pull out a pair of jeans, a baggy T-shirt and some old Nikes. I throw my hair up in a simple ponytail and strut outside to Jakim's Maxima.

I quickly get in the car. "What's up? What do you want to talk to me about?" I ask, getting to the point; I have no time to fool around. Tyrone will be here any minute, and I need Jakim to leave as soon as possible.

"Damn, you look nice, Shana. You got company inside?"

"Nah, I was just busy with some housework," I lie. "Why are you here?"

"Yo, I ain't gonna lie to you, Shana. On da real, I'm missing you so much right now. This shit is fuckin' killin' me," he straightforwardly tells me.

"Jakim—"

"Yo, all I'm asking you is to give me another chance. I deserve that, Shana, don't I?" he pleads.

I can't answer him. I'm at a loss for words. There are only two things on my mind: one, why is this ni*ggah hounding me like this, and two—Tyrone.* I love me some Tyrone, and having Jakim around isn't making things easy for me.

I glance at the clock radio on the dashboard. It's ten minutes to nine.

"Jakim, do we have to talk about this now?" I ask, becoming anxious for him to leave.

"Well, I do."

"Niggah, you gettin' pussy right now?" I bluntly ask. "Be straight wit' me."

"Wh-what?" he stammers.

"I said are you fuckin' other bitches right now?"

"What's dat got to do wit' us?" he asks.

"A lot, niggah; you must not be gettin' any pussy at the moment, because you're sweatin' me too fuckin' much right now. And to be frank, all this pleading you're doing with a sistah about gettin' back together...yo, it's turning me the fuck off!"

Jakim gives me a deadpan look. He remains quiet for a few seconds, and then he says, "It's like dat?"

"Yeah, it's like dat!" I say loudly. But then I soften my tone and add, "Jakim, I love you and all, but you gotta chill, baby. Why you rushing things?

Yo, if it's meant to be, then it will be. But you constantly show up at my door, unannounced and shit, worrying about my fuckin' business—you need to stop it; I'm starting to get mad about that. And don't worry about who I'm fuckin'. Do I be in your business every day about who's panties you're chewing into? Nah! I ain't wit' you like dat. You got all this time to play, and you stressing me like I'm your wife. C'mon, niggah, chill wit' dat shit. All you're doing wit' that pleading and pity shit is making me mad and wanna go out and fuck another niggah!"

"So, you fuckin' another niggah?" he has the nerve to ask after my little speech.

I roll my eyes and give him a perplexed look, as if to say, 'Niggah, is you serious?' But I just sigh. I look at the time again. It's five minutes to nine.

"I'm sorry, Shana. You're right," he says sounding all apologetic and shit. "I'm out."

I get out of the car, but this niggah has the nerve to follow me to my front door and shit. I'm like, 'What da fuck!'

"Shana, I ain't mean to piss you off and shit, but—"

"But what, Jakim?" I shout out of frustration. "You're doin' it right now!"

"C'mon, why you screaming on me like I'm some brand new niggah! We've been together for two years. And it's hard for me to picture you being wit' other niggahs."

"Well, get used to it," I sarcastically reply.

Just as I'm about to say something else, I peep Tyrone's shiny, black BMW creeping from around the corner. *Oh-my-God. Why is this happening to me?* But Tyrone, being the street-smart man that he is, keeps it moving down the street. I'm a bit relieved. A few moments later, I hear the house phone ringing.

"Jakim, it's getting late, and I'm tired. I don't feel like discussing us right now. Can you please leave? I gotta answer the phone," I say to him nicely.

"You know what? I'm out. Peace, Shana," he says, throwing his arms up in the air and stepping backwards as he takes one last look at me.

I watch him walk to his car. The house phone has stopped ringing now, but when Jakim gets off my block, the phone begins to ring again. I rush inside and pick up. "Hello?"

"Yeah, he left?" Tyrone asks.

"Yeah, baby, he's gone."

"You dressed?"

"Nah, not yet, baby. But give me like twenty minutes, and I'll be ready," I kindly tell him.

"Aiight. I'm gonna be parked around the corner just in case Jakim comes back around. And wear something with easy access, 'cause you know I'm 'bout to tear dat pussy up tonight, right?"

I smile and let out a slight laugh. "Aiight, baby. Maybe I'll wear a skirt." I hang up and throw open my closet door, looking for something sexy and decent to wear. I would have been ready if Jakim hadn't stopped by.

I can't find a decent skirt to wear. Fuck it, I'll just throw on some tight fitting jeans. I call Tyrone and tell him it's safe to pull up in front of my crib. I strut outside to his whip in my tight Guess jeans, leather, high-heeled boots and a baby soft, leather jacket.

"Hey, baby," I say greeting him with a kiss on the lips.

"Damn, what happened to the skirt?" he asks.

"Couldn't find nothin' to match with it. Maybe you gonna have to take me shopping."

"Maybe I will," he says smiling. "You ready to do this?"

"It's your night," I tell him, placing my hand on his leg and gently moving it toward his crotch.

"What was dat about wit' Jakim?"

"The usual—about him missing me and wanting to get back together. But I ain't hearing dat shit. I'm gettin' it too good right now. Umph!"

Tyrone chuckles. "Damn, I told Jakim to do him tonight and let you be."

"Well, he obviously didn't listen."

"Shit, dat's still my man, so I'm trying to help the niggah out and have him do him—make him forget about you. That way, when you break the news to him about us, it won't be so hard on him."

"I know, baby," I say, trying to get Jakim off my mind and think about getting some dick tonight.

"Fuck it," Tyrone mutters. He puts the car in drive and we slowly pull off.

7 SHANA

Take your time, baby," I whisper to Tyrone as we fuck in the back seat of his BMW. We're parked by the Verrazano Bridge in Brooklyn. It's going on one in the morning. I'm sitting down on his lap with his chocolate erection thrusting hard up inside me. I clamp my arms around his neck as he grips my butt tightly.

"Damn, you feel so fucking good, Shana."

There are about eight cars parked nearby. A couple parked right next to us observes us. We don't give a fuck who's watching. We continue on with our business.

Tyrone is about to make me cum. My body quivers as I move my hips back and forth. My jeans lay on the back seat beside me, and Tyrone's pants are around his ankles. His penis completely fills my vagina, expanding it to its fullest capacity. He kisses and licks on my hardened nipples. Then he plays with my butt and thrusts himself even deeper into me. The windows are all fogged up from our heavy breathing and the cold air outside, causing limited visibility. After a few moments, I feel myself becoming really excited.

"Give it to me, Ty, baby! Give it to me!" I cry out.

He shakes frantically, and I feel him bust off inside me. His neck snaps back, and his eyes roll to the back of his head. He squeezes my buttocks together tightly with his powerful hands. His dick feels even larger now. He raises his thighs with me still on top of him, making me almost hit my head on the car's roof. Now I feel myself about to cum. I tell him not to stop. He continues to thrust his hard-on deeply into me, making me climax explosively. I scream out and shiver rapidly. I'm out of control. I dig my nails into his back and rest my head over his shoulder. It feels so fucking good. "Damn, you got some good muthafuckin' pussy, Shana," he says. We remain close for a few more minutes. I just want his big dick to stay in me for a while.

"I needed that, boo," I say before kissing his earlobes.

"Jakim never gave it to you that good?"

"Yeah, but you're better. You be making me go into muthafuckin' convulsions and shit. What the fuck do you be feeding that thing anyway?"

"Brunettes, blondes, Asians, Blacks...you name it, he'll eat it."

"Just don't stuff yourself too much. I can't be having it getting too fat on me, 'cause then the shit'll no longer be able to fit."

"Then I'll just force it in," he says.

"Please, it can barely fit now," I say laughing.

I get off the dick and start to put my clothes back on. Tyrone does the same. I wipe the sweat from my forehead and face, climb over the passenger seat and sit down. Then I roll down the window to let a little air circulate throughout the car; all that fuckin' made a bitch hot. With his shirt unbuttoned, Tyrone opens the back door and walks around to the driver's seat. "You ready to go?" he asks.

I nod. He starts up the car and drives it out of the parking spot.

He explains why he didn't come through after my second fight with Sasha. He tells me he was out of town on business for a few days. He slides his right hand up my leg and rests it between my thighs, controlling the steering wheel with his left. I place my hand over his, letting it rest there.

"You hungry?" he asks me.

I nod, and we soon pull into a twenty-four-hour burger joint near Coney Island. I can't stop looking at him. I think I'm falling in love. I try to keep my emotions hidden from him, still pretending that it's only about sex. The more I try, the more I desire him.

I start thinking about Jakim. We've been separated for almost two months now. He's constantly stopping by, bringing flowers and candy, and writing poems for me expressing how much he misses me. And even though he kind of pissed me off tonight, I still admire him and his ways. He really is cute.

Jakim claims he hasn't been with another woman in weeks. I know that's bullshit. He said if we get back together, it's going to be different—no more mistakes like before. He said he'll always put us first.

But what I have with Tyrone, I really don't want to give up. He's rocking my world day after day. Dick has never before been this good to me. I mean, Jakim did his thing, too, but damn, Tyrone works it like he created pussy. I don't have one bad thing to say about him when it comes to fucking. That niggah gets a ten *times* ten on my scale.

We head inside the burger joint. I'm starving now. It's kind of crowded for it to be this late. There's only one line and one cashier. I'm not too fond of lines, so I take a seat in one of the nearby booths. As Tyrone stands in line, I sit back and admire him. He's definitely a sexy man. He's sporting a lot of jewelry, including a diamond ring, a thick, diamond encrusted bracelet and a thin, leather jacket.

I notice a few men on the line clocking me closely. They whisper to one another and look my way. I don't even smile back—especially since Tyrone is right behind them.

The line soon starts to shorten. Tyrone is up next to order. A group of four young brothers walks into the burger joint. They're very loud, and I know one of them. I'm very surprised to see him again. I used to talk to him when I was a freshman and he was a junior at Jamaica High School. His name is Terry. We dated for a few months, but I broke up with him because I felt I needed to move on. He tried to get back with me, to no avail. Eventually, he moved down south and got some girl pregnant. We remained friends over the years; sometimes he would hook a sista up and wire me some cash when I depleted my funds. He would call and write, and he even sent me pictures of his newborn baby girl, Riana.

The last I heard from Terry, he had gotten into some beef wit' his baby mama, and some other shit went down with him, too. I haven't heard from him since. That was two years ago.

I try to turn my head, hoping that he doesn't recognize me. He gets on the back of the line with his buddies. I want to get up and change booths, to not be so easily seen. I mean, it's good to see him again, but I feel that now is not the time to be reminiscing about back in the day...it's too late; he already saw me.

"Shana?" Tyrone turns around to see who's calling my name. Then he looks at me. I give him a faint smile and remain seated.

"Oh, shit, Shana, it *is* you," Terry says. "What's up, girl? I ain't seen you in a minute." He comes at me with open arms, expecting a hug. I want to ignore him, but I really can't. His boys continue standing on the line and watch. I glance at Tyrone as he continues waiting to place his order. I'm nervous, but I can't pinpoint the reason why. Tyrone's not my man, and Terry is just an old boyfriend from my past who just so happens to be in the burger joint tonight. All of a sudden, Tyrone's eyes dart straight in his direction.

"Damn, you're still looking fine as ever, Shana" Terry says.

"Long time, Terry," I reply, leaving just enough room between him and I.

Before I can even look back over at Tyrone, he's already standing behind Terry. My eyes widen. Terry turns around, and he looks like he's seen a ghost. He takes a quick step back, bumping into me slightly. His boys, still on line, curiously stare on.

"Tyrone," Terry murmurs.

"Yeah, muthafucka, it's me. Where you been, and where the fuck is my money?!" Tyrone shouts.

"Look, I ran into some problems," he tries to explain.

I'm dumbfounded. *How does Tyrone know Terry?* They went to different schools, and every time I saw Tyrone and Jakim together, I never saw Terry.

Terry looks scared shitless, and his movements make him look so pussy. He glances over at his boys, who are also lost. Then he glances back at me, and he sees by the look on my face that I'm just as clueless as every-one else in the place.

"Tyrone, look—"

"Shut the fuck up!" Tyrone shouts, interrupting Terry's explana-tion. He clenches his fists tightly and stares into Terry's eyes without evening blinking. He's mad.

"Tyrone—I—man...you see, what had happened was..." Terry didn't even get to finish his sentence. Tyrone just knocked him across the head with a closed fist, causing Terry to stumble back against the table. Everyone's attention is now on the situation. Tyrone then pulls out a gun and starts repeatedly hitting Terry over the head with it. I begin to scream as Tyrone continues to pistol-whip him right in front of me.

"Tyrone, what the fuck are you doing?!" I shout. He pays me no mind. Terry's boys start to rush to his aid, but when Tyrone turns around and points his gun at them, they all freeze.

"What the fuck y'all gonna do—help out your pussy- ass boy?" he shouts, aiming the gun directly at them. Everyone in the place starts to panic; some run out of the restaurant, while others duck behind tables and counters. Terry's three friends don't know what to do with themselves as they stare down the barrel of Tyrone's nine millimeter in terror. I also don't know what to do, so I just stand there, watching one of my ex-boyfriends get beat down by someone I'm fucking. Terry now lies across the table, beaten and bleeding. He looks helpless.

Tyrone walks back over to Terry and continues to terrorize him. He pushes the barrel of the nine millimeter to his temple and threatens to shoot him if he doesn't come up with his money soon. Terry begs for his life.

"I'm giving you till next week. I want my fuckin' money, or I'm gonna blow your fuckin' brains out!" Tyrone shouts.

He then shoves Terry down onto the floor. I remain completely silent. Terry looks up at me. One of his eyes is badly bruised and closed. His nose looks like it's broken, and blood covers his mouth, chin and neck. He's a fuckin' mess.

"C'mon, Shana!" Tyrone yells, grabbing me by the arm. I stand there, contemplating if I should get in the car with him. "C'mon, Shana, get in the fuckin' car!" he calls again.

I'm so scared, and I can't help but feel sorry for Terry. What has he gotten himself into—getting tormented and beat down by a street thug, a street thug that I'm fuckin'? Back in the day, Terry was on the varsity foot-ball team. He was voted *Most Likely To Succeed*. He was even on the debate team. Now his life is looking like shit.

Tyrone begins blowing his horn repeatedly. I can hear sirens in the distance. I want to comfort and help Terry, but my mind is telling me to get in the car with Tyrone. I look around nervously.

"Shana, if you don't get your fuckin' ass in this car, then I'm gone, bitch!" he shouts at the top of his lungs now. I need to leave the scene; I can't afford to stay and hang around, not knowing what I may be getting myself into. The cops might arrest me, thinking that I'm somehow associat-ed with what just happened to Terry. They might want to interrogate me.

I jump into the car. Tyrone doesn't even give me a chance to shut the door all the way before speeding off down the street doing sixty. For the next ten minutes, he drives like a mad man, accelerating up to eighty miles per hour on side streets until we hit the parkway. He remains quiet, not even looking at me or trying to explain what just happened until we're a few miles away. I want to say something, but I keep my mouth shut.

"You love me?" he suddenly blurts out.

My eyes get big. *What the fuck is he talking about? He's not going to explain what just happened? He just nearly beat my ex-boyfriend to death in front of me...and what's with the you-love-me question?* I remain silent. I can't answer him. I'm too scared to.

He continues speeding, now going over seventy miles per hour on the Belt Parkway. I tightly place my hands between my legs. I want to say something, but I don't.

"Look, I'm sorry about what happened back there, but that was just business. Don't let it interfere with what we have. You cool?" he asks, actually sounding concerned. He rests his hand on my thigh and begins to massage it lightly.

"I'm cool," I quietly reply.

He gives me a quick smile. I feel really uncomfortable right now. I don't move his hand off my thigh, even though I want to. He starts to slide his hand between my legs, placing it over mine, but I stop him.

"C'mon Tyrone, you expect me to be feeling romantic after what just happened?"

"Shana, don't worry about it. That's *my* business."

"I used to go out with him. Did you know that?"

He slows the car down. "You was fucking that asshole?"

"That was a long time ago, and where do you know Terry from anyway?" I ask. I can't hold the questions any longer. I need to know something.

"Look, all you need to know is that we did business together, and he owes me a lot of money," he meagerly explains.

Tyrone isn't too big on giving out information or letting you know his business. He's a very discreet niggah. As I recall from what Jakim told me, Tyrone would disappear for days, maybe weeks at a time back in the day, and nobody would know a thing regarding his whereabouts. He would just suddenly turn up in the neighborhood again, with no explanation. Now, at only twenty-two, he has a decent-size bank account, his own crib and drives a fancy car. He is both feared and respected by everybody he comes in contact with.

I can't turn myself away from him. Even after what went down tonight, I know I'm going to still be involved with him. Tyrone is like a drug, and he's also my supplier. I know he can be violent at times; it's just the way he is, and it comes with the job. But he never flips on me, and that's the main thing. Even when I was with Jakim, when he came around, he always treated me kindly and with respect. To be honest, I wanted to get with Tyrone before I ever got involved with Jakim. But Jakim and I hooked up, and I let my little crush on Tyrone fade away—until now.

Tyrone wants to drop the subject and just forget about it—what's done is done; so like his bitch, I remain quiet and drop it. He doesn't give a fuck about me and Terry dating at one time. We leave it at that. My fear turns into lust; he can definitely hold it down. He's a true, die-hard, rough-neck thug.

We park in front of my crib for a few minutes. Tyrone tongue kisses me goodnight and I step out of his car. After getting inside, I take a quick shower and go straight to bed.

It's been three days since Tyrone beat Terry down in that all-night burger joint. I keep the incident to myself, telling no one about it. Yesterday, Tyrone surprised me with a gift. He bought me a diamond bracelet from Tiffany's in Manhattan. I nearly cried when he clamped it around my wrist. He refused to tell me the price of the bracelet.

I flaunt the expensive bracelet in front of Naja and Latish. We're over Naja's crib now, chilling and playing cards. Naja lives with her man, Bosco. He's one of Tyrone's business associates. Naja likes the bracelet so much that she says she's going to press Bosco into buying her one; he makes enough cash to afford it.

"So what's up with you and Jakim now?" Latish asks, all up in a bitch's business.

"What do you mean what's up with me and him? We're still cool," I reply.

"But I thought you said you was planning on getting back together with him?" Naja chimes in.

"Please, girl, I got it good on both sides. And Jakim can wait it out a little longer...it's my decision," I say.

"Why you messin' with that boy's head, Shana? You know he loves you too much, and you're out fucking his man. That's some cold shit," Latish says.

"First of all, Latish, he fucked up with me, and I'll give my pussy to whoever I wish. Jakim don't own this," I say pointing down at my shit, "This is my treasure...I just lent it to him for a little while."

"Now you know you're frontin'," Naja loudly says. "Jakim had you in love. It was always Jakim this, Jakim that. I love me some Jakim. Y'all relationship is like an emotional rollercoaster."

"Please, ain't like y'all never cried over no dick," I say.

"Yeah, I be crying," Latish says, "when the dick be hitting my spot just right." Naja and I laugh, and we slap each other five. "Yo, I got with this niggah named Bent," Latish adds. They call him that because when he gets hard, his shit bends three inches to the side, looks like he got a hook at the end of his shit. But anyway, he can work some muthafuckin' pussy, g-i-r-r-l. That niggah be hooking on to my shit, and be dragging me all across the room with his hook dick."

"You are so stupid," Naja says.

"So, Shana, let me ask you a personal question: who got a bigger dick—Jakim or Tyrone?" Latish says. I hesitate answering her.

"Yeah, for real, whose is bigger?" Now Naja wants to know.

"Why y'all wanna be all up in a girl's business?" I say. "They're both big."

"Tyrone!" they shout in unison.

"What makes you think it's Tyrone?" I curiously ask.

"Because I can see it in your eyes, plus you ain't gotta answer; the way you've been carrying on about Tyrone, I'm surprised you just don't marry the man and have his babies," Naja says.

"And leave a fine man like Jakim out in the cold? Girl, you must be crazy. You gonna fuck around and have some other ho pick up your left-overs, Shana," Latish cautions.

I could never trust Latish around any of my men; she'd fuck them in a heartbeat. I wonder how I've managed to befriend and stay cool with her for so long. And I still have my doubts about her and Jakim being together. Sometimes the way she looks at me makes me feel so uncom-fortable, like she knows something I don't.

"Shana, what's the deal with you and Sasha? Y'all been friends for so long—ever since the eighth grade," Latish suddenly brings up.

"Fuck her!" I flatly say.

"I heard she tried to cut you," Naja says.

"Yeah, on Jamaica Av a few weeks back. Can you believe that shit? She's gonna get hers one day," I say.

"Well, I saw her the other day in the mall with some guy. She told me you actually started the whole thing," Latish says.

"You gonna believe that bitch's lies? She set me up with the ugliest person y'all could think of and expected to me to be on my best behavior with the muthafucka. That bitch knows my standards. Then she had the nerve to beef about it in front of my crib the next day and shit, so I had to slap her!"

"Y'all just need to kiss and make up," says Naja.

"I just wanna beat her ass again! Can we just drop the conversation about that dumb bitch? Damn, stop stressing it. Just fuck that bitch and let it be!" I shout.

The room is quiet now, and Latish and Naja just stare at me. They're upset over my outburst.

"Look, I'm sorry about that. But y'all know y'all are still my girls, right?" I say apologetically. They begin to relax, and we get back to our friendly game of cards and girl talk.

The next morning, I get a call from Jakim. He wants me to accompany him to the studio in Flatbush, Brooklyn. He practically begs me to come. It's going on eleven, and he says he'll be here around one to pick me up. I'm not even upset with him anymore.

I hear a knock at my bedroom door. My Aunt Tina peeps her head into my room. "Wake up, sleepy head," she says.

"What you want?" I ask.

"What you doing tonight?"

"Why you wanna know?"

"Because I got tickets to the Baller's Jam at the Manhattan Center."

"Say, word?!" I holler, jumping out of bed and running up to her. "That shit's been sold out for weeks! How the fuck did you get tickets?"

"I got my ways, girl."   *She definitely does.*

Every major playa in the city is going to be there tonight. My girls and I have been trying to get tickets for weeks without any success. Artists from Def Jam, Arista, Bad Boy and Roc-A-Fella will be attending this party, so you know I have to be up in there somehow. I want to kiss my aunt.

"So, you rolling tonight or what?"

Like she had to ask. I never gave it a second thought. "Of course I am," I reply. My aunt can get just about anything. She doesn't care who she has to suck or fuck. She knows that what she has between her legs is precious and she uses it to her advantage, making men buy, beg, borrow and steal to give her the world. I wonder why she's still living with my moms and me, when all she has to do is fuck the right man and have him buy her a house.

I remember her Italian boyfriend, Eddie, who owned a car dealership. He owned ten different lots in eight major cities across the country. He bought her a brand new car one day—a white BMW 740IL—a fifty-three-thousand-dollar car. She wrecked it in three weeks, totaling it. She ran a stop sign and crashed into a city bus. She suffered a fractured hip, sprained ankle and a few cuts and bruises. Her friend, Ebony, who was in the car, too, walked away with minor injuries. Eddie wanted to kill her. Needless to say, they broke up and he ended up paying for all the damages. The car, the insurance, everything was in his name.

My aunt fucked up big time with that one, but she recovered and moved on to the next luxury dick. During the three weeks she had that car, we had a ball driving around. She even let *me* drive it a few of times.

"Be ready by eight. Kendell is coming to pick us up at nine," she says.

"How many people are going?"

"Just you and me."

Damn, I wish I could bring Naja and Latish with me. I quickly get over that thought. I need something to wear; nothing in my closet is going to cut it tonight. I want something special—an eye catcher that's sexy as hell. I want all the males at the party to crave me. I need to get my hair done, too. I know Sandra will hook me up and fit me into her busy schedule. She's my homegirl. She'll definitely look out. She works at a hair salon on Merrick Boulevard.

It's now eleven-thirty, and there are lots of things that I have to rush to get done before going to this party. I call Sandra up and explain my situation to her. She tells me to come in around five. She won't be too busy around that time. I need to go shopping. I only have two-hundred dollars. I saw this phat dress in Macy's at Green Acres Mall the other day. The price tag said three-fifty, and I have to give Sandra sixty-five to do my hair—not to mention spending-money for tonight. Although I can always con some guy into buying me drinks, I think it's always good to have my own little cash stashed away in case of an emergency.

Damn, why did my aunt wait so late to tell me she had tickets for this event? Now I have to run around and get things done like a chicken with its head cut off.

I can ask my moms for some doe; Danny's always giving her

money, or I can ask Danny myself. I know he's here; I saw his truck parked outside. I know Tyrone could front me the cash, but I think about how long it might take him to get over here. Besides, I really don't feel like seeing him; he might try to mess up my plans.

While taking a quick shower, I think about my options. I decide to ask Danny for the money. I step out of the shower and wrap a small towel around myself. I walk into the living room, still glistening, with my hair still wet. I remember Jakim once told me that a female looks her best when taking a shower, and coming out with the water still trickling down her skin. Watching me bathe used to turn him on. We'd fuck on the bathroom floor afterward.

I want to see if my being wet and coming out of the shower will have the same effect on Danny as it did on Jakim. He's on the couch watching TV. I go and stand directly in front of him.

"Where's my mother?" I ask as his eyes study every inch of my body.

"She's in the bedroom," he says in his sexy voice. I walk to my mother's bedroom. I carefully peek inside and see that she's asleep. I smile and quietly shut the door back. I look back at Danny. His eyes never left my body. He plays it cool, though.

"Danny, I need a big favor from you," I soothingly say.

"What is it, baby girl?"

I take a seat next to him on the couch in my short, wet towel, which stops at mid thigh. I place my hand on his lap and gaze into his eyes. "I need to borrow three hundred dollars," I say.

"That's a small favor here," he replies. He reaches into his pocket and pulls out a wad of hundreds. I try to keep cool, but being next to him with all that money in his hand, combined with him looking so good, near-ly makes me lose control and jump on his dick. I want to take him into my mouth and suck his dick so good that he'll forget about my mother and work his miracles on me. I want to drop this towel to the floor and show him how young and lovely my body is. The sight of my naked body does won-ders for all of my old boyfriends; they never got tired of it. I only got tired of them.

"Here you go, baby girl," he says, handing me four hundred-dollar bills. "Here's an extra hundred just in case."

God, I hate my mother for having such a wonderful and fine man. He could hit this morning, noon *and* night! I give him a quick kiss on the cheek and get up from the couch. As I slowly stroll down the hallway to my bedroom, I do the craziest thing: I drop my towel down to the floor, giving Danny a clear glimpse of me from the back—butt naked. I bend over to pick up the towel with my legs parted slightly and retreat to my bedroom. I don't even turn around to see his reaction; I already know what it is.

Who needs a job? I'm getting dollars from the fellas left and right. I throw on my blue Guess jeans, my blue and gray Georgetown sweater and my fresh, new, beige Timberlands. I pull my hair up in a ponytail and put on a little lip gloss. I call Naja to see if she wants to go out to the mall to do a little Saturday afternoon shopping. She doesn't pick up her cell phone. Then I call Tyrone, but he's not home. I page him, but he doesn't get back to me.

The doorbell rings at twelve-thirty. It's Jakim. I've totally forgotten about promising that I'd go down to the studio with him and chill for the day; I've been so excited about the party tonight. "You ready to go?" he asks standing in the front doorway.

"Shit, Jakim...I forgot about this afternoon," I tell him, feeling badly about it.

"What you mean you forgot about this afternoon? I just spoke to you about it two hours ago!" He's pissed.

"Yeah, but something came up."

"Like what?"

I turn around and see that Danny is all up in our business, so I calmly step outside and shut the door.

"Look, Jakim, I promised my Aunt that I would help her with something today. She reminded me about it right after I hung up with you."

"That's some cold shit, Shana. You got me all excited about spending the day with you, and now you wanna blow me off to go and hang out with your aunt?"

"It ain't even like that, Jakim."

"Why are you doing this to me? Why are you playin' me?"

"I'm not doing this on purpose," I tell him. Then it came to me. Jakim could take me shopping. I know he wants to go down to the studio and all, but with a little coaxing, that could easily change. I lightly press myself up against him and give him a gentle kiss on the lips. "Look, baby...you want to hang out with me today?" I say sweetly in his ear.

"You know I do, Shana."

To put my plan into effect, I lick the corner of his ear and whisper, "Can you ride me around then? I need to take care of a few things." I place my hand over his heart and feel it beating rapidly. I knew the ear thing would excite him.

"But I was planning on going down to the studio today," he says.

"Well, can it wait?" I ask snuggling up to him. "I need a ride, baby." I can feel him caving in, so I turn up the pressure by cupping my hand over his dick, and again I whisper softly in his ear. "You miss my lovin', boo? Do me this favor, and I promise to repay you tomorrow night—with interest."

"How long you gonna be?" he asks.

"Does it matter? You're gonna be spending the day with me."

"All right, then. Let me make this quick run to Greg's crib to get my shit. I'll be right back."

"Don't take too long."

He rushes to his car, hard as a rock. He's still my heart. I watch him pull off before turning to go back inside the house. I see Danny peeping at me through the window, and I chuckle. I walk back into the house and head towards my room. Danny's eyes stay on me the whole time.

Jakim comes back at around two to pick me up. We go straight to the mall, and I purchase a phat, Malte Jersey dress. I also get a few skirts and some shoes. Jakim shops around with me. He helps me pick out a few things, too, and he even takes me to get something to eat. By the time we're done, it's going on four o' clock. I still have that five o' clock appointment to get my hair done.

"Shana, you must think I'm stupid," Jakim suddenly blurts out as we drive down Sunrise Highway.

"What?" I ask, stunned by his words.

"You doing all of this shopping and shit, and now you about to go and get your hair done—who you seeing tonight?" he asks irately.

"What are you talking about, Jakim? I told you, I'm hanging out with my aunt tonight."

"You told me she asked you to do something for her."

"Yeah, to hang out with her," I quickly reply.

"So you gotta get all dressed up and shit?"

The day was going so good, and now here he comes with this atti-tude. I promised myself that I wasn't going to get upset today—especially over no bullshit. I glance out of the car window and turn back to Jakim, flip-ping the script. "Look, muthafucka, did you or did you not forget that we are separated, as in no longer together–apart? I can see or fuck whoever I want, so don't come to me with your bullshit attitude worrying about my business. You ain't see me get all up all in your business when you was fuck-ing that bigheaded bimbo down the block."

Jakim grips the steering wheel and says, "Look, Shana, all I'm say-ing is stop teasing me. I'm sorry about that, but I feel I've been punished too long for it. I'm no fucking puppet! You just can't keep stringing me along whenever you feel like it. You always talk about *your* feelings...shit, what about mine?"

I don't even answer him, still trying to keep that promise I made to myself. I study Jakim as he focuses his eyes on the road. He looks so cute, reclining in his seat with one hand on the steering wheel, looking like some thug or gangsta. I continue to study him for a few more minutes. "Jakim, I will always love you, no matter what. But right now, I just need some time to myself. And I'm not going to lie to you—yes, I'm seeing other people. Maybe someday we'll get back together, and maybe we won't. But we'll have to let time take care of that."

"Well, I'm still in love with you, Shana. And I'm still missing you, so fucking much that it's hurting. And if we can't be lovers, I feel that we can't be friends."

The rest of the ride to the hair salon is mostly quiet, with bits of small talk here and there. When we arrive to the salon, I tell him I'll catch a cab back home; there's no telling how long I'm going to be.

I walk into the salon and see six patrons and only four ladies doing hair. I see my girl, Sandra, finishing up with a customer. Sandra is a beautiful woman in her mid twenties with two kids. I met her through my mother, when she used to do her hair. She waves at me, and I walk over to her.

"What's up girl?!" she hollers.

"What's up with you?!" I holler back. We exchange hugs, and I take a seat in the empty chair next to her station. After about ten minutes she finishes up her client's hair, and then she gets started on mine. I just want a perm. We gossip as she begins to work on my hair. She tells me what's going on around the way and with her life. She's finally dumped her man, who she was with for three years. She caught him cheating on her with her cousin, who he'd gotten pregnant. Damn, talk about drama.

"I whooped that bitch's ass, Shana. How she gonna play me like that and fuck my man behind my fucking back?"

"I would've killed the bitch," I say, just to be talking.

Sandra always has news or dirt on other people. That's one of the main reasons why I go to her—to get the low-down news on other people. She brings up my beef with Sasha, curious about what's going on with that. I explain to her what, when and how it all down. She's a hundred percent on my side. "She was in here the other day," she informs me.

"Fuck that bitch!"

I get done around a quarter to seven. I pay Sandra her usual fee, plus a twenty-dollar tip. Once again we hug, and we promise to hook up some night and go out to the club. Then I call myself a cab.

I'm dressed around eight and ready to go to the Baller's Jam. I'm looking so fly in my new dress. It shows every curve of my phenomenal body. And my butt is looking too good from the back; it's like an onion–

guaranteed to make a niggah cry. I move my hands over my body and look at myself in the mirror. "Girl, you are looking too good," I say praising myself.

I'm home alone, waiting for my aunt to arrive with her date. I sit quietly on the living room couch watching television. It is now eight-thirty. Naja gives me a call, and I tell her about my plans for tonight. She's hating, and she wants me to beg my aunt for another ticket. I tell her that I received the last one. Tyrone calls, too, but I don't pick up. He leaves a message.

It's ten after nine when my Aunt Tina comes to pick me up. Her date is driving that new Range Rover. She's dressed in a beige leather mini skirt and a blue, sheer, mesh shirt. "Shana, you ready?" she asks, looking at me from head to toe.

"Been ready," I say.

I meet her date outside. He's not all that cute, but you could work with him. He's stocky, about 5'8", has a thick beard and is wearing two dia-mond earrings. He has braids and is sporting a very nice, gray Italian suit. His name is Kendell. My aunt says he's an A&R for Arista records.

We arrive to the Baller's Jam a little after ten. The crowd of people outside is ridiculous. Every make and style of car is parked out on the street—Lexuses Benzes, BMW's, Porsches, Town cars and stretch limousines. The crowd tries to get in; they even attempt to rush the door, but security is strapped and not having it.

We drive by a barricade for VIP only. We get out of the truck and

Kendell escorts us to a private entrance. He gives several people dap, which lets us know that he is well known.

"Damn!" I hear someone shout out. I know the mystery person is talking about me.

We enter the party, and the first person I bump into is Jay-Z, holding a bottle of Moet. My eyes light up with excitement. Oh-my-god! He is too fine.

He marvels at me and says, "Damn, shorty! You got a license for dat?" I know he's referring to my body.

"You willing to find out?" I counter, smiling at him. My aunt notices him, too, and she scurries over with excitement, asking for an autograph. I tell you, Latish and Naja would be hating right now if they knew I ran into Jay-Z. Aunt Tina is all over him, smiling and flirting, while I stand off to the side thinking about how much of a groupie she is.

The place is jam packed with celebrities, athletes, fans, managers, producers...and of course, groupies. The DJ is doing his thang, mixing vinyls from Jay-Z to R-Kelly. Kendell buys me a drink. I glance around the club. There are so many fine men in the house, I feel like a child in a candy factory.

"Can I buy you another drink?" a fine gentleman asks. He's dressed down in Armani, has short, curly hair and is fine enough to be related to Denzel Washington, my future husband. Denzel just doesn't know it yet. Anyway, he has gorgeous brown eyes and the softest looking lips.

"It depends," I reply.

"Depends on what?" he asks.

"Depends on if you tell me your name."

"Barry Jones." He takes the half-empty glass of Alize out of my hand and places it down on the bar. "Let's get rid of this old drink. Allow me to order you a fresh one."

He orders me another drink and pays the bartender. He then escorts me over to the VIP area, where P. Diddy is sitting at a table.

"So, I never caught your name," Barry says.

"That's because I never threw it at you."

"So, are you going to pitch it to me before this party is over?"

I pause and gaze into his lovely brown eyes, while wondering how big his dick is. "Its Shana," I finally tell him.

"You are beautiful, Shana. Have you ever thought about a career in the entertainment industry?"

"No, not really."

"Well, if you do, here's my card," he says, placing it in my hand. "I'm a music manager," he adds.

I stuff the card into my purse and sip on my drink. We move to the floor and talk and dance for about an hour. He eventually asks me back to his hotel. He says it has a Jacuzzi, twenty-four-hour room service and satin sheets. It's tempting, but I decline   Aunt Tina's having a good ol' time, forgetting that she came with a date. Men were approaching her left and right.

I'm totally exhausted by two a.m. I take a seat in the lounge and nearly fall asleep. I've danced with and talked to so many men, and now I can barely keep my eyes open.

I feel someone plop down beside me. I open my eyes and see Kendell hunched over with his elbows resting on his thighs.   "S h a n a, what up with you?" he asks.

"Huh?"

"A couple of the fellas are throwing a little after-party at the

Sheraton, and they want you to roll along."

I give him a blank stare. He places his hand on my lap and just lets it rest there like it's a fuckin' truck stop. I glance around, looking for my aunt, but she's nowhere in sight.

"So, you rollin' with us or what?" Something in his tone tells me to turn down his offer.

"Nah, Kendell, I'm gonna pass. I'm too fuckin' tired," I explain.

He looks at me disappointedly and tightly grasps my leg. He then starts rubbing my inner thigh with his fingers. I see him look over and nod at one of his homies.

"But yo, mad heads are rollin' with us, including your aunt. I'm sayin', we got like fifty people coming. We got the liquor, the weed and the music." He moves his hand slightly up my inner thigh, easing his fingers near my precious kitty kat.

"Kendell, do I look like one of these groupies to you?" I suddenly blurt out.

"Nah, Shana, why you ask that?" he says looking smugly at me.

"'Cause you got your hand on my thigh, reaching for my shit like I owe you something. And I would appreciate it if you'd move it." He slowly and carefully moves his hand; he doesn't want to look like a fool in front of his boys. If he had jerked it away too quickly, they would have known that I shot his ass down. "And no, I'm not rollin' to no hotel with y'all," I add.

By the expression on his grill, I know that he's not too happy with my answer. "If you ain't rollin', then take the subway home, stupid bitch!" he whispers in my ear before getting up and walking away.

No he didn't! I thought. I really want to slap the shit out of that ignorant muthafucka right about now. I don't give a flying fuck who he is.

That muthafucka doesn't have a right to disrespect me. I get up and search for my aunt. I'm ready to go home. What Kendell just said to me has me too fuckin' upset. I'm about ready to fight up in here.

I see my aunt standing next to Kendell, arm-to-arm. I quickly step over to her and that bastard. His boys are also standing nearby. They see me coming over and start smiling ear to ear.

"I see you've changed your mind," Kendell's ignorant ass says.

"No, fuck you! I came over to get my aunt," I say, pulling her to the side.

"What's da matter?" my aunt asks.

"Your new man's a dick-head, and I'm about ready to leave."

"But I'm about to go over to the after-party with Kendell," she replies. "Plus he's our ride home."

"Fuck him, Aunt Tina! I'll take the subway home," I shout out, loudly enough for that asshole to hear. He shoots me a dumb smirk as he stands there drinking with his wack-ass crew.

"I'm not taking the subway," Aunt Tina states.

"Kendell tried to hit on me," I say.

"Shana, stop. You're fucking lying! Why you gotta hate on me because my man got money and can get us into fine places? Every niggah in da world don't want you."

I'm in shock! *Did this niggah brainwash her?* Kendell and his crew, having obviously heard my aunt's words, are in a huddle laughing at me. I am so furious that I could kill that muthafucka.

"I'm going with Kendell. You can leave by yourself, Shana," Aunt Tina says.

I want to smack her, too, for being so naïve and stupid. She gets a rich piece of dick and thinks the muthafucka is gonna treat her like she's the Queen of England. She was better off with the last loser.

Aunt Tina walks her sorry ass back over to Kendell, as he continues drinking, laughing and carrying on with his boys. He throws his arm around my aunt and flips me the bird. My temper's at the boiling point. It's all good, though.

I go over to the bar, pick up someone's unfinished drink and walk toward Kendell. "If you got something to say, then say it, you dumb bastard," I say, standing directly in front of him now.

"Get away from me, you dumb bitch," he replies.

I throw the drink in his face and slap him so hard that everyone within thirty feet of us hears it. "Who's looking like the dumb bitch now?" I yell.

"Shana!" my aunt shouts. Kendell, looking shocked as hell, wipes the drink off his face. His boys chuckle; they know what time it is. My aunt helps him get cleaned up, all the while glaring at me, stunned and very angry. I flip her the bird and proceed to storm out of the place, while hearing Kendell rant and curse. I feel so fucking good.

I take the subway home, even after getting about ten offers from guys willing to give me a lift when they saw me leaving the club. I've had enough for tonight, and I'm no longer in the mood for male attention.

I get home around four in the morning. I see that there's a message on the answering machine, and I press the speaker button.

"Hello, Shana, it's Naja. Sorry I'm calling so late, but I thought you might want to know as soon as possible...Terry's dead. They found his body last night. Call me when you get this."

I stand there frozen. I replay the message to be sure I heard her right—I did. My ex-boyfriend is dead. First the incident with that asshole at the club, now coming home to hear that someone I know and once cared for is dead...Terry is dead!

JAKIM 8

"Aaaaaahhh, baby....just like dat! Fuck me, baby!" Latish cries out as I fuck her in the ass. That's the way she wants it—raw, fast and straight up the ass.

I don't give a fuck. I'm taking out my frustration over Shana on her. I'm upset that Shana keeps blowing me off. I want her so bad, but since she's not giving up the pussy, I'm going for the best option—Latish. She happily accepts me, with open arms and spread legs.

I thrust my dick hard and fast into her. I repeatedly smack her on the ass and pull at her hair. She grips the dresser, holding onto it tightly. I'm in a zone, and Latish is loving every minute of it. She also likes it rough—especially when I leave bruises.

"Cum in my ass, Jakim. Fuck me and cum in my ass, niggah!" she pants and shouts.

"You want me to cum in your ass, bitch!"

"Yes, give me dat dick, baby! Ooh, you feel so good." She throws her ass back on me, and my nuts slap up against her. I simultaneously cup one of her tits, pull at her hair and pound my dick into her.

As we continue fucking, I glance at my reflection in the mirror. Beads of sweat are dripping down my forehead and I look possessed. Latish grips the dresser tighter and arches her back a bit more, telling me to put it deeper in her ass. We've been going at it for a good twenty minutes. We're in sync.

Several moments later, I feel myself about to explode. I wild out and come in her butt. She loves it. I pull out, take a few steps back from her and pass out on her bed. Sprawled out on my back, I stare up at the ceiling, huffing and wheezing.

"I love it when you cum in my butt," Latish says plopping her naked ass on top of me. I just smile. She rubs her bare tits against my chest and nibbles on my right ear. Then she sticks her tongue in my ear and moves it all around. I chuckle, and she moves her hand down my body and gently grips my dick, massaging my balls with her fingers. I moan.

As I lay there, she begins fondling me from head to toe. "Damn, Latish, don't you ever get enough?"

"Shit, I'm always horny. I need a niggah who can keep up. You know what I'm sayin'?"

"I hear you."

She starts to suck on my nipples and then goes down on me for the third time tonight. Do I stop her? Fuck no! I continue to lie there, feeling her warm, moist mouth engulf my semi erection. I watch her head move up and down. She's sucking my dick like a porn star. I just lie there, enjoying the moment. She sucks me for a good fifteen minutes more, giving me a full erection again. *Damn!*

"Ooh, I knew I could it get back up again," she says smiling at her work.

"You definitely do a good job," I tell her.

She moves forward and mounts me gently, sliding her animated pussy down my pole. She lets out a slight grunt as she clutches my chest and closes her eyes.

I grip her hips and push myself up in her, causing her to cry out as she digs her nails into my chest. Her tits move freely and wildly about as she bounces up and down against my pelvis. God, I love it when she tightens her muscles, making it feel like her pussy has caved in on my dick. I clutch the sheets and begin to shout. "Damn, Latish! SHIT!" She continues to fuck me rapidly.   "I'm gonna cum!" I yell out.

"Dat's right, muthafucka! Cum for me! You know my pussy is good!" With her nails still digging into my chest, she gyrates her hips frantically in a forward and backward motion. She grinds hard on my dick, and I reach out and grab on both her tits, squeezing those shits tightly. Latish gazes down at me, sweating and panting. Then she says, "You know Shana never gave it to you this good, right? Say it! Say I got the better pussy. Say I fuck you better, niggah!"

"Hells yeah, you fuck me better," I say, feeling my nut coming. "SHIT! Don't stop."   She smiles and begins to move faster. Her hips rocking against me cause my toes to contract, and I twist up my face. I know she's enjoying this.

"Cum in me, Jakim!" she screams.

"I'm...CUMMING!"

"Dat's right, baby. Fuck me! FUCK ME!" She continues to ride my dick like a jockey on a prize-winning horse.

I groan and grunt, holding on to her bare hips. "Oh, yeah! Oh, shit! Oh, yeah! I'm cumming...oh, yeah!" I scream out. I grip her hips tighter and finally feel myself explode in her. I know I look like I'm catching seizures and shit, as I shake and jerk beneath Latish.

I'm sweating profusely now, panting and wheezing as Latish stares down at me with my dick still resting in her pussy. I smile. I'm done.

We relish the moment. That was some good fucking. Latish leans forward and starts kissing me on my face, and then she shoves her tongue in my mouth. We passionately kiss for several moments. She gets up off the dick and collapses on her back beside me.

All I can do is just lie here and try to get my energy back. Shit, I'm really done. "What time is it?" I ask.

Latish sucks her teeth. "Why, you wanna leave?" she says angrily.

"I'll chill for a minute."

Latish begins to nestle against me like we're a couple. She softly runs her fingers up and down my chest and kisses me on the neck. "Stay da night with me, Jakim. Please..." she says coyly.

"I can't," I gently reply.

"Why not? You plan on hookin' up wit' Shana later?" she asks in an irritated tone.

"Nah. It ain't even like dat. I'm supposed to meet up with Tyrone and Evay later tonight," I explain to her.

"So, take me wit' you," she pleads.

"C'mon, you know how it is; people talk," I say with a sigh.

"So fuckin' what, Jakim?" Latish gets up and swings one of her legs over my torso, straddling me. "So I'm just a fuckin' hoe to you?" she says peering down at me.

It would be rude to tell her the truth, that yes, that is exactly what she is to me. And if I tell her that, that's the end of the pussy. Besides, I'm not trying to get cut off at such a critical point in my life. If I was back with Shana, yeah, I would've told her the truth—straight up—not giving a fuck. But I'm single and horny, and she satisfies my sexual appetite completely.

"Nah, Latish...I don't see you like dat," I lie. "You know I got feelings for you, but I ain't trying to get involved right now. Give me a few weeks to get my head right, and we'll see what's up."

"I know you're not waiting for Shana to come around...please tell me you're not."

"It ain't about Shana," I lie again.

"It better not be," she warns.

"What does that mean?" I say looking at her suspiciously.

"Nothin', boo. It ain't even nothin' for you to stress over. I just got jealous, dat's all."

"Yo, y'all bitches and y'all emotions," I say getting up off the bed. But deep down I feel that Latish is keeping something from me.

I start to get dressed. Latish just lays there with an attitude. "Jakim, If we did get together, I would be so faithful to you. You know dat, right?" I just look at her without saying a word. "I know you probably look at me like I'm a slut and shit, 'cause I do what I do. But if I had a man like you in my life permanently, this would be all yours and you wouldn't have to worry about nobody else getting at it. I like sex a lot, Jakim, I ain't gonna lie. But I love being with you and shit. You make me feel so good, baby."

I start to wonder where all this is coming from. Back in the day when we fucked, we just fucked; there weren't any feelings involved. She never got like this. But now it's like she's on some aggressive-possessive type of shit. It wasn't a problem before when we fucked and I simply got on my way. Now she's on some wanting-to-know-my-business twenty-four-seven shit.

"Yo, I'm gonna call you," I tell her.

Her face saddens, but she keeps her composure. "Aiight, call me, fuck me, whatever," she dryly replies.

"Yo, what's up wit' you?"

"Nothin, just fuckin' go!" she says sucking her teeth.

I have no more words for her. I grab my jacket and bounce.

I pull up in front of a social club in Canarsie, Brooklyn, around eleven. I see Tyrone's BMW parked out front, gleaming in the night. I walk in casually, looking around the place for my peoples. The relaxed crowd is made up of city workers and single folks, out to mingle and have a good time in this so-so spot on Rockaway Avenue. I spot Tyrone at the end of the bar, chatting with some girl. He sees me and gestures for me to come over.

"Ja, what's good?" Tyrone says throwing his arm around me. His female friend looks at me and smiles. "Jakim, this is Lisa. Lisa, this is my boy from way back in da day. We grew up together. This niggah is like my fuckin' brother."

Lisa extends her hand toward me. "Nice to meet you," she says.

"Same here," I reply, shaking her hand. "Where's Evay?"

"Dat fat fuck. He should be on his way soon," Tyrone says. "Yo, what you drinking?"

"Get me a Hennessy and coke."

"I got you."

I grab a seat on one of the barstools and wait for my drink. The bartender, a middle aged, bald, black man, takes his sweet time with my drink.

I begin a conversation with Lisa. She's mad cool and pretty, too. She's brown-skinned with braids and resembles Sanaa Lathan a bit. She's wearing a tight skirt and stilettos, and her tits are mashed together under a brown halter top. I have to admit that I'm attracted to her.

"Jakim, huh?" she says looking at me inquisitively.

"Yeah, dat's me."

"Tyrone told me a lot about you."

"Oh, really?" I say turning to look at Tyrone, who's wearing a devilish grin. He shrugs his shoulders and calls out to the bartender.

"What did he actually say about me?" I ask.

"That when you come in, I'll definitely like what I see—and he was right," she says smiling.

I smile back at her, blushing a little. "I know you must get this a lot, but you know, you look like—"

"Sanaa Lathan?"

"Yes. Y'all could be sisters." She laughs. I take a sip from my drink and continue chatting with her. Tyrone comes up and gently nudges me in my side, indicating that he wants to speak with me alone for a minute. "Excuse me, Lisa," I say apologetically.

"No problem," she replies.

I follow Tyrone to the back where the restrooms are located. "Yo, I hooked you up, son," he says.

"What you mean?"

"She was on me earlier, sweating a niggah. But I put her on to you—told her dat you were comin' through in a few and y'all could link up," he informs me.

"Oh, word?"

"Yeah, niggah. You know we brothers. You my dawg. I know how fucked up you feel about Shana, you know what I'm sayin? You can never call me selfish. I'm lookin' out for you first, 'cause you deserve it. I'm helping you get through this."

I chuckle. "She ain't a prostitute?"

"Nah, niggah. She good. Yo, go get dat number. I got another surprise for you later on."

"Damn, niggah—what, it's my birthday or somethin? You Santa Clause now?" I joke.

"I'm in a good mood, Jakim. Fo' real."

I walk back over to Lisa and we continue to talk. I know she's feeling me. She's very flirtatious, always touching and feeling on me in a playful manner. I rub on her thigh subtly as I down my fourth drink for the night. She doesn't leave my side...and Tyrone is getting drunker by the minute.

Around one in the morning, Evay comes trotting in the place. He looks nervous and edgy. He walks up to Tyrone and acts like he doesn't see me. "Tyrone, I gotta holla at you fo' a minute," he says.

"Evay, what's up? You don't see a niggah?!" I exclaim.

"Oh, Jakim, I didn't even recognize you." He moves toward me and gives me dap, but the look on his face is nonchalant. He continues to talk to Tyrone. They eventually step outside for more privacy.

"What was that about?" Lisa asks.

I shrug my shoulders and move closer to her. "So, what turns you on?" I ask, forgetting about Tyrone and Evay.

"The way you look at and talk to me," she says passionately. I just grin.

After about fifteen minutes, I start getting curious about Tyrone and Evay. "Excuse me for a moment," I say to Lisa.

"Not a problem. I was about to leave anyway," she states.

"I'll walk you to your car." She collects her things and follows me out the door. When we get outside, I see Tyrone and Evay talking by the BMW. I take a closer look, and it appears that Evay is in tears. Then I see Tyrone suddenly smack the shit out of Evay. "Yo, yo, Tyrone, what's up?!" I holler, briskly walking toward them.

"Jakim, this ain't none of your business," Tyrone chides.

"But what's da deal with Evay? Why you smackin' him up?"

"Dis niggah's a fool, dat's why."

"Yo, Ty, let me expl–" Tyrone slaps the shit out of him again before he can say anything else.

"Shut da fuck, up!" Tyrone shouts. I'm clueless. I look over at Lisa, who just stands there staring, looking unaffected by the whole thing as she waits for me.

"Yo, Ja, walk Lisa to her car. I ain't going nowhere. I'm gonna finish talking to Evay," Tyrone says flatly.

I'm reluctant to leave. Evay just stands there like a big baby, allowing Tyrone to smack him up. I slowly make my way back over to Lisa. I glance over my shoulder at Evay. He looks so pitiful.

I walk Lisa a block away to her car, a silver Honda Accord. We stop and gaze at each other for a moment. "Look, what happened back there, that's y'alls business. I'm only interested in you." She reaches into her purse and pulls out a pen and a piece of paper. She quickly jots down her number. "Call me," she says placing her number in my hand. "We can have fun together." She leans forward and gives me a kiss on the lips.

I watch her get in her car and drive off. I quickly make my way back to Tyrone. He's alone when I get there. "Where's Evay?" I ask him.

Looking very annoyed, he says, "I told that bitch-ass niggah to get da fuck from out my face and go somewhere, before I end up really hurting his ass. But anyway, niggah, you got dat number or what?" he adds, his expression doing an instant three-sixty.

"Yeah, I got dat number," I say.

"My niggah. I'm tryin' to hook you up wit' some pussy, son. Lisa's a bad bitch. I know her pussy is off da hook. But c'mon, niggah, ride wit' me," he suggests.

"What about my car?"

"Leave it—ain't nobody gonna fuck wit' it." I get in the car with Tyrone without asking any further questions. He throws in a Jay-Z CD and drives north up Rockaway Avenue.

"Yo, what was dat shit about with Evay?"

"Nothin', he just a fuck-up sometimes. Don't stress it, Jakim."

I don't. I just ride along with him and let it be. It's his business. I'll probably talk to Evay about it later on anyway. I'll leave it alone tonight, since Tyrone's acting like it's my birthday.

We drive to Bed-Stuy, and he pulls up to that same three-story brownstone on Decatur Street with the three beautiful ladies. "What we doin' here again?" I ask.

Tyrone smirks and steps out of the car. Once again I follow him back up the steps and inside the building. The front door is already unlocked, and we proceed on. We walk down the hallway and into the living room.

"What's up, ladies," Tyrone says. Mandy, Sweet and Milk are all

present. They've all made it back safely from their drug runs. Sweet is seated on the couch, smoking on a cancer stick. Mandy is lounging on the floor
against the couch, munching on some cookies. And Milk just sits in a La-Z
Boy chair, in a pair of pink panties and a skimpy, blue T-shirt. All three of
them are watching television.

"Hey, Jakim," Milk says greeting me cheerfully.

"What's up, love," I happily reply.

Tyrone throws one arm around my shoulder. "Niggah, I noticed
you clockin' my bitches hard the other day when they got undressed." I
smile sheepishly. "Yeah, niggah, I saw you lookin', gettin' all excited and
shit. Dey do look good," he adds. I remain silent. "Go ahead, Jakim—pick
one."

"What?"

"Go ahead, choose a bitch. You know you wanna fuck one of 'em,
niggah. Pick one," he says persuasively. "Or do you want all three at once?"

I chuckle. "Damn, Ty, you tryin' to bury a niggah."

"I know you ain't scared of no pussy. Stop being modest, niggah,
and get your dick sucked or somethin'," Tyrone says. "Milk, c'mere." Milk
gets out of the chair and walks toward us. She stands in front of me and
Tyrone while the other two ladies continue watching TV. "He's cute, right?"
Tyrone asks her.

"Yeah, he's really cute," Milk responds, smiling flirtatiously at me.

"You wanna fuck him?"

"I'll do more than fuck him," Milk says seductively.

"There you go, niggah. Do you," Tyrone says egging me on. "Or do
you want another bitch? Mandy, you c'mere, too." Mandy gets up from the
floor and joins us. "My niggah here wanna get wit' you—you down?" Tyrone

asks her. She immediately nods. "See, niggah, I'm hookin' you up wit' that threesome. You ever had a threesome before, Jakim?" Tyrone asks me.

Honestly, I never have. I dreamt about it, but Shana, she wasn't down with rubbing up against another woman. She always claimed that she was strictly dickly. I can't front, though; I'm truly excited about the offer. Mandy and Milk, damn, they're gorgeous. And it has been a few hours since I got mine, even though being with Latish is enough. But the idea of a threesome has me on cloud nine.

"Yo, y'all, take this niggah upstairs to the master bedroom, and do y'all thing. And please, don't take it easy on my man; he knows what he's doing," Tyrone says before walking over to Sweet, who's still seated on the couch. Mandy and Milk grab me by both my arms and lead me up the stairs.

As soon as we enter the master bedroom, they're all over me, shedding my clothing and molesting me. Milk pushes me onto the king-sized bed and pulls down my jeans. My dick is in her mouth in no time.

Mandy takes care of me up top. She sucks on my nipples, chest and neck, and then slowly straddles my face, lowering her shaved pussy onto my lips. I eat her out for about ten minutes, as she gyrates her thick, bare hips against my jaw. "Aaaaaahhh...Aaaaaahhh....mmmmmm..." she pants and moans, pressing her hands against my chest.

Milk is doing her thing below, deep-throating my dick like a porn star, and then tea-bagging my nuts in her mouth. She raises my legs in the air, cocking them back like I'm a bitch. Then her mouth and tongue go from my balls to the center of my ass. Her tongue penetrates my asshole gently. I squirm and wiggle from the intense sensation. I have to stop eating Mandy out; I'm distracted by this new feeling. This is my first time ever getting my salad tossed.

Mandy raises herself up off my face and gently starts licking my chest. Then she begins sucking on my dick while Milk continues to eat out my ass. "Ooh....my God," I cry out like a bitch. "SHIT! Oh SHIT! Oh...my...God!"

I clutch the bed sheets tightly, closing my eyes with my legs still cocked back. Milk is showing me no mercy. She twirls her tongue around in my ass and I want to jump up, but Mandy holds me down as she sucks my dick like a fuckin' vacuum.

This pure bliss goes on for about fifteen minutes. I know Tyrone must hear me downstairs. Milk is the first to straddle me; she comes down on my dick and lets out a loud scream. She places her hands on my stomach and slowly starts to ride me. Mandy straddles my chest, facing Milk, and they begin to tongue each other down and fondle one another's breasts. I push on Mandy's back as I fuck Milk. Moments later, Mandy jumps on the dick and I begin fuckin' her, while Milk sucks on her nipples.

We fuck in position after position, rolling around on satin sheets and getting sweaty like there's no tomorrow. I fuck both hoes in the ass and ram my dick down their throats repeatedly. When it's all said and done, I come in Milk's mouth and without hesitation, she swallows my babies down her throat.

Moments later, I watch the two of them go at it, eating each other out in the sixty-nine position. With a bottle of Moet in my hand, I sit back and enjoy the show.

I pass out on the king-sized bed about an hour later. I wake up around seven in the morning between Mandy and Milk, who are still naked and nestled against me. I have a wicked hangover. I almost consumed that entire bottle of Moet. I have to force myself out of the bed.

I quickly start getting dressed. Both ladies are still asleep and look like they're not getting up any time soon. I make my way downstairs and see Tyrone passed out on the couch with Sweet. They're both ass naked. I know he had a good time last night.

I gently nudge Tyrone, trying to wake his ass up. I need to get home, and my car is still parked in Canarsie. "Get up, Ty...I need to get to my car," I quietly say. He moves around a little and grumbles something, but he never opens his eyes. "Tyrone, yo, I need a ride," I persist. "Wake your ass up."

Finally, he opens his eyes and looks up at me. "Yo, Jakim, it's too fuckin' early in da morning for this shit. Take a cab home or somethin'."

"What?"

"Yo, take a hundred out my pocket. I'm too fucked up to drive." I sigh irately.

Sweet wakes up. "I gotta pee," she says. She climbs over Tyrone and, still naked, walks to the bathroom. I can't help but stare at her—especially her backside. Her ass puts J-Lo's to shame. *I shoula got at dat, too.*

After Sweet is inside the bathroom, I walk over to Tyrone's jeans on the floor and take five twenty-dollar bills out of one of the pockets. There's a wad of cash, almost twenty-five hundred.

"Yo, I'm out," I tell Tyrone. He doesn't even budge. He's sound asleep again, snoring like an old man. As I prepare to make my exit, I hear the toilet flush. Sweet steps out of the bathroom and glances at me, smiling.

"You leaving?" she asks.

"Yeah," I reply, studying her rawness.

"You coming back, right? Next time you come through, maybe you and me can fuck."

"Hey, no doubt," I say beaming. She makes her way back over to the couch and lies next to Tyrone.

I step outside and pull out my cell phone to call a cab. The screen tells me that I've missed three calls. I'm shocked when I see that two of them are from Shana. I quickly check my messages. The first one is from Latish, claiming how much she misses me and wants me to call her back whenever I get the message. I delete it quickly and go on to the next one, from Shana.

"Jakim, when you get this, please give me a call. I need to talk to you. If you want, you can come by the house. But call me...bye."

Shana has rarely called my phone since we've been separated. I try not to get excited; she might just want something from me—probably money or a ride somewhere. I know it's not the dick. I try not to stress myself thinking about what she wants. I call a cab, and it arrives in ten minutes.

During the ride, I contemplate giving Shana a call back. I want to know what's up. But I decide against it. Why give her the satisfaction of calling her back right away, when she's constantly blowing me off? Fuck that. I got enough ass in one day to hold me over for a week.

Shana is still on my mind when I get to my car. I start thinking about whether she needs me for something really important, an emergency. I know I have to put my ego to the side and give her a call back. I love her too much to put her on hold and ignore her.

I call Shana when I get home. She picks up. She seems upset about something. I'm baffled when she tells me about Terry's murder. I didn't know the guy all that well. I just know that he and Shana dated for a short time, and he was a few years older than me.

We talk for hours, and I listen to her cry like a baby. As always, I promise that I'm here for her whenever she needs me. I know it's a promise that I'll always keep.

SHANA 9

Numerous bitches are at Terry's wake. I've come with Naja to pay my respects. Terry has so many women shedding tears over his death that it's unbelievable. His baby mother—well, the only one I knew about before today—flew in from North Carolina. He actually had four different baby mothers and six kids. He cheated on all of them, and he was engaged three times.

His mother flew in from Trinidad. She's hysterical over her son's death. I'm surprised that she even recognizes me when I greet her.

I'm dressed in a black skirt and cream blouse; wearing all black is not my thing. There are a handful of mourners dressed down in all black, but the majority of people attending the wake are in everyday attire. Naja stays by my side and even holds my hand for comfort.

It's an open-casket wake, and from where I'm standing, Terry looks peaceful in his gray, three-piece, pinstriped suit. We go up to view his body, and I nearly break down in tears. It hurts me to see him like this, but it disturbs me even more to think that I'm probably fucking the prime suspect in his murder. But no one knows for sure who killed Terry. He was found in an abandoned car shot three times, once in the neck and twice in the chest.

"You okay, Shana?" Naja asks me as she wipes away my tears with her free hand. I nod and continue gazing down at him. He was my second love. We finish paying our respects and head toward the back.

"How you doing, Shana?" a slim, dark-skinned gentleman asks as he approaches Naja and I. At first I don't recognize him. But after a few seconds I do and greet him with a hug. It's Terry's best friend, Terrance. It's been three years since I've last seen him. He looks different; he's cut off his braids. We look each other over for a moment, and then he breaks the silence. "I miss him. That was my fucking boy."

I give him another hug, comforting him as best as I can. I'm speechless. I haven't told anyone that the last time I saw Terry he was getting beat down by Tyrone in a burger joint, while I just stood there and watched. I dread the memory of that night.

I feel my tears about to flow freely again as I hold Terrance in my arms. Back in high school, he and Terry were inseparable; they did everything together. Terrance was messing with Sasha, and Terry was my sweetheart. We had some wild and crazy nights together.

"Do they know who killed him?" Naja asks.

"Nah, the police don't have any suspects right now," Terrance says. "The crew is wilding out, though; they about ready to murder somebody."

When he said 'the crew,' he meant Terry's cousins and their boys. They're a rowdy and ruthless bunch of hoodlums and thugs. When we were together, Terry would always talk about his cousins and how wild and fucked up they were. He told me that one night they robbed a gas station clerk and shot him in the foot so he couldn't chase them as they just walked out with armloads of his stuff. They went to school about ten percent of the time, and when they were there, all they did was fight, harass other students and gamble in the hallways.

Terrance leaves us to go and view the body. He appears reluctant; it's tearing him apart to have to see his boy lying there dead. I just stand there with my arms folded across my chest, trying to relax myself.

Sasha arrives with a few friends. When I see her enter the room, I start to cry; all of this drama is too much for me. I start to reminisce about the past, on how things used to be. Now everything is changing.

Sasha looks over at me. I meet her gaze...there will be peace between us tonight; Terry's death sets our differences aside. I start to smile at her, but it's just not happening; I remember that the bitch tried to cut me.

Naja comes from out of the bathroom. She sees Sasha and asks, "You ready to go?"

I nod. *Everything is gonna be all right.* We head for the exit, saying our goodbyes to friends and acquaintances that we pass along the way.

When we get outside, I see a group of young men, talking and smoking. I throw my hand over my mouth after recognizing three of them. One of them looks my way and taps the other two on the shoulder. Now they're all looking at me. Scared, I hurry by them, rushing my ass to the car with Naja close behind, trying to keep up.

"What's da matter, girl?!" she shouts, sounding out of breath.

"Nothin'," I say.

When we get in the car, I quickly lock my door and slump down in the seat. I peep out the window at them as we drive by. They're still watching me. They're the three guys who were in the burger joint the night Terry got his ass whipped. I know they know my face. I'm so fuckin' petrified.

I look like I've just seen a ghost when Naja pulls up in front of my place. She keeps asking me what's wrong. I blame it on the wake, give her a hug and get my ass inside the house. My mother's home, thank God; I wouldn't feel too safe being alone in the house tonight.

Jakim stops by the next morning. He tells me he's sorry about what happened to Terry and tries to console me. It feels so good being in his arms. I want to tell him about what happened in the burger joint, about how I was there and witnessed everything up close. But I can't. I also want to confess to him everything that's been going on with Tyrone and me. My common sense tells me not to. I don't want him to start flipping and possibly have another fucked up incident on my conscience.

Jakim holds me in his arms as we lay propped up against a few pillows on my bed. He massages my shoulders, plays with my hair and whispers comforting words in my ear. He tells me that everything's gonna be all right. I turn around and give him a quick kiss on the cheek. I stare into his lovely brown eyes and then give him another short kiss on the lips. "Do you still love me?" I ask him.

"Of course I do," he quickly answers. We start tonguing each other down. He holds me tightly, and the taste of his tongue heats my panties. I want to feel him inside of me. I kiss all around his neck as he explores my body with his hands. He pulls off my jeans and I unbutton his shirt, tickling his chest with my fingers. We're completely naked in no time. He climbs on top of me and slowly reintroduces himself to something he's been missing for a while. "Jakim!" I cry out, as he slowly starts stroking it.

"Everything is going to be okay, Shana. I promise," he gently says. I just close my eyes and give him my body. It feels so good, but then I start feeling guilty about being with Tyrone.

"I miss you so much," Jakim adds.

"Aaaaaahhh, I miss you too, baby," I softly reply. I grip his back and wrap my legs around his waist as he thrusts himself into me. "Fuck me, Jakim! Fuck me!"

"I got you, Shana." Jakim begins kissing me passionately. "I never wanna let you go again."

The sex is raw, fast and very pleasing. It's so good, and when he comes inside me, it feels like Mount St. Helen has erupted between my thighs. Jakim holds me in his arms after we're done and we both fall asleep.

Jakim wakes up in the afternoon, naked and happy as ever. I'm already dressed. "You okay, baby?" he asks getting up from the bed.

"I need you to leave, Jakim," I say.

"Why? What's the matter?" he asks, coming toward me still undressed.

"I can't explain why. I just need for you to go."

He just looks at me and then begins to search for his stuff, as I stand near the doorway watching him. "You know, Shana, I don't fuckin' get you. Let me know what's happening between us, because you're buggin' me the fuck out right now," he says fastening his jeans.

I remain silent. It's not that I don't want to answer him; I just can't because I don't really know what's going on with me. After he finishes dressing, he storms by me, almost knocking me down. He goes to the door, turns around and gives me a cold look. "You're fuckin' someone else, aren't you?" I don't answer.

Later that evening as I'm walking home from the store, Tyrone's black BMW pulls up to the curb beside me. I freak out and start to quickstep, nearly jogging to my house. Tyrone gets out of the car. "Shana, hold up. I wanna talk to you!"

I'm in no mood to see him right now, but hearing his voice makes me stop in my tracks; my body numbs like I'm playing freeze tag. I press the bag of groceries I'm carrying to my chest and slowly turn around to see that he's already a few feet behind me. He looks serious, maybe a little too serious. I just stand there, watching him approach me. I'm not scared of him; I just don't know what he's capable of doing.

"Shana, I just wanna talk to you," he says in a low and calm voice. "C'mon, let's go for a ride." He extends his hand out to me.

"But I gotta take this bag of groceries home," I say.

"It can't wait? This is really important."

"No, Tyrone, my mother is really waiting on this stuff," I say taking two steps back.

"All right, then let me give you a ride to your crib." I knew he wasn't going to take no for an answer, so I get in the car.

During the ride to my place, Tyrone remains quiet, focusing his attention on the road. I just stare out of the passenger window. I want to ask him if he had something to do with Terry's death, but I'm hesitant to do so. We pull up in front of my house, and I slowly begin to step out of the car. He grabs me by my coat and says, "Shana, promise me that you're gonna come right back. This is something really important."

I nod and he releases his grip on me. Once inside, I place the bag of groceries on the kitchen counter, walk back to the front and peer out of the window at Tyrone's car. I'm reluctant to go back out there, but I promised him that I would return. My mother comes out of her bedroom wrapped in her bathrobe, ready to light a cigarette. I know she just got finished riding Danny's dick; her hair looks atrocious, plus I see him lying on her bed as I quickly look past her into her bedroom.

"You got my stuff?" she asks.

I point to the kitchen as I go back to peering out of the window. "What you looking at?" she asks.

"Nothin'. I'll be back," I tell her as I exit out the front door.

I cautiously approach Tyrone's car. I'm a bit nervous; I don't know what to expect. I get in on the passenger side and close the door.

"What's so important, Tyrone?" I ask.

"I haven't seen you in a few days."

"I've been really busy."

"C'mon, let's go for a quick ride," he suggests, turning the ignition and starting up the car.

"Go where, Tyrone? I got things to do today. I can't be driving all over Queens and Brooklyn with you."

"Shana, why you trippin? Is it because of that fool's death?"

"It might be...you tell me," I say folding my arms across my chest.

"You think I was the one that smoked him, don't you?" Tyrone says turning off the car.

"Well the way you beat him down the other night was a clear sign that you two didn't get along." I turn away from him and look out the window, watching a few kids play- wrestling on someone's front lawn.

"Shana, look at me...look at me!" he shouts. I slowly turn back around to face him and look into his eyes. "I didn't smoke Terry. Believe me, yo. And if you're thinking that I did, then get the thought of it out of your fuckin' head," he says.

"Well, if *you* didn't, then who did?"

"I don't fuckin know! That niggah had enemies."

"Terry?"

"Shana, let me tell you something about your boy: Yeah, he owed me money, and didn't pay up. But he owed a lot more money to people who are far more vicious and dangerous than me. Why da fuck do you think he got up and just left for North Carolina—to get out of paying his debts. Yo, your boy Terry was foul!"

I don't believe him. Terry wasn't that kind of person. He was an honor student for God's sake! He was one of those pretty boys who got manicures, shopped more than me and got his haircut twice a week. I remember one time he got pulled over for speeding, and was so nervous speaking to the police that he started stuttering.

"Shana, why you trippin' over his death anyway? Ain't like y'all was still together."

"That's not the point. He was my friend. How much did he owe you anyway?"

"Yo, Shana, I don't wanna discuss that sorry mutha-fucka's debt right now. Let it be."

"Why?"

"Shana, just let it be!"

I hate when he omits vital information about himself, his life and his experiences. I mean, I'm fuckin' him; the least he can do is open up some. And if he *didn't* do it, I'm sure he knows who did. Tyrone knows almost every thug, killer and hood in Queens and Brooklyn.

I peer over at him. I know he knows something; he just isn't saying. I don't know what it is with him. I just can't figure him out...maybe he isn't meant to be figured out.

"Shana, look, I'm falling in love with you, and I would never do anything to hurt you," he says leaning forward, placing his hand on my thigh.

He presses his lips against mine, trying to pry my mouth open with his tongue. I feel his hand deep in between my legs. "Tyrone, not now," I beg, slowly moving his hand away.

"What's da matter? You don't want me?"

"It's just that I got a lot on my mind right now, Tyrone. I just need to be by myself for a while."

He slowly moves back into his seat. "Shana, don't be stressing over your ex's death. I'm sayin', life moves on, and I wanna move on with you," he says taking my hand in his. I know this is a side of Tyrone that people rarely see—a sweet, loving and romantic Tyrone—not the usual, shoot-'em-up hood roughneck. I'm now starting to believe every word he's said to me. He leans forward again to try to give me another kiss. I go along with this one. His phone goes off, breaking the spell. He looks at the number and places the phone back on his hip. He gives me a quick peck on the lips.

"I gotta go, Shana, this is important," he says restarting the car. "I'll give you a call some time tonight."

I step out of the car and watch him pull off. The temperature has dropped rapidly. I'm shivering and wonder if this is a sign. I run back into the house, where I will remain for the rest of the night.

It's been two weeks since Terry's wake, and my escapades with Tyrone are becoming more frequent. I've even stayed a few days over at his place. He has the gift of gab; he could talk the panties off of a nun. He makes me dinner, takes me shopping and even eats my pussy out for hours.

I've stopped asking questions about Terry's death. It's obvious that Tyrone isn't ever going to break and say anything anyway, so why keep trying? I've taken his advice and gotten over it.

After several more days pass, I go out shopping with Naja and Latish. We're looking for outfits to wear to a party tonight. Tyrone gave me five hundred dollars. We head out to Fifth Avenue in Manhattan. When we're done shopping, the girls and I decide that it would be best for everyone to get dressed over at my place.

By evening, we're all buggin' out, talking and watching *Boyz N the Hood* on cable in my room when Latish asks, "So Shana, what's going on with you and Tyrone? I mean, y'all been pretty tight these past few days...."

"We're doing our thang," I reply.

"So, is it really over between you and Jakim?"

"No, he's still my boo."

"Shana, you know you're playing with fire, right!" Naja says shaking her head.

"Please, Naja, I got the heat under control. And like I said before, Jakim and I are not officially together again, so I can spread my legs for whoever I want to," I say, laying back on the bed and parting my legs.

Latish starts laughing. "G-i-r-r-l, you crazy!"

As I prop myself back up into a sitting position, the doorbell rings. The girls look over at me. I shrug my shoulders; I'm not expecting company.

"Could it be Tyrone's sexy ass?" Latish teases.

I go to see who's at the door. I look out the window and see Jakim's car parked outside. I sigh and slowly open the door.

"What's up?" he says stepping inside the front door.

"Why you here?" I ask.

"I'm sayin', I ain't been through in a minute," he replies taking off his coat and leaning forward to toss it onto the arm of the couch like I've asked him to stay.

"Well, me and the girls are about to go out tonight, so you can't stay long."

He probably wants some pussy tonight. He got a little taste of it again and wants seconds. I know he's horny; I can see it in his eyes...antsy muthafucka. He moves in close to me, placing his arms around my waist and tries to kiss me on the neck. I pull away from him, smelling the liquor on his breath.

"What's da matter? A brotha can't get no love from the woman he loves?"

"Jakim, you're drunk. Go home."

"I'm not drunk, boo."

I grab his coat off the couch and pass it to him. He comes toward me again with open arms. I push him back. Hearing laughter coming from my bedroom, he quickly turns his head in that direction. "Who you got in there with you?"

"My friends, Jakim."

He moves past me, hurrying toward my bedroom. I follow him. He pushes open my bedroom door and sees Naja and Latish sitting on my bed, half-naked and getting ready for the party tonight. Startled, Naja runs and covers herself with a towel hanging over the back of a chair, but Latish remains seated on the bed in her panties and T-shirt.

"Sorry, ladies," Jakim says.

"Hi, Jakim," Latish says with a broad smile on her face.

"Jakim, get out of here!" Naja screams out, embarrassed that he saw her with nearly nothing on.

"Jakim, can you please leave!" I yell.

He walks back into the living room, stands by the door and says, "I'm sayin', Shana, when you and me gonna really get together and hook up again?"

"I don't know, Jakim." He starts to say something but thinks better of it and walks through the door. I lock it behind him and go back to my bedroom with the girls.

"G-i-r-r-l, he got it bad for you. You need to let the brotha be," Latish says laughing.

"Let's just forget everything and get ready for this fuckin' party tonight," I say.

It takes each of us two hours to get dressed. Naja spends nearly an hour in the bathroom, and Latish takes more time applying her make-up and doing her hair. We finally leave my house at ten o' clock.

We arrive at the Executive around ten-forty. The Executive is a popular club in Queens located on Linden Boulevard. Every Saturday night there's something going down there. Famous rappers and other celebrities frequently stop in to get their party on. The line is getting long, so Naja hurries to park her four-door, blue Pontiac.

It's our night, and we're dressed like divas. I'm wearing a blue, belled Lurex herringbone mini skirt, knee-high boots and a cream turtle-neck sweater. Latish is wearing a mini, too, but not as fly as mine. Naja is wearing a denim skirt and a pair of knee-high boots, similar to mine.

We step up to the line, and it seems like every male is breaking his neck to howl and whistle at us. And of course, once again, the bitches are hating.

Once inside, we hear the speakers blasting Biggie. The club is nearly filled to capacity. "I'm at da bar," Latish says.

Naja and I stand around for a moment. One guy blows me a kiss. I don't catch it. It was probably tainted with his chapped lips. I know he's heard of ChapStick.

Beside the sprinkling of a few ugly men, there are a number of cuties in the place. One guy with a bald head catches my attention. He's looking too good. As I'm eyeing him, a guy with a fucked up bowl cut and bucked teeth walks up, trying to holla at me. He offers me a drink. I refuse his offer. He smiles. I shoot him down with an ice cold stare. Then he tries to talk to Naja, and she turns his ugly ass down, too. Now he has the nerve to try to talk to Latish. She's nicer to him than Naja and I were. He buys her two drinks, and then she tells him to fuck off.

I go crazy when my jam, *Lifestyles of the Rich and Shameless* by Lost Boyz, starts blasting over the speakers. I love this song. I grab the nearest cutie and start grinding up on him. The muthafucka doesn't have any rhythm, so I dismiss him and move on to the next fine man who isn't cursed with having two left feet.

"My name's Charlie," he whispers in my ear. I give him a strange look; I don't care to have his name. I just want to dance. "So, what's your name, beautiful?"

I look at him and say, "Goodbye!" and move on to the next guy. Naja is laughing, as she and Latish saw everything.

The third guy is really cute. He has curly hair, brown eyes, a goatee and a nice build. We're grooving together nicely. He's real smooth, and he keeps his mouth shut. My joint comes to an end, and I need to take a breather. We head to the bar, and he offers to buy me a drink. He doesn't say anything; he just uses hand gestures.

"Damn, boo, don't hurt nobody tonight," some idiot shouts as he passes by. I just ignore him.

I give the bartender my order. Then I take a seat on one of the stools next to my male company. He's definitely fine. He pulls out a wad of hundreds to pay for my drink. I wonder why he isn't talking. I mean, now when I want a guy to talk, he doesn't say a word. I smile at him and sip on my drink. "So what's your name?" I finally ask.

"C-Cory."

"You're not getting yourself a drink, Cory?" He shakes his head no. "So, Cory, you not gonna ask me for my name?"

He hesitates to speak. "Wh-wh-what...i...i...is...yo-your...name?" he finally stammers out.

I cover my mouth with my hand. *Holy shit!* It took him almost a minute to ask me my name. He just looks at me as I start to chuckle, with tears of laughter forming in my eyes. He's cute and all, but the speech impediment ruins it. I gulp down the remainder of my drink.

"Ca-ca-ca-ca-can—I—I—b-b-b-b—buy—yo-you— a-a-a-an-an-another—one?" he asks.

The lady sitting next to me is cracking up. I shake my head no. I don't even tell him my name.... Oh-my-God! The cutest guy in the place, and he has a serious speech problem.

"Shana," I blurt out. I've decided to be nice.

"H-huh?"

"Remember you asked me for my name? Well, my name is Shana,"

I say.

He is so fine; he deserves to know my name, even though he can't talk for shit. Latish and Naja come over, admiring Cory. They stare him down, looking all in his grill. "Damn, he's fine!" Latish whispers in my ear, unaware of his little flaw.

I kind of still want to get with him; what he lacks in words, he makes up for on the dance floor. I pass Cory my home phone number and he passes me his. Then I give him a kiss on the cheek and whisper in his ear. "I'll call you and we'll hook up later, aiight?" He smiles.

Latish is drunk as usual. She's slumped over at the bar as Naja gets her groove on with some fine brotha with dreads. I go on a search for the ladies room. "Fuckin' bitch!" I hear someone say after bumping into me as I make my way through the tight crowd. I can't see who said it; I'd scratch their fuckin' eyes out. I blow it off and continue to look for the bathroom.

Three ladies enter as I'm running the comb through my hair in the bathroom mirror. I pay them no attention, and I begin to freshen up.

"Your name's Shana?" one of the girls walks up behind me and asks. By her reflection in the mirror, I see that she's about my height, with chinky brown eyes, cornrows and an attitude. She's beautiful—almost as stunning as me.

"Why? Who wants to know?" I say turning my head slightly.

Her girls have her back. They surround me, one to my left and the other one to my right. I know this situation far too well. We used to beat bitches down in Jamaica High School like this, catching them when they went into the bathroom. We called it 'the web' because it was impossible for a girl to run or escape. You had to accept your ass whooping. Now, here I am, being put in the same predicament. The pathway to the door is blocked by the short and stocky girl to my right.

"Stay da fuck away from my fuckin man, bitch!" the chinky-eyed girl shouts.

"Excuse me," I reply, "I don't even *know* your fuckin' man."

"Yo, Chinky, fuck this bitch up!" the girl on my left yells. She's tall, with a red scarf wrapped around her head. I shoot her down with a wicked stare.

Chinky, I know the name; it travels around the way. Chinky is supposed to be this ruthless bitch from the Jamaica housing area, AKA Forty Projects. She runs with a ruthless crew. They're known for slashing bitches with box cutters across their faces, leaving permanent and disfiguring scars. Almost every girl who comes across her fears her, like she's God almighty! They call her Chinky because of her eyes; they're small and slanted, like she's Chinese. And it's like every niggah is sweating her. But I've only just heard about her. I've never met her—until now.

"Bitch, do not fuckin play stupid with me," Chinky shrieks as she reaches into her right pocket.

"Who is your man?" I demand to know now.

"Tyrone!"

"What?" *I can't believe it.*

"Yo, fuck this bitch up, Chinky," the tall girl on my left shouts. I'm about gettin' tired of her ass.

"Dat's my kids' father, and I know you fuckin him!" Chinky says, staring at me with ice-cold eyes.

"I didn't even know Tyrone had any ki—"

"He got two by me, bitch!" she yells.

My first instinct tells me to just throw the first punch and set it off.

Why waste any time? I'm about to become a victim in this club tonight. Both of my homegirls are outside partying, and they have no idea that I'm about to get jumped.

My situation goes from hectic to critical when Chinky pulls out a small box cutter. The tall girl to my left does the same. Here I am, about to get my shit sliced because Tyrone neglected to mention that he has two children by this crazy bitch. I pray for someone to come in the bathroom and help me out. Now is a good time to have Sasha by my side; she can definitely throw down. I clinch my fists and prepare for the worst.

"Fuckin bitch!" I scream out and lunge at Chinky with the quickness, hitting her on the head before she can even attempt to cut me with that box cutter. Both her partners come to her aid, but I manage to knock their weapons out of their hands. Thank God! However, I fall to the floor, and now I'm getting stomped and kicked by all three.

"Fuck dat bitch up! Fuck dat bitch up!" I hear one of them yell. Chinky grabs me by my hair and drags me all across the bathroom floor like I'm some kind of rag doll.

"Get off me, bitch!" I say kicking my legs wildly about.

I manage to kick Chinky in her shin, crippling her for a few seconds, but I can't get her two girlfriends off of me. I look around for one of the box cutters while I'm getting beat down, and I see that I knocked one under a bathroom stall next to the toilet. I try to reach for it, but the tall bitch is too strong. She yokes me up with some wrestling move.

The short and stocky bitch gives me a serious scratch across the eye. Chinky retrieves one of the box cutters and comes swinging. The tall one holds me from behind. I throw up both my legs and start kicking at her. There's no way my face is going to be looking like a jigsaw puzzle. I scream and kick frantically now. The music in the club is so loud; I'm sure no one can hear me screaming for help.

I manage to kick Chinky in her face, striking her across her mouth with the heel of my boot. The tall bitch finally lets me go, seeing Chinky's mouth coated with blood. Chinky throws both of her hands over her mouth and begins to scream. She's in some serious pain. But that doesn't stop the other two from fuckin' me up on the floor as I lay in the fetal position.

They go buck wild on me. I've never hurt so badly in my entire life. These bitches from Forty Projects are stomping, kicking, punching, slapping and even spitting on me. I know for sure that they must have yanked out a handful of my hair. I'm nothing but a helpless bitch. What seems to have gone on for hours has really only lasted for about three minutes. Security finally arrives.

It's a big scene. It seems like the entire club is in the ladies bathroom. Everyone wants to see what's going on. The club's security tries to get everything under control. They try to give Chinky medical aid, but she's shouting and cursing me out something terrible. "It's on, bitch! I'm gonna kill dat fuckin' bitch! I'm gonna kill dat stupid fuckin' bitch!" she yells, still bleeding from her mouth.

"Whatever, stupid bitch!" I shout in return as security holds me back from attacking her again.

They order everyone out of the bathroom. The crowd parts, making room for our exit. I see Naja. She looks stunned. "I know dat ain't my girl, Shana! Shana, what happened?!" she says. Then she looks at Chinky and her girls with fire. "I'm gonna fuck you up, bitch!" she shouts at Chinky.

It takes about twenty minutes for everything to return to normal. Unfortunately the club is shut down for the night and the police are called.

Eight squad cars arrive at the scene. EMS workers come for Chinky. They have to fight with her to put her in the ambulance, and I have to ride down to the precinct with those other two bitches who tried to jump me. Naja says she'll follow me down to the precinct. It looks like she'll have to drag Latish's drunken ass along...*I should have just left with Cory when I had the chance.*

It's around eight in the morning when I finally leave the precinct. I gave the police my version of what happened in the bathroom. They still have those two stink, nasty bitches in custody for assault with those razors.

Naja and LaTish are waiting for me. They look dog-tired, having sat almost all night on those hard, wooden, nasty and dirty benches in the precinct. I give them both a hug. I explain everything to them in the car as Naja drives me home. She's so fuckin hyped; she's ready to kill Chinky. I'm really okay, though, except for a few bruises and scratches. But Chinky caught the worst of it. I busted her fuckin' jaw with the bottom of my boot, knocking two of her teeth out. I let her know that she was fuckin' with the wrong bitch!

My real beef is with Tyrone. He should have told me that he was fuckin' with Chinky, and that he fathered two of her children. But Naja says on the way home in the car that the bitch was probably lying about Tyrone. She's straight up trifling anyway. I know I have to get to the bottom of things. I plan to have a few words with Tyrone as soon as possible. I don't care if I have to go to his apartment and knock down his front door.

After Naja pulls up to my house, I give her another hug and thank her. She tells me to call her soon. We're going to handle this situation, even if we have to get a crew together and go to Forty Projects to whip that bitch's ass.

I go in the house and see that my aunt and moms are already up cooking breakfast. They notice the bruises and scratches on my face and become hysterical, shouting, "Shana, what the fuck happened to you?!"

I tell them about my brawl with Chinky and her crew. They're ready to start making phone calls and hunt Chinky down. I have to love them for that, but I tell them it's not necessary.

My moms fixes me a plate of grits and fish. She tries to pamper me the best she can, treating me like I'm still her baby girl.

The next morning, I take a cab over to Tyrone's apartment in Rochdale. I've already tried to call his house number and his cell, but he didn't pick up either.

I bang on his door for about five minutes until his roommate, Evay, comes to the door with no shirt on. "Why you come bangin' on my door so fuckin' early in da morning like you da police or somethin'?!" he hollers.

"Where's Tyrone?" I say storming by him, making my way into the apartment.

"He ain't here."

"Then where is he?"

"He's been gone for a week—went out of town to do business with some peeps."

I don't believe him. He could be covering up his man's whereabouts. Tyrone practically tells him what to do. He controls him like he's a worthless, brainless zombie.

"I'm sayin', Shana, he bounced some time yesterday, him and this other dude. You know dat niggah don't really tell me shit."

"Whatever!"

I go into Tyrone's bedroom and look around. His bed is still made.

I search his closet and see clothes missing, along with a small duffel bag he always keeps in the corner on the floor. I guess Evay was really telling the truth.

"C'mon, Shana, you know you can't be in here while he's away," he pleads.

"I'm his woman; I can go anywhere I fuckin' please," I chide.

He just looks at me, with his sorry ass, standing by the doorway. "Do you know this bitch named Chinky?" I ask him. The expression on his face tells me he knows something.

"Chinky?"

"Yeah, Chinky. You see my fuckin' face? That bitch tried to jump me in a club the other night."

"Word!"

"Yes, word. So is Tyrone still fuckin' with her?"

"Nah, Shana, I don't know nothin' about that," he says, looking down at the floor.

I'm heated. "Dat bitch told me that Tyrone is the father of two of her kids."

"Word, she told you that?"

"Yeah, I wanna know if it's true or not."

"C'mon, Shana, that's his business. I can't be telling you his business like that when he ain't even here."

"Why not?"

"Ty's my man. He trusts me."

I just stand there staring at him, thinking about doing the impossible. Evay knows what's up with Chinky and Tyrone, but he fears Tyrone so much that he won't tell me. You cannot live with a man and not know some details about him. I just want to know something. I go up to him and gently grab a hold of his dick through his dirty sweats. I slowly massage his shit with my hand and softly whisper in his ear. "If you tell me everything I need to know, I'll suck your little dick right here in this room." He looks at me and starts grinning as his dick gets hard in my hand. I force a phony and seductive smile, squeezing his dick tighter. He cracks like a walnut.

After he's done singing like a bird, telling me everything I need to know, he drops his sweats to the floor, exposing himself and waits for his reward. I look down and laugh. His dick is a little bigger than I thought, but I'm still not sucking it. And it nearly turns my stomach, just seeing him naked, with his fat belly hanging over his dick. I'd have to lift up his gut just to get to it. It's not happening—not in this lifetime. He remains standing there, waiting for my precious lips to touch his shit. I just sigh and walk off, leaving him standing there harder than the man of steel himself.

"Shana, what's up?" he says chasing me to the outside corridor, pulling up his sweats. He then grabs my shoulder from behind.

"Don't touch me!" I scream, knocking his hand away.

"I'm sayin', you ain't gonna suck my dick?"

"Hell no, muthafucka! What do I look like to your ass?"

"Oh, that's fucked up, bitch!" he shouts, looking like he wants to knock me the fuck out. But he knows better if he loves and values his life.

"You ain't nothin' but a triflin'-ass hoe—stink-ass bitch! You ain't all dat!" he continues to shout as I wait for the elevator.

I flip him the bird and give him a nasty look. Then to tease him, I stick out my tongue seductively, lick my lips and grab one of my breasts. He's beyond furious, and he goes back to the apartment and slams the door behind him.

It's true. Tyrone is the father of two of Chinky's kids. And come to find out, she's also two months pregnant by him, which means he's still messing with her. The way Evay was explaining it, Chinky is his wifey—his main hoe. If that's the case, then what the fuck am I to him? Evay told me they've been together for seven years now. He also told me that Tyrone has another eighteen-month-old boy by some ho out in New Jersey. My ass is so hurt. First Chinky, now this.

When I arrive at my crib, Jakim is waiting out front. We embrace hello. Shit, his boy is playing me out, and he's in love with me...but I'm in love with his boy. This is like some Jerry Springer shit.

I mean, at first it was just a sexual thing with Tyrone, but then I let my feelings get involved. I should have just kept it sexual. But the dick was too good.

Jakim asks me if I want to go for a ride. I say yes. I need to get out of here, go some fuckin' where. Anywhere is better than here. We end up at the studio in Flatbush, Brooklyn.

I sit on one of the spinning stools, listening to Jakim rhyme on the mic. He has true talent. He's with a group called The Queens Magnificent. Me, personally, I think the name is corny.

Listening to Jakim rhyme actually makes me feel good and makes me forget about everything that's going on with Tyrone. Heck, I even get on the mic, singing and acting like I'm some diva.

After leaving the studio, we go back to his crib in Jamaica, Queens, by Baisley Park. Jakim lives with his father. His mother is a struggling actress and lives in Los Angles. He sees her maybe five or six times a year, including Christmas, Thanksgiving and birthdays. He showed me a picture of her once. She's beautiful.

We retreat to Jakim's room, where I fuck the shit outta him. I end up spending the night. The following morning, I tell myself to leave Tyrone alone and focus all of my time and energy on Jakim. Easier said than done.

SHANA 10

It's three days before Thanksgiving. My mother plans to have dinner at our house with family and friends. The last family function we had, two of my uncles got into a fistfight over a woman.

It's been almost two weeks since I've heard from Tyrone. Jakim and I are hitting it off, though, but nothing is official yet.

The girls and I went out partying last night. I met a few cuties, but they weren't anything to make a big fuss over. I didn't get in the house till six this morning.

I'm still in my skirt, blouse and stockings when I wake up with a wicked hangover to the sound of bedposts knocking against my mother's wall. She's moaning and calling out Danny's name. I try to go back to sleep, but hearing them having sex in the next room is keeping me awake. I wonder if the dick is really that good. I get out of bed and go into the bathroom to take a nice hot shower.

I'm in the shower, washing every detail and inch of my body. I let the water cascade off my nipples, down between my legs. I think I hear movement in the bathroom. I peep from behind the curtain and see Danny standing over the toilet, butt- ass naked, taking a piss. My eyes widen as I gaze down at his dick. *Damn, he's hung*. I can now understand why my mother was howling so loudly. He continues to pee like I'm not even there. I know he feels me watching him. "You left da bathroom door open," he nonchalantly states.

"Oh," I reply.

"It's cool," he says. I take a deep breath. I'm in shock, and I'm starting to get aroused. "You all right?" he asks, looking over at me as I continue to peek at him from behind the shower curtain.

"Yeah, I'm cool."

"This doesn't bother you?"

"Nah, it don't, it really don't." God, he has a big dick. I watch him shake his dick and flush the toilet. He goes over to the sink, washes his hands and then starts to brush his teeth. I continue looking at him like I'm not in the shower with the water still running.

"You gonna be in there all day?" he asks.

"Oh, no," I respond awkwardly. I turn off the shower and step out of the tub, dripping wet. Danny glances over at me and smiles. I reach for my towel. I'm not uncomfortable being naked in front of him. I want him to see me naked. I stare at him as I continue to dry myself off. He just stands there watching me, hard as a rock.

My heart begins to beat rapidly. My pussy is moist and I can feel my nipples hardening. I want some dick. I want him in me, and I want to taste him and feel him in my mouth. I couldn't care less if he's dating my mother at this point. All I know is they're not married; that leaves the door open for plenty of opportunity. And temptation is just burning in me something terrible. "Where's my mom?" I ask.

"In da room, sleep." I continue to look at him as he stands at the sink with his dick in full view. That shit is just hanging, looking big and black. I know he wants the same thing I want; if not, then he would've left the bathroom a long time ago. I want him so bad that my pussy is just throbbing with excitement. I slowly continue to dry myself off. I throw one leg up on the toilet and wipe myself from toe to thigh in a sensual motion. He smiles as I tease him by wiping the towel in between my pussy, letting out a soft moan. His smile has turned into a sinister grin.

"What's all dat about?" I teasingly ask as I look at his dick.

"It likes what it sees." His dick has to be about nine and a half inches long. "But what's all that about?" he says looking down at me.

"What? I'm drying myself off. Is there a problem with that?"

"Don't know a woman to dry herself off like that, all sexy and shit."

"Well, it's the way I do it. I take my sweet time with whatever I do."

"Word?"

"Word!" My eyes are focused on his dick. My pussy is getting wetter by the second. I swear I got a river flowing between my legs. It's either now or never. I take a seat on the toilet and spread my legs, exposing everything. I lean back slightly and start fingering myself.

Danny is hyped. "It's like that!" he says, all excited and shit.

"If you want it to be," I say, slut that I am. Danny locks the bathroom door and comes back over to me. He gets down on his knees, buries his face between my legs and starts to eat my pussy. "Mmmm...see, nice and clean for you," I say to him, playing with his dreads as he eats me out on the toilet.

I start to moan loudly. His tongue action is fierce. He sucks on my pussy, sticks his tongue in my ass and kisses all in between my thighs. He has to tell me to shut up a couple of times. Afterward, he bends me over the toilet. When he puts his dick in me, it takes everything in my power to not cry out. The dick is so fuckin' good. SHIT!

He makes me cum quick as hell, but he's not done until he lets off a roaring nut up in me, gripping my but and making me hit my head against the back of the toilet.

After we're done, I throw on a towel and duck in my room. Am I feeling guilty about what just happened? Hell no! In fact, I'm looking forward to round two. And it was the way I dreamed it would be—even better. My mother is such a fuckin' lucky bitch to be getting dick from a man like him on a regular.

Jakim stops by early in the evening. He's in the mood for some pussy, but I protest; I got mine just this morning, but like all men when they don't get any pussy, he catches an attitude. He tells me he "got needs," so I tell him to go and get his needs taken care of somewhere else. He tries to persuade me to give him a blowjob, but that's a no. My mind is still on Danny and how good that dick was.

On the day before Thanksgiving, I hang out with my girls, Naja and Latish. We do a little shopping on Jamaica Avenue and go to the movies afterward. I get my hair and nails done, since we're having family and friends over.

My day is going so good, till Detective Briscoe from homicide approaches me. He and his partner have been waiting for me in front of my house in a black Caprice. I'm carrying three shopping bags filled with gifts and clothes, about to get ready to go out tonight with Naja. But my plans change as soon as he steps to me asking questions.

"Excuse me, are you Shana Banks?" Detective Briscoe asks. He's about 5'9" and a little stocky, wearing a leather jacket, glasses and a beard.

His partner follows him, stepping out of the car with a cup of coffee in his hand. He's taller and younger, and he's also wearing a leather jacket. He's sporting a goatee and a gold earring in his ear.

"Who wants to know?" I ask.

"I'm Detective Briscoe–Homicide. This is my partner, Detective Rice. We would like to ask you a few questions about the death of Terry Miles."

"What?" I'm stunned.

"We would like for you to come down to the station with us, Ms. Banks," Detective Briscoe says.

"Am I under arrest?" I ask.

"No."

"Then I don't see any reason for me to roll with y'all."

"Ms. Banks, we can do this the easy way or the hard way. It's your choice," Detective Rice states.

I just stare at the both of them. Tomorrow is Thanksgiving Day, and here they are coming to me with this bullshit. I know nothing. I'm not even sure if it's Tyrone who killed Terry. I sigh and agree to go with them. There'll be no need for officers to come and break down my front door over some silliness.

They escort me to their car. The ride is quiet to the 103rd precinct.

I sit in the back seat, wondering how soon it will be over.

When we arrive at the precinct, the detectives escort me into a small, grayish bare room with a wooden table and two chairs. They leave me there to sit for about twenty minutes. I'm nervous as hell.

Detectives Briscoe and Rice finally enter the room. "Ms. Banks, I want to ask you a few questions about your boyfriend, Tyrone Sorbs," Detective Briscoe says, taking a seat in the chair opposite me.

"He's not my boyfriend."

"Then what is he to you?" says Detective Rice.

"Just a guy I'm fucking," I bluntly say.

Detective Rice puts out his cigarette in the ashtray on the table and peers at me. "The reason you're here, Ms. Ba—"

"Damn, would you please stop calling me Ms. Banks! Fuck!"

"Okay, *Shana*, the reason you're here is that witnesses placed you at the scene on the night Tyrone Sorbs assaulted and nearly killed Terry Miles in a fast food restaurant," Detective Rice informs me.

"What?"

"Your lover is our prime suspect in this case," Detective Briscoe says. "Do you know of his whereabouts?"

"I haven't seen or heard from Tyrone in weeks. He just fucks me, then leaves, fucks me, then leaves."

They want to know how long we've been going out and how long I've known him. Who are his friends? Do I know where he hangs out? I'm surprised they don't want to know how long his dick is, too.

After spending about forty minutes with them, I start to get really agitated and annoyed. "Look, am I gonna be placed under arrest?!" I yell out.

"No," Detective Rice says.

"Then can I just fuckin' leave? I don't know nothin' about Tyrone. He don't tell me shit about his life. We just fuck and that's it!"

Detective Briscoe, becoming annoyed with my attitude, waves his hand and announces, "Let her go!"

Detective Rice looks reluctant to do so; maybe my beauty is the highlight of his day. "Come with me," he says.

Before I step out the door, Detective Briscoe stands up and says, "Shana, if he contacts you, you call us." He passes me his card.

How am I supposed to get home? I see Tyrone's roommate, Evay, in the hallway, handcuffed to a chair and sitting slumped over, looking like he's feeling sorry for himself. I turn my head, not wanting him to notice me. I wonder why he's here.

Detective Rice offers to give me a ride back home. I accept. He tries to rap to me in the car. He has some nerve. They wasted a good portion of my day, and now he thinks I'm gonna give him my phone number. Fuck him!

As soon as I get home I take a hot shower, to get that precinct smell off me. When I get out of the shower, I check the answering machine. Naja left two messages. In the first one, she says that she and Latish are coming over for Thanksgiving. In the second one, she tells me to be ready by nine. We're going out once again.

When I call Naja back, her boyfriend picks up. God, I hate hearing his voice; he sounds like a little kid. The niggah is twenty-seven and talks like he's thirteen. When Naja finally comes to the phone, she sounds tired and exhausted.

"Were you having sex?"

"Yeah, I gotta get mine, too. What's up?"

"I need to talk to you."

"About what?"

"Just get over here, girl. This is important."

"Shana, you can't tell me over the phone? Shit, I'm in the middle of some good dick here."

"Then break his dick off in your pussy and bring it with you," I say.

"Now, see, you're wrong, bitch. Just give me a half hour. I'll be there soon."

"Hurry, girl."

After hanging up the phone, I throw on my house robe and go into the kitchen to make myself a snack. My mind is on Tyrone and his situation. He told me himself that he had nothing to do with Terry's death. And I somewhat believed him. But then again, he's been out of town for a while now. Maybe he's on the run.

I walk into the living room with a cheese sandwich and a soda, turn on the television and plop down on the sofa. It's times like these that I feel like getting high–just rolling myself a phat ass L. The house is quiet– a little too quiet. It feels like I'm in one of those horror movies, where the young female is home alone and there's a killer stalking around town. But there ain't any serial killers in New York, much less in Hollis, Queens. The only thing out here is gangs, chicken- heads, wannabe thugs, playas and fake-ass bitches.

When Naja finally arrives, I tell her about the two detectives that came to see me. I tell her I was with Tyrone when he beat down Terry. Naja goes crazy, thinking that Tyrone actually killed Terry. Then she asks me why he did it. I tell her it was over money.

"Bitch, why didn't you tell me this before?" she asks, looking upset.

I have no explanation for her. I guess I was just too scared to tell anyone before now. Naja tells me to leave Tyrone alone from now on, but I can't do that; I feel that he really needs me...wherever he is. I tell her I'm too in love with him to let him go. She looks at me like I'm crazy. Then she starts asking about Jakim and what's going on with him. I tell her the truth–about the sex, and how we talked about maybe getting back together some-day. I even admit to her that I still love him, too.

The bitch calls me confused. She says I don't know true love from good dick, and asks me how I could care for that asshole, in light of the Chinky incident.

Naja's wrong; I do know what true love is, and I know what it feels like to be in love. I tell her that I really *am* in love with both Tyrone and Jakim, and a girl still gotta get her freak on every once in a while. It ain't like I'm married to either of them. She keeps warning me to stay away from Tyrone and get back with Jakim. But once again I disagree; I don't feel ready for that yet. And as for that dumb bitch, Chinky, the ho can't be trusted.

I'm tempted to tell her about Danny, but I decide to keep my mouth shut about that one. That's too much information to be exposing right now.

Naja stays over at my house for the remainder of the evening. We change our minds about going out. Instead we rent movies, call Latish and help my mother prepare for Thanksgiving dinner.

That little meeting with the detectives will be kept a secret between Naja and me. She made a vow not to tell anyone about what I've told her. I trust her.

It's Thanksgiving Day, and more than twenty relatives and friends are coming over. My day is all planned out. First I'm going to have dinner with my family, and then my girlfriends and I will head out to Newark, New Jersey, where there's a huge party jumping off tonight. We are definitely going to that.

My moms cooked mashed potatoes, string beans, rice and peas, macaroni, collard greens, yams, roast beef, stuffing, ham, fish and turkey. She also baked five sweet potato pies and one large chocolate cake. Even though my moms acts ghetto sometimes, she can definitely cook. My grandmother was one of the greatest cooks in the South, and she passed that gift on to my mother.

By two, my uncles, Jimbo and Jimmy, arrive. They're the two who got into that fistfight. My mother said she would throw them both out if they don't behave themselves this year.

My cousin, Pamela, shows up with her third husband in four years, and my cousin, Sharice, shows up with her three bad-ass little boys. My Uncle Leon is with his gold-digging girlfriend. That bitch has on more jewelry than Mr. T from the A-Team. Then there's my Aunt Samantha, who's more promiscuous than me, my mother *and* my Aunt Tina combined. She's wearing some old fashioned, eighties fishnet stockings, bamboo earrings, a mini skirt and a sultry attitude. My perverted Uncle Penny and my always-staying-drunk Uncle Lake are on the scene. And last but not least, my cousin Jade is here. She's from Forty Projects, and she is my girl. She's a few years younger than me, but she can hold it down. I could go on and on about my dysfunctional family.

My Uncle Penny keeps trying to hit on Naja, talkin' 'bout she got pretty legs. He's an embarrassment. Then my other two uncles, Jimbo and Jimmy, try to get into Latish's pants. She plays along, flirting with them. They're my family and all, but those two are disgusting. They're both unemployed and would fuck anything with a pulse and a pussy between its legs. I admit, though, they're attractive men, but they have no kind of ambition at all.

"Damn, g-i-r-r-l, why you lookin' so fine, wit' yo beautiful self?" my cousin Ellis says to me. He just walked in a few minutes ago. I chuckle and give him a little smile. I think he's funny. He just came up from Delaware with his butt-ugly girlfriend, Shannon. That bitch is so ugly, she makes dogs scream and howl. But my uncle loves and sports her around like she's a prize-winning trophy.

"Shana, get your perverted Uncle Penny away from me," Naja pleads.

"What da matter, girl? You don't like to have a good time?" my crazy, nasty and drunk, Uncle Penny says to Naja. There's a cup of whiskey in his hand.

"Uncle Penny, will you please leave my friend alone?" I beg him.

"What da matter, Shana, she a lesbian or somethin'?" he asks looking at her strangely.

"Oh, no he didn't. Shana, do something with him before I have to smack him," Naja says.

"I will, just go in my bedroom," I say. She walks away looking over her shoulder, to make sure Uncle Penny doesn't follow her. I start pushing him in the opposite direction, assuring her that he won't come anywhere near her. But you can't blame my uncle entirely; Naja is wearing a tight-ass mini skirt that stops at mid-thigh, hooker heels and her cleavage is showing in a low-cut top.

Minutes later, Naja comes to get me with this bugged out expression on her face. "Shana, come here and look at this shit," she says, leading me to my bedroom.

I follow her. I can't believe my eyes when I reach my bedroom and open the door. I see Latish making out with my uncles, Jimbo and Jimmy, on my fuckin' bed. Is *she crazy?* "Bitch, you crazy?" I shout, startling them.

"Oh, shit, I thought y'all locked the door," Latish says rising up from between them, looking surprised.

I'm about ready to kill that bitch along with both of my uncles. Naja stands at my side, just shaking her head in disbelief. Latish's skirt is hiked up, her shirt is unbuttoned and her hair looks a wreck. Both my uncles have their pants off. I step into the room and slam the door behind me. All three of them just look at me, probably too shocked to say anything.

"Shana, let me explain," Latish says awkwardly.

"Explain what—that you're a nasty bitch?!"

Both of my uncles retrieve their pants from off the floor. I feel like I'm about to vomit. It's a horrendous sight, and it caught me totally off guard.

"Shana, I'll wait for you out in the hallway," Naja says leaving the room.

"First of all, y'all need to get the fuck up out of my room!" I shout. "And second, y'all need to get the fuck outta this house!"

"C'mon, Shana, we were just having some fun," my Uncle Jimbo says buttoning his jeans.

"Not in *my* fuckin' house and especially not in *this* fuckin' room. All three of y'all must've been smoking crack!"

My mother walks into my room, with Naja following not too far behind. She looks around and immediately knows what's going down.

"I know both of my brothers must be crazy to have thought that they were going to fuck in my daughter's room."

"C'mon, sis, it ain't even like that," Uncle Jimmy says.

"And Latish, I'm surprised at you; I thought you had much better taste than these two."

"But Ms. Banks, they paid me."

"What?!" my mother and I shout simultaneously.

"Y'all think I'm running some fuckin' brothel in my house?" my moms continues to shout.

By now the whole family hears all the ruckus going on in my room. They gather around the door and peer inside to see what's going on. My mother's going crazy, throwing things at her brothers and trying to smack them across their heads. Naja's holding her hand over her mouth, trying to hold back her laughter. Latish, embarrassed, just rushes out of the room. I follow her. She reaches the front doorway, and I grab her by the shoulder and spin her around.

"Where you going, bitch? This shit ain't over!"

"Shana, I'm sorry, but they forced me to."

"My uncles ain't force you to do shit!" I yell with my fists tightly clenched, feeling about ready to knock this bitch out for disrespecting me in my own home.

She looks petrified. I decide not to hit her. It wouldn't even be worth it. But she now has two strikes against her—one for fucking my man,

even though they both deny it, and now this. Just one more and I'm definitely going to fuck this bitch up.

"You know what...everyone get the fuck out!" my moms shouts
walking into the living room. I turn to look at her. She's about to blow a gas-
ket.

"C'mon, sis, don't spoil it for everyone," Uncle Jimmy says walking
up behind her.

"You shut the fuck up. I'm 'bout to kill both of y'all," my mother
threatens.

Before I can even turn back around, Latish is already out the door
and gone. Then Naja comes up to me and says, "G-i-r-r-l, your family's crazy.
I'm gone. You still down for tonight?"

I just look at her. Minutes later, everyone starts collecting their
things and leaving the house, one by one. My moms, mad as hell, retreats
to her bedroom. Thanksgiving is officially over, and once again, her brothers, Jimmy and Jimbo, have ruined it for everyone.

Everyone is finally gone, leaving my mother and me to clean up
everything. There are tons of dishes that need to be washed, the living
room is in shambles and there are crumbs everywhere. Plates and cups are
on top of the TV, coffee table and stereo—not to mention my room—that shit
needs to be disinfected, sterilized, washed and sprayed down.

Jakim comes by later. He sees how upset I am and tries to comfort
me the best he can, but it's just not working. He even volunteers to help me
and my mother clean the house. When I tell him about Latish, he has nothing good to say about her. He calls her a nasty slut.

After all the cleaning and rearranging is done, Jakim and I settle
in my room for the night, where I thank him personally. I softly kiss him on

the neck as I unbutton his shirt. Then I slide my hand down to his crotch and squeeze gently. He moans and closes his eyes. I slowly undress him until he's butt naked. I push him down onto my bed—on new bed sheets of course—and tell him to watch me undress. He smiles up at me. I slowly come out of my skirt, panties and bra. He's hard. I run my hands across my body and approach him as he grips his erection. I climb on top of him, straddling him, as he slides his dick into me. I gasp and start to ride him, my palms flat against his chest. I lean forward and whisper in his ear. "Baby, I never stopped loving you."

"Same here; I still love you," he replies.

"Fuck me," I gently say.

He grips my hips and goes to work, thrusting his pelvis back and forth, causing me to pant and cry out. "I love you, Shana!"

"Hold me," I cry out as I fuck him, bending forward and laying my breasts against his chest as he holds me in his arms.

"I got you, baby. I got you," he assures me.

"Thank you."

"Shana, I'm gonna love you forever." I feel wanted and needed. Still on top of him, I start to cry, and he holds me all night. I feel safe with him. I believe in him. And I'll never stop loving him.

11 JAKIM

I can't do it anymore. I want to stop jumping from woman to woman and be with Shana. She makes me happy. It looks like we're finally getting back together again. Thanksgiving night was the best. I didn't want to leave her side. Since we started fuckin' again, all I do is think about her night and day. Yo, I'm in love.

I cruise in my Maxima, singing along to a song by Method Man on the radio. I'm on my way to meet Tyrone at a lounge on Merrick Boulevard. It's a cold Saturday night, and I'm in a good mood. I asked Shana if she wanted to come along, but she declined.

My phone rings. I look at the caller ID, and I sigh as I glance at the number. It's Latish. *I gotta cut this bitch off.* I can't risk my relationship with Shana by fuckin' wit' this bitch. I reluctantly answer the call. "Yo, what up?"

"Jakim, I wanna see you," she says.

I think on what Shana told me about Latish being with her uncles. She's a freak. "Yo, we need to talk," I say.

"Talk about what? I wanna see you tonight."

"Well, that can't happen. I'm busy tonight."

"So tomorrow night then...please," she begs. "It's really important."

I think about it. "Aiight, tomorrow night. I'll come through around
nine."

"Okay. So who you seeing tonight?" she asks, prying into my business.

"Yo, I'll see you tomorrow night," I say and hang up.

Fuckin' bitch. I need to cut her loose. Her pussy is good and all, but
it just ain't worth it. My perverted mind contemplates fuckin' her one last
time before calling it quits.

I race to meet up with Tyrone. I'm excited and can't wait to break
the news to him about Shana and me. I want to tell him that he was wrong.
I was persistent and got what I wanted. He wants me to move on and forget
about Shana, and think that it's all right to find 'em, fuck 'em and forget
about 'em. That's his playa theory.

I park a block away from the Midnight Lounge. It's crowded
because there's a two-for-one special on drinks till midnight. That always
brings out all the ladies and drunks. I parade past the crowd lined up outside like I'm a celebrity. I'm definitely on cloud nine. I get to the door and
see that they're charging ten dollars for admission. But Tyrone put me on
the list. He's partial owner of the lounge, so that gives me special privileges.
Security recognizes me and lets me slide right on in without a hassle.

I navigate my way through the dense crowd and head toward the
back. The bar is swarming with customers, ready to take advantage of the
discount for the night. The Midnight Lounge is a cozy and snug, two-level

joint, and there's a DJ every Friday and Saturday night. Spongy red sofas and spherical dark blue glass tables are situated throughout the place. The lighting is dim and the music is contemporary.

I make my way up the spiral staircase, passing a very voluptuous woman in a black, tight mini dress. She throws me a quick smile and continues on down the stairs.

Tyrone is in a private section on the second floor in the back. It's his VIP area. He has bottles of Cristal, Hypnotiq, Moet and Belvedere on the table. He's sitting with his arm around a beautiful Dominican woman with thick red lips. "My niggah, Jakim, came through," he says, standing up as I approach him. He gives me dap and a quick, manly hug. His companion glances up at me and smiles.

"Yeah, you know I had to come through to celebrate your birthday—happy birthday, my niggah," I say.

"Good lookin' out, Ja. A niggah twenty-three today. Can you believe that? We gettin' old," he says, picking up an empty glass and a bottle of Cristal to pour me a drink. "Here, my niggah. It's my birthday; we gettin' twisted tonight."

I take the glass and quickly down the Cristal. Tyrone sits back down and puts his arm around shorty. "I'm surprised you came alone," he says.

"Yeah, you know, I'm chillin' tonight," I reply.

"Niggah, fuck dat. We got plenty of bitches in here. And it's a good thing you *did* come alone—look around."

I look around and see that he isn't lying. The lounge is overflowing with women, and they're all looking fine. Tyrone pours me another drink, and I down that one, too.

We sit around at the table for a moment, drinking, talking and flirting with the ladies. Tyrone is really having a good time. He's dressed like a rap star, sporting a lot of jewelry, mostly platinum and diamonds. And he's clad in a denim Sean John suit and a Yankees cap, tilted low over his left brow.

By midnight our table is surrounded by beautiful women. Milk and Sweet also come through. They're both dressed like they just came from a porno shoot.

Tyrone is a big Jay-Z fan, and he's already had the DJ playing his records back-to-back for about an hour straight. The bottles of Moet and Cristal are quickly being consumed, and the women are getting frisky and horny.

"You having a good time, Jakim?" Tyrone shouts over the loudspeakers.

"Fo' sure, niggah," I shout back. I have a beautiful woman under my arm and a bottle in my hand.

"Yo, you look really happy. What, you got some pussy earlier?" he asks.

"Somethin' like dat," I reply smiling.

"Word?! You fucked dat shorty I hooked you up with in Canarsie?"

"Nah, I ain't holla at that yet."

"Niggah, what...you need to get at dat."

"I might."

Tyrone shakes his head in disbelief. "Yo, get on your job, Jakim. She a bad bitch fo' real."

"I know."

"So, what's wit' the jolliness? I know it ain't 'cause it's my birthday," he continues before glancing behind him. "Yo, I can't hear shit wit' these fuckin' speakers blasting in my ear. Walk wit' me outside. I need to smoke anyway."

We get up and walk outside. When we get a few feet from the entrance, Tyrone pulls out a cigarette and places it between his lips. He quickly lights it and takes a long drag. He remains silent for a moment. "So, who is she?" he asks.

I can't hold my excitement in any longer. "Yo, I'm getting back with Shana again," I blurt out.

"What?"

"Yeah, son. We've been talking, and we trying to do our thang again. I spent da night with her on Thanksgiving."

Tyrone looks at me with disdain. "Jakim, what I told you about dat bitch!"

"Ty, she ain't a bitch," I protest.

"Yeah she is. Can't you see, niggah? She fuckin' wit' your head. She's fuckin' playin' you! Niggah, you get one whiff of it again, and your ass is pussy whipped. C'mon, son, you got plenty of bitches to get with, and you keep running back to her triflin' ass."

"Yo, it ain't even like dat. We love each other. See, you wouldn't understand something like dat. You out here too busy being a playa...niggah, you don't know what love is anyway," I counter.

"Niggah, love is turning you into a fuckin' fool. How you know she ain't out here fuckin' wit' da next niggah! Yo, dat bitch gonna break your heart again. You need to leave her alone, Jakim."

"Man, you sound like you hatin' right now...what's up wit' dat? I thought you was gonna be happy for your boy."

"I'll be happy once you leave dat bitch alone! You need to call Lisa and get wit' her ass."

"Fuck Lisa! You fuck her then, if it's dat good!"

"Niggah, fuck you! I'm tryin' to look out for you, and you out here playin' *Love Jones* and shit. Dat bitch don't give you no respect, so why you keep sweatin' her? She don't give a fuck about you, niggah. She probably already fuckin' da next niggah. But he dissin' her and she got you on the rebound. Get your head out your ass, niggah. Shana ain't nothin' but a two-dollar ho!"

I quickly punch him in the jaw, and blood spews from his mouth. I reacted without even thinking. He called my woman a ho, and I couldn't let that fly.

Tyrone spits blood from his mouth and then glares at me. "You know what, niggah? I'm gonna give you a pass on dat one. It's my birthday, and you my boy. But you ever touch me again, and I'll fuckin' murder you. I don't care how long we've been boys." He walks away, dabbing at his mouth.

"Ty..." I call out, but he doesn't respond. He walks back into the joint without saying another word to me.

I feel guilty, having attacked him like that. It's his birthday, and I can't let the night end like this. I know I'm in the wrong, despite what he called Shana.

I go back into the lounge. I want to apologize to Tyrone. I head back upstairs and find him on the couch with his arm back around the Dominican woman. He gives me a blank stare. I stand silently in front of the table for a moment. He smirks and then whispers something in the Dominican woman's ear. She glances at me and then does the unexpected. She leans over sideways into Tyrone's lap, indicating that she's about to give him a blowjob in the crowded club. I watch her head bob up and down. Tyrone just throws his arms across the back of the couch and relaxes while looking at me.

"Don't apologize, Jakim. Shit happens, right? You can't help but be who you be. You in love, then you in love. Dat must be some good-ass pussy for your bitch-ass to keep running back to it!" he yells out for everyone to hear. "Fuck it! Get caught up, niggah. I don't' give a fuck! Fuck dat bitch and be married. Turn a ho into a housewife."

"Niggah, fuck you!" I chide and walk off. Fuck him and his birthday. I tried to do right by him, and he's hatin'.

I walk out of the club, wishing it didn't have to go down like that—but it did. "Jakim, wait up!" I hear someone shout as I approach my car. I turn around and see Milk running up to me in a pair of stilettos. "What you want, Milk?"

"He didn't mean dat shit back there," she says in his defense.

"Fuck him!"

"You know he's drunk, Jakim. He's just showing off and acting stupid. He's jealous because he knows he can never find what you have with your girl. I think it's nice that you're in love. I wish I had a man in love with me," she says.

"Yeah, well, you're a cutie; I'm sure you'll find someone."

She smiles. "Here, take down my number and give me a call one day—in case things don't work out with you and your girl...or if you wanna have some fun again."

I take her number, and that little dog in me starts telling me to fuck her tonight. I'm having flashbacks of our threesome. But Shana soon comes to mind, and I realize that for me to become a better man for her, I need to change my promiscuous ways and stop feeding into temptation and lust all the time. God knows Milk is definitely tempting, with her sexy white ass. She's wearing a short, scanty mini skirt, with a split that almost goes up to her ass. Staring at her petite figure, I slowly back away from her. "I'll think about it," I say.

"You do dat, baby, wit' your fine self," she says and struts back into the club. Scandalous, some women can be. She knows I'm trying to get back with my girl, and she's still throwing the pussy at me. I shake my head and get in my car.

The following afternoon, I'm chilling with Evay on Farmers and Linden. We just came from the liquor store, getting ourselves a bottle of Hennessy and a two-liter of coke. We sit in my parked car, talking and getting tipsy.

Evay was looking stressed out, so I suggested that we get a bottle and chill. He got arrested a few days ago, but the cops didn't have a charge on him. The only reason 5-0 fucked wit' him was because he and Tyrone are associates. And Tyrone isn't playing it cool with either of us, since smacking Evay up and dissing me at the lounge.

I take a swig from the bottle and pass it to Evay. "Yo, dat niggah better stop playin' himself, Jakim. I swear, if he puts his hands on me again...I swear, I'll kill dat muthafucka. He thinks it's funny—embarrassing me in front of his peoples. We supposed to be boys. He touches me again, and I'll kill him. I swear, Ja...watch."

I know it's the liquor talking; Evay's no killer. He's as harmless as a fly. "Niggah, don't stress it. You know how Tyrone is. He's a showoff."

Evay passes the bottle back to me, but before I can put it to my lips, my cell phone goes off. It's Latish. D*amn that bitch.* "Evay, give me a few minutes. I gotta take this call," I say. He steps out of the car. "What up?"

"What time you coming by tonight?" Latish asks.

"Latish, I said I'll be there! Damn!"

"I just wanted to make sure, dat's all. I miss you, baby."

"Yeah, whatever. Listen, stop calling me," I chide.

"But....Jakim, I like you a lot, and despite what everybody thinks about me, I really wanna be with you. I'll change just for us to be together."

"Yo, I'll talk to you when I get there." I hang up.

Evay comes back to the car a few minutes later with another bottle of brown juice. He's getting twisted; he has a lot of shit on his mind.

"Yo, Evay, I gotta make a run real quick. I'm gonna holla at you later," I say.

"Aiight, Jakim." He strolls off down the street with the brown paper bag containing the liquor clutched in his hand. I watch him through my rearview mirror as he disappears around the corner. I start up my car and head to Latish's place.

I get there around five. My gut is telling me to leave, but I don't. I step out of my car and know that I have to break the news to Latish about Shana and me getting back together. I walk up to her door and ring the bell. Moments later, Latish appears in her panties, bra and stilettos. There's a broad smile on her face. I swear my dick just jumped. "Come in," she says hospitably.

"Latish, we need to talk," I manage to say.

But she pulls me inside by my jacket, not giving me a chance to explain myself. "Just come inside. We can talk downstairs," she says cheerfully.

I follow her downstairs. The living room is dimly lit with sweet scented candles. I know she just wants to fuck. But I tell myself not tonight or ever again. I want to be in a serious, committed relationship with Shana.

Latish comes up behind me and puts her arms around my waist, pressing her breasts into my back. She then slides her hands gently underneath my shirt and moves them soothingly up and down my chest. I moan slightly, appreciating her soft, womanly touch.

"I wanna please you tonight, baby," she whispers with sensitivity. "I wanna make love to you."

I let out a helpless sigh. "Latish–" She abruptly turns me around and pushes me down onto the couch.

"Ssshhhh..." She presses her index finger against her soft, glossy lips. I stare up at her as she begins taking off her underwear. She stands stark naked in front of me in her stilettos, and her petite, dark form shimmers in the candlelit room. It's a wonderful view.

Latish slowly and seductively struts up to me. She then straddles me and begins fondling and kissing me tenderly. Moments later, she's down on her knees in between my legs, pulling away at my belt.

Stop her, I tell myself. *You're in love with Shana. This can't happen tonight.* Latish pulls out my dick and starts stroking me lovingly. I moan as her warm, soft hand slowly moves up and down my shaft. I close my eyes, enjoying her gentle touch for the moment.

Pussy, I tell myself, *is going to be my downfall if I don't end this affair now.* With my jeans lying around my ankles, I feel her mouth, lips and tongue sucking and nibbling away at my nuts. She's tea-bagging me, and definitely teasing and making it hard for me to say what I have to say. She kisses all around my shaft while playing with the tip of it. "You like when I suck your big black dick?" she says pleasingly.

I remain quiet. Her lips slide down on the dick, and she starts slobbing me down like a porn star. "Ummmm," I mutter, overwhelmed. *Fuck, why am I so fuckin' weak?* I let her continue to suck my dick for about five minutes. "Latish...stop!" I finally cry out.

She stops and looks up at me. "Excuse me?" she says.

"I said stop," I sternly state.

"What's wrong, baby?" she asks, looking at me with concern.

I push her away from me and reach down for my pants. "I can't do this no more."

"What da fuck you talkin' about, Jakim?" she asks with a bit of disdain in her voice.

"I can't do this wit' you anymore." She's not trying to hear me, and she moves toward me again, wanting to continue where she left off. But I'm adamant about what I just said. I push her away from me, harder this time, and she falls back on the floor on the palms of her hands. I continue. "You and me, it stops right now. I'm not doing this wit' you anymore."

"But Jakim...what's wrong, baby? Don't I suck your dick real good? Please, let me know what's da matter? What do you want from me?" she pleads.

I look down at her and try to break the news gently. I can no longer disguise the truth, so I just come out with it. "I'm back with Shana again. I'm in love with her," I confirm.

"What? Niggah, stop fuckin' playin' with me," she says glaring at me.

"Latish, you're cute and all, but Shana comes first in my life," I calmly explain to her.

"You stopped me from suckin' your dick to tell me this fuckin' bull-shit?! Niggah, you're playin' yourself!"

"Yo, it is what it is. That's why you and me, it can't be anymore."

Latish stands up, her face contorted with anger and frustration. "Jakim, you a fuckin' fool! Why are you goin' back wit' dat bitch? Niggah, she doesn't love you. I love you, baby. Please, don't do this to me." Her tone has gone from angry to desperate.

"Latish, I don't love you. I love Shana. We had our thang, and it was good while it lasted. But from now on, you need to stay away from me."

"No...please," she cries out. She tries to throw her arms around my neck in an attempt to win back my love or something. But I bitterly push her away. "Latish, stay da fuck away from me, please."

"Oh, so it's like dat, huh? You gonna dis me for dat trifling bitch. I'm here giving myself to you, and you gonna dis me for dat bitch. FUCK YOU, JAKIM!" she shouts. "Niggah, you ain't shit, and Shana ain't shit. If she cared about you, then she wouldn't be out there fuckin' your boy, Tyrone, every chance she gets...and you tryin' to wife that dumb bitch"

I glare at her. I know I must have heard her wrong. "What da fuck you say?" I ask grimly.

She gets up close to my face. "Niggah, you fuckin' heard me: Tyrone is giving dat big black dick to your bitch lovely every-"

SMACK! I strike her out of sheer rage. Latish grabs the side of her face and looks at me with shock. "Niggah, is you fuckin' crazy?!" she screams out. She then comes charging at me, swinging like a mad woman, but I toss her light ass against the couch.

"You lying bitch!" I shout.

"Niggah, you're lying to yourself if you think Shana ain't been getting da dick like that. And your boy is the one who's feeding it to her. But you're so stupid, and your head is so far up your ass dat you can't even see it. They playin' you, Jakim. He smilin' in your face, and she keeps fuckin' leading you on and shit. I hate to be the bearer of bad news, but Shana is in love wit' Tyrone. You just da rebound niggah, 'cause Tyrone's been dissin' her lately."

It's all hard for me to swallow...Latish has to be lying out of pure jealousy. And she has a reason to lie; Shana found her in bed with her two uncles.

"If you don't believe me, ask around. Talk to Evay. Shit, he was there at the club when Shana left with Tyrone to go back to their apartment to fuck his brains out."

I'm stunned, and at the same time seething with rage and anger. But my anger soon turns into hurt and shame. I try to compose myself in front of Latish as she sits naked on the couch, surveying the damage that she's caused.

"Baby, I forgive you for hitting me," she says rubbing the left side of her face. "It ain't nothin'. Now dat you know da truth about your girl, let me take care of you da way you deserve to be taken care of." She leans back against the couch and spreads her legs slowly.

I look at her with contempt. "Fuck you! You don't even have a fuckin' clue." With that, I leave her apartment.

I spend the next few hours getting drunk with Evay in the park on Jamaica Avenue and 202nd Street. It will soon be midnight, and I'm tipsy. Evay, being the chatty niggah that he is, runs his mouth to me about everything—making Latish's accusations concrete.

"Yeah...she fuckin' dat niggah...Ja...she been fuckin' him...fo' a minute...now.....Ja," he informs me in his slurred speech. "I wanted to tell you...but ya know...shit fucked up, son. You my...man and all...and I wanted to tell...ya...fucked up, Ja."

I take a swig of the E&J straight. The more I think about the two of them together, the more I want to get my piece and gun 'em both down. I feel so disrespected. "Fuck dat!" I hurl the bottle across the park and walk hastily to my car, with Evay right behind me, staggering.

"Go handle...ya bi-bizz-nez, son. Ya know....what I'm..sayin?"

I start my car and head straight for Shana's crib. We get there in seconds, since she's only a few blocks away from the park. I'm a bit inebriated, but nevertheless, I get out of my car and stagger to her front door. "SHANA!" I scream. "SHANA, COME DA FUCK OUTSIDE!" I kick the door and continuously ring the bell. I want *someone's* attention tonight, and I'm determined to get it. "YOU FUCKIN' BITCH! Why you do me like dis? You fuckin' my boy, huh?! FUCK YOU! I'll kill ya ass!"

Finally, I see lights come on in the house. I stagger back and gaze at her crib like it's about to transform or something. The front door opens, and Shana's aunt comes out in a bathrobe. "Jakim, what the hell is wrong with you? Boy, is you crazy?" she reprimands. "It's late."

"Tina, where's Shana? I wanna see her."

"Jakim, are you drunk?"

"I'm fine, Tina...just call dat bitch outside." I stagger to the door, but Tina pushes me back.

"Go home, Jakim, before I call the police on you. Shana's not here anyway."

"Tell dat bitch dat I wanna see her."

"I will. But you need to go home and get you some sleep."

I stare at Tina for a moment. She's guarding the door like a secret service agent, adamant about not letting me pass. "Yo, you her aunt...let me...know...my shorty fuckin'....wit' my boy?"

"I don't know," she flatly states.

"Fuck it....all y'all...some bitches anyway."

"Jakim, please go home," she pleads.

I don't say another word. I turn around and proceed back to my car with Tina watching me from the steps. When I get in the car I take a look at Evay, who looks like he's asleep. But he isn't. With his eyes still closed, he asks, "Ja...you took care...of...dat fuckin'...bitch?"

"Fuck her!" I drive off.

Evay crashes at my crib for the night. But I can't sleep. My mind is constantly on Shana fuckin' Tyrone. I grip my .45 handgun as I sit on my couch, staring at a picture of Shana and me together. It kills me to think that she loves another man more than she does me.

Do it, kill that bitch. She dissed you, son. Niggah, she never loved you. You got played, son. How she gonna fuck your man behind your back like that? That bitch never respected you. Tyrone's probably fuckin' her better than you ever did. Handle that bitch, and take care of your boy. Don't let 'em walk all over you. That was your pussy. Don't let another man take away what's yours and what you love.

"Fuck her!" I scream. "Fuck dat bitch!" I jump out of my chair and fire a live round into the wall, wishing it was Shana's fuckin' head.

Two days have gone by, and I'm a bit calmer. I still haven't run into Shana or Tyrone. It has to be God's doing, because if I did, I would have probably murdered them both on sight. But I still want revenge.

12 SHANA

I lay on my back with my legs spread in the air, as Danny sticks his tongue so deep into me that it feels like a hard dick. I clutch his dreads and moan, before glancing at the time. It's three in the afternoon. My mother had a doctor's appointment, and she took Danny's jeep and left him here with me, which wasn't a bad idea. His whole mouth just swallows up my sweet pussy. I tell him to lie on his back, and then I take him into my mouth, sucking his huge dick down to the balls. He grunts as he lays butt naked on my bed. He has the body of a god. I suck him off so well that he makes me stop, pulling my head away.

"Lay on your back," he orders, and I quickly obey. He gets on top of me and slowly pushes his big dick inside me, which causes my legs to spread wide open because his frame is so large and muscular. I passionately scream out, feeling his dick ramming and swelling in me. My juices flow with every stroke. He calls me his little wildcat, because I stay scratching up his back when we be fucking. He doesn't care, because my mother be doing the same thing when they go at it.

We're into it for about fifteen minutes, sweating, bumping and grunting. He starts tearing it up from the back and I grip the headboard tightly. Suddenly we hear a car door slam. "Shit!" Danny shouts. He jumps out of the pussy and runs to the window. "It's your mother. Get dressed!"

I dash from the bed, run to my closet and quickly throw on a pair of blue jeans and a T-shirt. Danny rushes out of my room naked, forgetting his clothes, and runs into the bathroom. I shove his clothes under my bed and start spraying air freshener around my room to get rid of the smell of sex. I hear my mother coming down the hall toward my room. *Damn, she moves quickly.* I hop back in bed and pick up the phone, pretending to be talking. I hear the shower come on in the bathroom. My pussy is throbbing hard because I didn't get to finish.

My mother walks into my bedroom. She sees me chatting on the phone. "Why you home so early?" I ask.

"The doctor's office wasn't that crowded," she replies peering around my room. "Who you on the phone with?"

"Naja."

"Where's Danny?"

"You don't hear him taking a shower?"

"At three in the afternoon?"

"That's *your* fuckin' man," I say before going back to my fake conversation with Naja.

She's looking strange and acting like something is wrong with her. She insisted on going to see the doctor alone this afternoon. Come to think of it, she's been acting strange all week. "You all right, ma?" I ask.

"Yeah, everything's okay, Shana."

I just shrug my shoulders and continue on with my phony conversation. My mother leaves my room and slowly closes the door. I hang up the phone as soon as she's gone. I hear her banging on the bathroom door calling Danny. That muthafucka is actually taking a shower. He could have quickly gotten dressed in the bathroom and pretended that he was taking a shit or somethin'. I swear, men don't think nothin' like women. They do things backwards. They just be *looking* to get busted.

I look out into the hallway and see my mother standing in front of the bathroom door. Danny finally comes out with a towel wrapped around him. He's dripping wet. "Hi, baby," he says giving her a quick kiss. "When you get home?"

"I need to talk to you," my mother says.

I start to think about how he's going to retrieve his clothes from out of my bedroom. I know he didn't take an extra set with him in the bathroom. He walks toward my mother's bedroom, with her leading the way. He looks at me like he doesn't know what to do. I point to the bathroom, hoping he gets the signal that I'm going to put all of his clothes in there after they get in the bedroom.

The second they're out of sight, I grab every piece of Danny's clothing. I run out of my room and throw everything on the bathroom floor. Minutes later I hear movement in the hallway. Curious, I open my door and see Danny still in a towel. He's coming my way. I step out and point to the bathroom. There's no need for him to come into my room. A few seconds later my mother comes out of her bedroom crying. I get nervous, wondering what could be wrong. Does my mother know I'm fuckin' her man? If she had any suspicion, she would have confronted me about it. My mother doesn't play when it comes to her boyfriends. She'd be ready to scratch a bitch's eyes out in a second, and then cut her man's dick off. You best believe she would be up in my face like I was some stranger in the street, fighting for her man, daughter or no daughter.

I follow my mother as she goes into the kitchen. "Ma, what's wrong?" I ask.

She just ignores me and takes a seat at the kitchen table. Danny, now fully dressed, comes into the kitchen. "Muthafucka, what you do to her?!" I scream.

"I gotta go," he says calmly and collectively.

"Wh—what the fuck happened?" I yell, glaring at Danny. Feeling lost, I follow him to the door. I grab him by his shirt and ask, "What did you tell her?"

"I ain't told her shit about you and me. She's dealing with a different problem," he says and walks out the door.

I walk back into the kitchen, where my mother is still sobbing at the table. I pass her a few pieces of tissue and take a seat next to her. "Ma, what's the matter? You okay?"

She takes a deep breath. "Shana, I'm fuckin' pregnant!" she announces.

"What! It's Danny's?"

"Of course!"

"Damn! So what he say about it?"

"He told me to go and have a paternity test taken; then he'll probably take care of it if it's his."

"What?" I can't believe it. My mother is pregnant. And that muthafucka has the nerve to try and deny being the father when he's running up in her twenty-four seven. I try to comfort her, but I feel guilty since I just finished fuckin' him a few minutes ago. "So what you gonna do? You gonna keep it or what?" I ask.

"I don't know...maybe," she softly replies.

"How far along are you?"

"The doctor told me five weeks." She dries her tears and I pass her some more tissue. I bring her a glass of water and walk her to her bedroom. I stay with her for the remainder of the day, making sure that she's okay. Damn, being pregnant must be really fucked up. You get fat, moody, lose your shape, not to mention the cramps and no longer fitting into any of your clothing, while constantly being tired and sleepy. Shit, having children definitely isn't for me. Kids can wait!

Christmas will soon be here, which means gifts. I sometimes receive cards with money inside. The most money I've ever received in a card was five hundred dollars from a man who used to ride the bus with me every morning when I was in high school. I'd never met him, but he used to gawk at me every morning on the bus, while probably getting a hard-on. A week before Christmas, he approached me, giving me a white envelope with *Please read, sexy,* written across it.

I arrived at school and opened the envelope during my third-period class. There were five, crisp, hundred-dollar bills inside of a Christmas card. I nearly fainted when I saw the money. I opened the card, and it read:

Dear sexy,
I don't know your name, but you can know mine. It's Kyle, and I'm

forty-five. I watch you every day on the bus, and your beauty has just blown me away. You're the most beautiful woman that I've ever laid eyes on. I know you're young, but age doesn't matter when it comes to beauty like yours. Give me the chance, and I'll marry you in a heartbeat. What's mine in this world, I'll give to you in the blink of an eye. I give this money to you just to prove that I'm for real. You're definitely worth a lot more, but this is all I can afford. The next time you see me on the bus, please speak. And remember, Kyle's my name.

He also wrote his numbers down. I ripped up the card and kept the money. *How stupid can you be, giving a total stranger you never met, five hundred dollars?* I remember thinking. From that day on, I took a different bus to school, I didn't want to risk running into him. I used the money to buy Jakim a leather jacket for Christmas and a few outfits for myself.

I'm on Jamaica Avenue doing my Christmas shopping with Naja. "So what your moms gonna do?" Naja asks after I tell her about my mother's condition.

"She don't know. She might have it."

"Damn, Shana, you might be having a little brother or sister."

"Yup!"

"How do you feel about that?"

"I don't know."

As we walk towards 165th Street, I can't help but wonder what I'd do if it was me. But I'm not trying to ruin my wonderful figure by having some fool's baby. I think my mother should get an abortion. Aunt Tina told her the same thing, but she's not for it. She loves Danny. And even though he's acting like an asshole, my mother isn't going to kill his baby.

Best of luck to her in trying to get me to baby-sit. I love my moms, but I have a life, and watching kids all day long is not a part of the plan.

As we walk down 165th Street toward the Coliseum shopping center, Naja points out a black BMW. "Ain't that Tyrone's whip?" she asks.

It is. I recognize the chrome, eighteen-inch rims and tinted windows. I know his car like I know my period. I haven't seen or spoken to him in weeks. I have a serious bone to pick with him about Chinky and my little scrap with her in the bathroom at the club. That bitch tried to cut me because of him. Then there's the thing with the detectives coming to speak to me about him.

"You wanna go the other way?" Naja asks as we stand there staring at his car.

I think about it. "Nah, I wanna ask him some questions," I tell her, while walking toward his car.

"C'mon, Shana, it's Christmas; you don't need to be dealing with this shit right now! Deal with him some other time."

I ignore her and continue walking straight toward his car. There's some dude sitting in the passenger seat. Tyrone is nowhere in sight. "Where's Tyrone?" I ask him.

He leans forward in his seat, which is reclined far back. "Damn, boo, why you lookin' for him when you've already found me?" he says.

Naja comes and stands behind me, disappointed by my decision. "Where's Tyrone?" I ask again.

"He's in the record shop," his friend answers. "But I'm sayin', boo, what's your name?"

I walk toward the record shop with Naja close behind me. But I stop at the glass door when I look inside; he's chatting with some hoochie-looking female. She's smiling and laughing, and all over him like flies on shit.

"C'mon, Shana, fuck him! You got Jakim back in your life now," Naja tries reminding me. She's right. Jakim and I are bonding again, but seeing Tyrone chatting with that girl has set me off. Here I was a minute ago ready to curse him out, but catching feelings when I see him talking and huggin' up on someone else. Once again I'm confused.

"C'mon, let's go," Naja says pulling me by my arm away from the record shop. I want to resist, but I don't. I want to approach Tyrone, smack that bitch and tell her to get the fuck away from my man. I want to curse him out, hate him and try to still love him at the same time. I also want the truth from him, about his relationship with Chinky, his children and us.

We walk away from the record shop. I want to turn around and seriously confront Tyrone, but Naja encourages me to move along.

As we wait for the bus, Tyrone's car pulls up to the curb in front of us. I sigh and then turn my head. Naja sucks her teeth.

"Shana, I need to talk to you," Tyrone says from the driver's seat.

"What do you want?" I ask, feeling somewhat glad that he's showed up. He steps out of the car, wearing a black hoodie and a thick chain draped around his neck. His man remains in the passenger seat, staring at Naja.

"Naja, watch my bags," I say, placing them on the ground next to her. I try to calm my nerves. I don't know if I want to smack and curse him out or just fuck and love him. It doesn't matter that he's wrong. He is for me. He pulls me to the side out of everyone's hearing range. I back up against a brick wall. He stands inches from my face. "So, what's up?" he asks.

"What's up with you?"

"I was in jail for a few days," he states.

"Why?"

"You know why—because of that *Terry* situation. Fuckin cops trying to blame me for his murder. What you tell 'em, Shana?"

"I ain't tell 'em shit, Tyrone."

"You sure?"

"They asked me a few questions about you, and if I knew anything about your whereabouts. All I told 'em was we're just fuckin', and that's it."

He chuckles. "That's my girl. They ain't got shit on me because I didn't do it. I ain't touch that muthafucka since that night I was with you. You believe me, right?"

I don't answer.

"You believe me, Shana, right?" he repeats.

"Yeah, I do," I slowly answer.

He smiles and then has the nerve to ask, "Yo, you and Jakim got back together?"

"What?"

"Jakim tells me that you and him are fuckin' again. That's true?"

"Listen, I got with him because you wasn't around. I got lonely. But honestly, it's not even like that with him," I make clear.

"So, what you sayin', y'all fucked?"

I can't believe he's getting jealous. It makes me smile inside for a moment, knowing this.

"We did our thang, why?"

"So it's like dat. What about us?" he asks.

"What *about* us?" I sarcastically reply. "You actin' like we ain't together like dat. You don't call me. You don't come around. I thought you got bored with me."

"Shana, it ain't even like dat. Yo, let me take you and Naja home and we'll talk privately," he says.

"Nah, before we go anywhere with you, you need to answer a few questions," I tell him, "since you all in *my* business."

"Like what?"

"First off, who da fuck is Chinky?"

"What?"

"Don't fuckin' play games with me, Tyrone. That bitch jumped me in a club. She claims that you're her man, her baby daddy and shit!"

"Don't believe that dizzy bitch, Shana."

"Why not, it's the truth, ain't it?"

"Nah, we ain't together. Yo, fuck that bitch!"

"Tyrone, don't bullshit me; Evay already told me all about y'all. He told me y'all been together for seven years. And he told me you got some other bitch pregnant out in Jersey."

"Yo, you gonna believe that fat fuck, Shana?!" he shouts. "That niggah just jealous. And he likes you, you know...."

"But why would he lie?"

"Because he's hatin' on a brotha!"

"Nah, see, you need to take care of that bitch, Chinky. Her and her homegirls nearly sliced my face open, and−"

"I'll take care of it," he interrupts.

I stare at him with doubting eyes. I want so much to believe him; I've been hearing so many things about him, and it's hard for me to tell what's a lie and what's not.

"I'm not gonna lie, Shana. Yes, I do have kids by her. But we ain't together no more. I thought you knew this; everyone does," he says convincingly.

"What about that bitch in Jersey?"

"What bitch in Jersey? Shana, don't believe a word that fat muthafucka told you. I'll deal with him later."

"Shana, the bus is coming!" Naja shouts.

"We'll catch the next one." She doesn't look too pleased standing there, with Tyrone's friend trying to kick it to her. "What about that bitch I saw you huggin' up on in the store a few minutes ago?"

"Shana, that bitch ain't nobody; I just ran into her. We used to talk a while back. "

"So am I just another bitch in your life, Tyrone?"

He comes closer to me, so close that I can feel his breath on my skin. He pulls me against him, and his scent enters my nostrils. "Don't be letting these jealous muthafuckas out here brainwash you with all these stupid rumors. I want you to be my woman. It's about me and you."

"So why you never act like it, Tyrone? I mean, you're always leaving town without me knowing. I don't hear from you in two or three weeks, then—"

"Ssshhhh...come here," he says. He slowly presses his lips against mine. I know Naja is watching; I feel her eyes on me. I know she's pissed. But who cares? This is *my* life, and I know what I'm doing.

"I'm taking y'all home," Tyrone insists.

"I thought we were catching the bus, Shana?" Naja says looking perplexed.

"Nah, Tyrone's gonna take us home," I say with a smile, happy we've worked things out. Naja rolls her eyes and sucks her teeth. She snatches up our bags and throws them in the back seat of the car.

"Damn, boo, it's Christmas; Santa ain't bringing you no dick this year?" Tyrone's friend says looking back at her.

"Check your fuckin' mutt, Tyrone," Naja says.

"Chill, Pipe," Tyrone tells him.

While riding in the car, Tyrone is constantly checking me out through his rearview mirror, smiling. I smile and flirt back. Naja, seated next to me, is mad. She doesn't say one word during the whole ride home.

Tyrone pulls up to the front of my house. Naja gets out, and I give her my keys to go inside, to have a few minutes alone with Tyrone.

"So, what you doing tonight?" he asks me, both of us standing outside of his car now.

"Nothin', why?" I say, sounding like putty as he embraces me in his arms.

"I thought we could go out to dinner or somethin'."

"That sounds good. Then what?"

"Then we can chill over at my place. I'm about to evict that niggah, Evay, for good. I miss you, Shana."

"I miss you, too."

"I'll pick you up around nine, cool?"

"I'll be ready," I say, slowly backing away toward my front door, staring at him as he gets back in his car.

When I enter the house, I know I'll hear a few words from Naja.

"Why you playing yourself out like that, Shana?"

"What you talking about?"

"I mean, why are you still fuckin' with him? You know he's wrong for you."

"What, you're my mother now? You gonna preach to me?"

"No! I'm just trying to look out for you. You saw him huggin' up on that bitch in the store, *and* his baby mother tried to cut you in the club. Two detectives came to your crib asking you about Terry's death, after you witnessed him pistol whip Terry a while back over money. Tell me you don't believe he didn't do it?"

"He said he didn't."

"Open your eyes, Shana. Tyrone's putting you in bad situations. He's gonna get you hurt or killed. What happened to you, Shana? You were stronger than this back in high school; you could see right through a guy's bullshit. Now you're acting like a fuckin' floosy."

"You don't know what you're talking about, Naja. I can take care of myself."

"I'm telling you—leave Tyrone alone."

"Or what, Naja?"

"What about Jakim? I thought y'all were getting back together?"

"We were."

"So you just gonna let him go? You gonna dump him for Tyrone?"

I become silent, and I slowly turn away from her. She folds her arms across her chest, not once taking her eyes off me.

"You gonna play Jakim like that?" she continues.

"Fuck him!" I exclaim.

"Oh, that's wrong, Shana. You know he loves you! Now here comes

Tyrone, creeping back into your life after you ain't seen or heard from him in weeks. And you ready to go play make-up with him."

"Please, it's *my* life," I state.

"And you're just gonna dump Jakim for his best friend."

"So! I don't feel for him like I feel for Tyrone."

"You talk all this shit about Jakim being your love, your heart. You're playing with fire, girl, and it's gonna blow up in your face. You can't be switching back and forth between two best friends like that."

"Well, I'm not. I'm with Tyrone, now, and Jakim's gonna have to understand."

"You gonna tell him?"

"Yup!"

"You know he ain't gonna take that shit lightly," Naja warns.

"Yeah, I know, but he won't have a choice," I say.

Naja sighs, unhappy with my decision, but it's my life and it's what I want to do. Jakim is a sweetheart. It's just that when I'm with him, sparks don't fly for me. My panties don't get moist, and I don't get aroused like I used to when we're having sex. It's different with Tyrone. He's like a cigarette: you know it's bad for your health, but you still smoke it anyway.

I know I have to tell Jakim about Tyrone—if he hasn't heard already. But I don't know how. I do know that once I tell him, he'll be upset. That's the way life is; you have to accept the good along with the bad, the bad in this case, is that I'm screwing him over for his best friend.

All week it's been nothing but Tyrone and me. He took me to see a Broadway play, we ate at Sylvia's in Harlem and he took me shopping.

I know that what Tyrone and I share is love. And I'm the only female in his life. That's why I satisfy him orally, anally and give him whatever he wants.

It's a week before Christmas, and he's asked me to move in with him. He sends a small van to my mom's crib, and a few fellas help me move my things. I don't have much to move, except for my clothes, my shoes and my television.

When I tell Naja, she thinks I've lost my mind. Aunt Tina hates to see me go, but she understands. I can't pass up this opportunity.

Word around the hood is that Jakim finally knows about Tyrone and me, and he's threatening to cause Tyrone some harm. Tyrone doesn't take his threats to heart; he understands that the boy is hurt. I know I should've told Jakim about Tyrone. It probably would have been better for him to hear about us from my lips, rather than on the street. God knows how they put it to him...but now that he knows, it feels like a burden has been lifted off of me.

Christmas day is the best. Tyrone and I wake up around eight. We make love in bed, and then in the shower. We have a real tree set up in the living room near the balcony. I make breakfast, and then we tear open our gifts. I receive a diamond ring and necklace, a gorgeous white mink, a leather jacket, shoes, a Gucci purse and lingerie.

"Why so much?" I ask, a bit overwhelmed.

"Business been good this year," he replies smiling. I bought him some sexy, silk boxers, a coat, beige Timberlands and a ring.

After opening our gifts, we cuddle on the floor and watch movies together. Tyrone loves watching old black and white movies from the forties, fifties and sixties. He's kind of old school with the flicks.

Tyrone sends chills down my spine when he starts nibbling on and whispering romantic things in my ear, tickling my body with his fingers. My baby has me open. Being warm and romantic are special qualities that he hides so well—qualities his woman knows about.

Tyrone is also a very clean and meticulous person. He puts everything in its place. And he takes his time with whatever he does; he doesn't like to rush things—extra points in the bedroom. He's also smart. He has a collection of novels, biographies, autobiographies and non-fiction books. I've never met a black male who loves to read so much. Despite his street life, you'd think he was a Harvard student, the way he sometimes carries himself—in a very professional and well mannered way.

Some brothas out here try to hide their intelligence—if they have any. They think you must always act, talk and be rugged to survive in the streets. But it ain't even about that. Some of the most notorious kingpins were very intelligent and weren't afraid to show it. Shit, you gotta be a smart man if you don't wanna do twenty-five to life and want to keep your business. I've learned so many great things about Tyrone after moving in with him.

Tyrone wants me to try on one of the lingerie outfits he's bought me. I dash into the bedroom and slip into an animal print piece and some stiletto heels. I come back out into the living room, and by the gigantic smile on his face, I know I'm looking good. "Come here!" he orders. I obey.

At about eleven a.m., after our third sexual encounter, Tyrone's cousin, Aaron, stops by. He's a cutie, too, but my man is cuter. This is my first time meeting him, and by the way he looks at me, I know he likes what he sees. Tyrone tells me to go and get dressed because we're going out. As

I get dressed in the bedroom, he discusses business in the kitchen with Aaron.

I wear my new, white mink coat along with my diamond ring and necklace. I look and feel like a superstar when I step out of the car. We approach Lassie's, a very elegant and upscale restaurant, located on the lower east side of Manhattan.

"You're looking stunning tonight," Tyrone says as we walk hand in hand into the restaurant. I blush. I feel so proud being with him tonight. It's Christmas, and there's nothing that would make me happier than being with him today. I'm lookin' fine, and so is he, dressed in a black Armani sweater, black slacks and alligator shoes.

The waiter escorts us to our table. Tyrone made reservations for two. The patrons here are mostly white, old fogies. Tyrone, being the gentleman that he is, pulls out my chair for me. Then he takes his seat opposite me.

The environment is so welcoming and genteel, and I can feel the Christmas spirit all around me. Mistletoe is all over the place. A small band of three plays Christmas carols on their stringed instruments. Our waiter is wearing a red and white Santa hat. Even our table has a small Christmas tree as a centerpiece.

Tyrone leans forward and gives me a courtly kiss. "What's that for?" I ask smiling.

"Look up," he says pointing his finger toward the ceiling. I look up and see mistletoe hanging over my head. I chuckle and begin to blush once again. "Damn, you're beautiful...Merry Christmas," he says.

"Thank you," I reply shyly. My night can't get any better. I feel like I'm in heaven. I'm out with my dream man on a dream date. I have to pinch myself to make sure everything is real. I mean, a woman like me couldn't ask for anything more. We have our own apartment—a very nice apartment—and he has money to burn, so he's not cheap. He always dresses nicely and smells good, thank God for that. And the sex is Un-fuckin'-believable. I have no complaints. My life is the bomb!

After dinner, we go on one of those horse-and-carriage rides through Central Park. We start to make out in the carriage. He fondles me through my dress, and I bless him with that thing I do. It's a little breezy out, but it's not brick- ass cold. And the cool air feels good blowing between my open legs. This is the best day of my life.

After getting home, we chill in front of the television, watching more movies and sexing each other. I lay in his arms, and he holds and caresses me gently. I feel like Cinderella with Tyrone as my handsome prince in this spacious apartment, our kingdom. I feel that no man or woman can break up what we have. This is it. He'll be my man—or maybe my husband—for lIfe. No one can take away what we have.

13 JAKIM

Just thinking about Tyrone and Shana together puts me on edge.... I sit in my bedroom, holding a loaded .45 in my hand. It's getting late. I've been calling Shana over and over again, but to no avail. Either she's ignoring me, or too busy being with Tyrone to return my phone calls. And that drives me fuckin' crazy.

I feel dissed, betrayed and used. I'm hot, but sometimes my rage turns into hurt, and I get emotional. I'll even start crying like a bitch. I want us to get back together. I thought she wanted the same thing, too. I feel stupid after telling everyone, even Latish, about us reconciling our differences. The entire time, Shana was cheating on me with Tyrone. I feel like such a jackass.

Tyrone has to pay; he's grimy. And I've finally figured out his angle, his motive. He was pushing me onto other women, while trying to convince me to leave Shana alone. But behind my back, he was pushing up on her.

I want both of them to hurt. I should go back over to Latish's and

fuck the shit out of her. I want to get even. I'm so angry that I'm even thinking about getting Latish pregnant, just to make Shana jealous. But that
absurd idea flies out of my head quickly. It wouldn't be worth it.

I hear a knock at my door. I know it's my father. "You can come in,"
I say, quickly hiding the gun under a pillow.

"You okay in here?" my father asks opening my bedroom door.

"Yeah."

"Well, Evay is at the door for you. You want any company?"

"I'll meet him outside."

"Okay," he says closing the door.

My pops is cool. He isn't in my business too much. He likes Shana.
He used to tell me that she reminded him of my mother back in the day. He
and my mother divorced ten years ago. My father is in his early fifties. He's
still an attractive man, with salt and pepper hair, smooth brown skin and a
nicely trimmed goatee. He was a playboy back in the seventies and eighties, and he finally settled down and married my mother when they were in
their mid thirties. He used to school me on women. And when I was with
Shana, he'd preach to me on how to please, talk, handle and make love to a
woman. We talked about everything. But at this moment, I can't talk to him
about what's going on. I don't want him to talk me out of anything. I know
he'd probably tell me it's not worth it. But I'm crying, and I've never cried
over a bitch.

I get my nerves together and meet Evay outside. I notice that he
looks fucked up. "Yo, what da fuck happened to you?" I ask. Somebody
fucked him up pretty badly. His lips are split and swollen. One of his eyes is
bruised and closed shut, and he has a big bump on the right side of his
head.

"Your boy did this to me. Tyrone and his crew jumped on me last night. He threw me out of the crib and moved that bitch in with him. No dis-respect, Jakim."

"None taken—fuck her!"

"Jakim, he ain't right. How he gonna do me like this? Yo, we all grew up together, and he gonna violate me like this, Ja...over some pussy!" Evay cries out.

"Yo, don't worry about it, Evay. We gonna handle it. I promise you that," I tell him.

Evay is in bad shape. I think his pride and spirit is more damaged than anything else. Tyrone and his crew fucked him up pretty bad. He's a sight for sore eyes.

"Yo, come inside. We'll talk in my room."

As I'm about to walk into the house, my cell phone rings. I look at the caller ID. It's Latish. This bitch doesn't give up. I'm not in the mood to talk to her. But in a way, it feels good to be wanted.

Evay and I have a long talk, and we smoke, drink and get fucked up. He ends up falling asleep on the couch and doesn't leave my crib till the next morning.

I know that I have to confront Shana personally now. The bitch can run, but she can't hide.

SHANA 14

The night is young. My body quivers as I stare up at the bedroom ceiling. I bite down on my bottom lip and close my eyes, enjoying the moment, as my man devours me with his tongue.

The television is still on, but our attention isn't at all on the anchor person broadcasting what we see every day—crime, murder and corruption. I moan and clutch the back of his head, scratching and digging into his cornrowed hair. "Oh, baby," I cry out. Tyrone moves his hands up to my breasts, pinching and squeezing them. I can't wait to feel him inside me. Ever since I've moved in, our nights have been nothing but sex. We just can't get enough of each other. Naja continues to warn me that I'm making a big mistake, moving in with my sweetheart. She can't be anything but wrong I'm a woman now, and I know what's right and what's not right for my life. And right now, Tyrone is feeling so damn right.

"Oh, baby, turn off the television," I say restlessly. "It's starting to bother me." He reaches around the bed for the remote, not once getting distracted from eating me out. When he finally finds it beside me, he leans to one side, with his tongue still in me, and clicks off the television. The room becomes dark. The only light coming through our bedroom window is from streetlights and other buildings.

I moan and grunt as Tyrone continues to deeply penetrate me with his long, moist tongue. He moves it against my clit and sucks on my shit like there's no tomorrow. "Aaaaaahhh, baby, don't stop! You gonna make me cum!" I cry out, gripping the bed sheets and tightening my legs around his neck.

He sucks on my lips below, and then he moves his tongue down a bit and sticks it in my asshole. He puts his tongue so far up in me that I think it's stuck. With his tongue still inside me, he sticks two fingers in my pussy, causing my eyes to flutter. I begin to tremble and dig my nails in his hair again.

"Tyrone, shit...I love you!" The position I'm in is almost unbearable. He rapidly and simultaneously fingers me and eats out my asshole. I pant loudly. He's taking control of my body, and he's doing wonders with it.

Then for twenty minutes straight, he eats my pussy—so good that I want to pass out. Shit, he even kisses and sucks the back of my knees, which is a sensation I've never felt before; it's very ticklish and pleasing. He also hits my G-spot numerous times.

I'm so wet, and I just can't take it anymore. As I'm about to tell him to fuck me, his cell phone rings, causing him to be distracted from the pussy. He jumps off the bed and retrieves his phone from the nightstand. "Yo!" he answers. I turn and rest on my side, watching him. I can really see spending the rest of my life with him.

"Yo, Shana, I gotta bounce for a minute," Tyrone says clicking off his cell.

"What? Go where?"

"That was my boy. Some shit went down earlier, and I gotta go take care of it," he says throwing on his clothes, looking like he's in a rush.

"I'm sayin' though, why they can't handle shit for once without you, Tyrone?"

"'Cause this is business, Shana."

"I thought *I* was your business a few minutes ago." He gives me a sly, smug look. He walks up to me and says, "Don't worry, boo. When I get back, I'm gonna dig all up in that pussy for twenty-four hours non-stop—just me and you. I promise."

"Yeah, I know," I softly reply. He kisses me on the forehead and throws on his beige leather jacket. He makes his exit, leaving me naked, horny and alone. My pussy is throbbing somethin' serious, and it needs to be scratched. I hear the apartment door slam and become angry—angry with him and then myself. I should have fucked him earlier, and maybe I wouldn't be feeling like this.

I'm so wet down there that I've left stains on the sheets. I'm dripping with excitement. I need to be pleased. I throw a pillow between my legs, trying to turn my lust for some dick down a few notches. It isn't working. Tyrone has left me in a sexual fuckin' frenzy. It was getting so good before his fuckin' phone went off. Fuck whoever called him. They took my dick away for the night, just when I needed it so badly.

I toss the pillow across the room. I move my right hand between my legs and start massaging myself gently. I bury two fingers into my opening and moan lightly. I continue on with this for several minutes, but it's not working for me. I need something bigger. I curse myself for not having a dildo. But I never needed toys; I always had access to dick. Frustrated, I get out of bed and go into the kitchen, thinking that a snack might make me feel better.

I walk into the kitchen and look in the fridge for a quick, small meal. I see something that could be very useful to me right now—a fuckin' cucumber. I think about it. It's big enough, and it's definitely long enough. *Nah, I can't*, I say to myself. But between my thighs is telling me something different. Without a second thought, I snatch the cucumber from out of the fridge and stroll back to the bedroom with it.

I sprawl out across the bed and do the unbelievable. I place the cucumber between my thighs and slowly begin to penetrate myself with it. I moan as I push it deeper and deeper inside me. It's about nine inches long and the width is great. I continuously thrust it in, panting with each stroke. I'm thinking about Tyrone the entire time. I throw my head back against the pillow and cry out as I fuck the huge vegetable. It takes me about twenty minutes to cum with it, and I cum hard. I huff and gasp, letting the cucumber fall out of my hands while staring up at the ceiling. This was something totally new for me, and it was good, too.

Morning comes before I know it. I roll over to an empty space in the bed, a space where Tyrone is supposed to be lying, all snuggled up against me. But he hasn't come home yet. He's been gone since he left me horny and hanging out to dry last night.

I turn to the weather channel, and the forecast is snow. I cringe just thinking about it. I really hate the cold months. I love warm weather, because then I can sport cute outfits, like short skirts and halter-tops. Jakim used to hate what I came to school in sometimes. He'd always threaten to send me home to change, saying I was embarrassing him because all of his friends were clocking me. He'd play himself out and scream on me like I was a four-year-old. *Niggah, you're my boyfriend, not my daddy!* I'd tell him. Then we'd start arguing in front of everyone like two fools.

I cover myself with the sheets and blanket, exposing only my head. The room is cold, and being naked doesn't help matters much. It's twenty-five degrees outside, just a week after the New Year.

Tyrone and I celebrated the New Year lovely. He bought a few bottles of E&J and champagne and we stayed in, enjoying each other's company. Ten minutes to midnight, we went out on the balcony of our apartment, peering over our Queens neighborhood from the twelfth floor with a glass of champagne in our hands. He held me tightly in his arms as the cold air gave us a chill, and we waited for midnight to come....

"Five, four, three, two, one...happy new year!" we shouted simultaneously with our glasses raised in the air, hearing horns honking from below and people shouting from the streets. Tyrone gave me a gentle and very passionate New Year's kiss. "I love you, Shana," he said.

"I love you, too, baby," I reply.

Afterward, he carried me off to the bedroom and gently laid me down on the bed. Then we stripped naked and made love for the very first time this year.

They say that the person you bring in the New Year with is the person you're gonna spend your entire life with. I pray that that's so in my case, because Tyrone is definitely the kind of man I want to spend forever with.

In the afternoon, I go to get my hair done by my girl, Sandra, and of course, she has the latest gossip on everyone around the way. "Girl, let me tell you about so-and-so, and let me inform you on whatcha-ma-call-it." She just runs her mouth as I sit there listening, laughing and running my mouth right along with her.

"Shana, let me tell you somethin' about your friend, Sasha. Oh, sorry, girl; I meant to say your *ex-friend*, Sasha. You know she still fuck with that bouncer from the club, right?" I'm surprised. I thought she would have used him up and dumped him by now. "Well, they were arguing and fighting right out here on the corner the other day," Sandra continues. "She slapped him and spit in his face. Then he yoked her up and threw her down on the ground."

"Nah, you lying. Fo' real?"

"I'm serious. Someone had to call the cops on them two before it got worse out there. I don't even know why she's messing with him. He ain't cute."

"You telling me, but that's her man and her business." And to think that bitch trashed our friendship over some ugly, black, trifling brotha. He had money, yes, but no class. It all got started because she volunteered to suck his dick that night we went to the club.

She continues to talk and do my hair for the next hour. "Girl, I heard you moved in with Tyrone. Damn, y'all together like that?"

"Yeah, girl."

"Mmm, mmm, mmm...that's a fine man," she says, telling me something I'm already aware of.

"Word, Sandra, that niggah knows how to handle his business in and out of the bedroom. Shit, last night he had my toes curling like pretzels. That niggah's tongue felt so good."

"Word, he be going downtown on you like that?"

"Yup, whenever he can, and I don't even ask him for it. That niggah be like, 'Lie down on your back and spread your legs,' and I don't complain or say shit about it. I just let him do his thang."

"Damn, girl, you are so lucky. I have to practically beg my man to eat my pussy. But he ain't got shit to say when I be suckin' his dick."

"Then stop suckin' his dick," I say.

"Yeah, but that niggah's shit be tasting so good, and I love it when he gets hard in my mouth."

"Nah, see, you're a nasty bitch!" I say laughing.

"Shana, don't front; you know you be suckin' Tyrone off, too."

"Yeah, but it goes both ways between us. I don't keep doing him a favor and he's not returning it. Nah, it's fifty-fifty between us."

"Do he got a big dick, too?" she asks frankly.

"See, bitch, now you're asking too many personal questions."

"I'm sayin' though, I'm just curious. I know his fine ass gotta be packing somethin' lovely below...so do he?"

"You see me smiling, right?"

"See, I'm hatin' right now...but you go, girl." She remains quiet for a few minutes and focuses on my hair. I gaze at myself through one of the many mirrors in the shop.

Whenever I walk into this place, bitches stare and start hatin' on me, just because I don't need a weave. They be scoping me from head to toe. They're either impressed or envious of my style and looks. But I don't give a fuck about them because it's only about me. I got what I want in life—

a loving man, a little money, beauty, my own place and that good piece of dick that runs up in me almost every night.

"You'll be done in another thirty minutes," Sandra informs me as she presses my hair. "Have you heard from Jakim?"

"We're over, Sandra," I say letting out a huge sigh. I mean, I still love him and all, but I felt that it was time for me to move on."

"Yeah, with Tyrone...Jakim ain't beefing about that?"

"Yeah, he is, but I ain't run into him yet—to talk it out. I feel bad for him, but that's life...what you gonna do?"

"Girl, you got better dick in your life now. Forget about him and do you." I smile in agreement.

By two-thirty I'm done, and I'm lookin' even finer than when I walked into the place. I pay Sandra and tip her the usual twenty.

I take a taxi and return home around three. I'm hoping that my baby has gotten back, because I really want to give him some.

I walk into the apartment to find the place completely quiet. The first thing I do is turn up the heat; it's fuckin' brick outside...I hate winter with a passion. I come out of my coat and shoes and plop down on the couch, turning on the television. I have my hair and nails done, and a new outfit hanging in the closet, so this is definitely not the time for me to be sitting around this apartment. I want to go out with my baby tonight. I want to be in his arms. I want him to sport me around and have people say that we're a very cute couple.

The phone rings at four. It better be Tyrone. "Hello?"

"Baby, what's up, it's me," Tyrone says.

"Tyrone, where are you? You got me sitting here waiting and worrying about your ass," I chide.

"Yo, I'm up in the Bronx right now."

"The Bronx!"

"Yeah, I had to take care of some business that went down last night."

"I called you, and you didn't answer your cell. What's up?"

"Ain't nothin' up, Shana. I'll be home around eight tonight."

"Eight! Why so late?"

"C'mon, Shana, I don't need the stress right now. I've got too much shit to take care of tonight."

"I need taking care of, too," I tell him in my softest, sweetest voice.

"I know you do, Shana. That's why tonight, when I get home, I want you dressed in your finest and sexiest outfit, because I'm taking you out."

"For real? Where?"

"It's a secret, boo...you know I'm gonna look out for my lady love, right?"

"Yeah, I know. And I'm gonna look out for you, too."

He chuckles, causing me to do the same. I can't wait till eight to see my man. I look at the wall clock over the television. It's five after four—four hours to go. "Keep it warm for me, Shana; it's fuckin' brick out here."

"Don't worry, baby. It's staying warm till you get here to put it on fire."

He laughs. "You a trip, Shana."

"I love you."

"I love you, too," he replies, making my body temperature rise and my pussy run like Niagara Falls. I hang up, feeling like I'm on cloud nine. I want things to stay this way forever.

Eight he said. What am I to do till eight? I love my new home, but it isn't much fun staying in without Tyrone being here to heat things up with me. I can only watch so much television, and there's nothing good playing on the radio right now. It's too cold out for me to go drink and chill out on the balcony...it's too cold for me to be going outside period. I go through hundreds of CDs in our collection. Tyrone has everything from pop and jazz, to rap, hip hop and R&B. I want to listen to something smooth and romantic—sexual—something that will get me in the mood till my man arrives—something that will get me hot and horny.

I put on a Miles Davis CD and go into the bedroom with a glass of wine. I sit down on my comfortable sheets, wearing nothing but a sheer nightgown. The early nightfall of January is about to come. The apartment is steaming hot, and I set the thermostat to eighty.

I listen to the music of Miles Davis, thinking about my man. I want to feel his touch, his fingers exploring my body. I lie back on the comforter and spread my legs, placing my hand between my thighs. I begin touching myself; he told me to keep it warm, and I'm going to fulfill his wishes.

I continue to play CDs all evening, from Curtis Mayfield and Sade, to R. Kelly and Blackstreet. I'm so wet, horny and hot now that I almost feel like taking a step out onto the balcony for a little cold air.

I look at the clock on the nightstand. It's six twenty-five. Damn, I wish my man would hurry up and get back here. I don't want to get too started without him.

I decide to take a bath. I sit down in the tub to take a warm and stimulating bubble bath. The small radio in the bathroom is tuned to 98.7 Kiss FM, and a few scented candles are lit around the tub. I just relax in the warm water, soothing my thoughts and finding solitude.

About a half hour later, I step out of the tub, dripping wet. I reach for the towel and gaze at myself in the full-length mirror behind the bathroom door. I blow myself a kiss and slowly start to dry myself off. I begin to feel very aroused as I reminisce about my sexual encounter with Danny in my mother's bathroom. I put lotion on my skin and don my blue cotton robe. I look over at the bathroom clock. It is now a quarter past seven. I walk to the bedroom, open my closet door and pull out my mink coat. I throw it on the bed and grab my clear stilettos. I'll be completely naked underneath the mink, and I know Tyrone is going to love it; he won't have to waste any precious time stripping me down. All he'll have to do is jump in it. And we'll still have plenty of time to do our thing before going out tonight.

I walk around the apartment nude, with my mink coat placed neatly across the sofa and my stilettos off to the side. I'm very excited.

I sprawl out across the plush carpet in the living room now and watch cable TV. The doorbell rings at eight-fifteen. *Why would Tyrone ring the doorbell when he has his own key?* No longer dwelling on that thought, I jump up off the floor and throw on my mink. I slip on my stilettos and go to open the door without asking who it is. *Who else could it be but Tyrone?* I quickly open the door, flinging back one side of my mink coat so he'll be able to catch a good view of my naked body. I'm stunned when I see Jakim standing before me. Shocked, I quickly pull both sides of the mink together, clutching them tightly. "Jakim, what are you doing here?" I say.

"I'm here to see you," he replies, staring harshly at me. I take a step back into the apartment, releasing the door. I feel so embarrassed. He totally caught me by surprise. Jakim, raising his hand to keep the door from slamming shut, wedges himself between the doorway and the foyer.

"What's up wit' that? You gotta cover yourself around me now?"

he asks, seeing me clutching my mink tightly across my bare body. "It ain't like I never saw you naked before."

"It's different between us now. I was your woman before. I'm not now," I say, standing just a few feet away from him. He steps all the way into my apartment and lets the door shut behind him. I can see the hurt and pain in his face as he stands in the foyer, dressed in a black leather jacket, faded jeans and a wool Yankees cap. He glares at me with his fists balled. "What's up wit' us, Shana?"

"What are you talking about?"

"I'm sayin', you and Tyrone being together...what's up wit' that?"

I don't answer. I'm actually scared. I look into his eyes and see black. I remain still. I pray that he doesn't go crazy. I don't want to end up on the eleven o' clock news, with some reporter telling the city about a young girl being murdered in her apartment by her crazed and jealous ex-boyfriend. I love my life.

Everything is finally falling into place for me...finally going right. "Jakim, I still love you, but I feel it's time for us to move on with our lives separately," I calmly explain to him.

"What the fuck do you mean *move on?* I'm trying to be with you, Shana. I don't want anybody else."

"Well, I do. And no matter how much it hurts you, you have to accept the fact that I'm with Tyrone now—and we're in love."

"He don't love you!" he shouts. "You ain't nothin' but a show piece to him, Shana. I'm telling you, Tyrone ain't nothin' but a dog...all he's gonna do is fuck you, front like he really cares about you, then trash you like the rest of his hoes out there. I've seen him do it. He talks shit about you all the time."

"Then why he got me livin' in his crib? Why he bought me all of these things for Christmas? Please, Jakim, you don't know what you're talking about."

"Shana, you ain't nothin' but some in-house pussy to him! You think you're the only female he buys things for? Yo, I'm telling you, I grew up with him, and I know how he gets down. He don't love you, Shana. *I* do! *I* love you! *I* wanna be with you!"

"Jakim, please...I think you need to leave."

"Why you playing me out like that, Shana? You mean the world to me."

"Well, you shoulda thought about that before you got wit' them hoes around the way," I say.

"You gonna keep bringing that shit up! I keep telling you I'm sorry. You gonna let this one mistake ruin us? You just gonna throw what we had out in the cold like that? Shana, what about Thanksgiving night, when you said you never stopped loving me? Did you really mean it?" he says coming closer to me. "I love you so damn much. I'm hurting being without you. And I hate to see you with a guy like Tyrone, when I know what he's all about. You're my heart, Shana."

I see a few tears trickle down Jakim's cheek as I continue to clutch my mink tightly. Nothing he's saying makes any difference to me. All I keep thinking is that he hurt me. He was the one who fucked up our relationship. He's at fault—not me. And I feel he's lying, saying negative things about his friend just to break us up. Since Tyrone and I have been together, he treats me like his queen. He always puts me first, other than tonight, in which case he claims he's taking care of business.

Jakim suddenly reaches inside his leather jacket. I take a quick step back, thinking that he might be reaching for some kind of weapon, a gun maybe. I get scared. He comes closer, and I take a few more steps back away from him. I know he sees the fear in my eyes. This is the first time I feel threatened by him.

"Why you backing up?" he asks. I begin searching the room for a weapon. I feel stupid when he pulls out a small, black velvet case, gripping it in the palm of his hand. He gets down on one knee. He slowly opens the case. Inside is a diamond ring. "Shana, I want you to become my wife. Will you marry me?"

I become wide-eyed, and my jaw drops. I'm in total shock. The ring looks flawless...it's beautiful. I'm speechless, baffled even. I ease the grip on my mink, exposing my nakedness. I no longer care if Jakim sees me in the raw. Slowly placing my hands over my mouth, feeling like I'm about to cry, I gaze into his eyes and see that he's dead serious. He doesn't blink or turn his head; he just keeps his eyes fixed on me, waiting for an answer. "Jakim—"

"Please, don't say no. I love you too much to hear a no from you. I want to marry you, have kids and raise a family with you, Shana. I know I've made a mistake. But I promise you, if you become my wife, you will always be first in my life. I will always do right by you, Shana. I'm done with all the bullshit. Let's just put the past behind us and move on from here."

A tear slowly trickles down my cheek as I look down at him, still on one knee with the case in the palm of his hand. My heart pounds vigor-ously against my chest—he just proposed to me. "Jakim, I can't," I tell him.

He closes his eyes and opens them again. "Please, Shana, I've already made one huge mistake cheating on you and not putting you first. I don't want you to make that same mistake by saying no. I know we'll work things out together. I feel that strongly in my heart. I know you feel it, too."

"Jakim, this is too much for me to handle right now," I say sighing.

"All I'm asking is for us to be together, for you to be my wife."

"I can't, Jakim. I'm in a relationship right now."

"But Shana, you're making a big mistake—believe me, he ain't no good for you," he warns me with tears in his eyes.

This is hard, but I already know my answer. I have to say no. I can't hurt one man's feelings by marrying another one who already hurt mine. Yes, I still do love him, but I'm sticking with this decision.

Jakim gets back on his feet and slowly closes the case. He can't even look me in the eye now. He's definitely hurt by my rejection.

"I just can't right now," I say firmly.

He doesn't say a word. The silence between us feels a bit eerie. I want to run to the bedroom and put on something decent. I feel awkward standing here in only a mink and stilettos.

"Shana..."

"Oh, shit! What time is it?" I shout. I suddenly remember that Tyrone is supposed to be home soon. I dash to the living room and glance at the clock over the television. It's eight twenty-five. "Jakim, you definitely gotta go," I say.

"You break my heart, now you gonna rush me out," he replies. I don't know what else to tell him. I look at him just standing there, probably feeling sorry for himself or envying his boy.

"Tyrone's about to come home soon," I inform him. By the look on his face, I know he isn't too thrilled about hearing his name right now. But I had to warn him.

"Fuck him! I got a few words for him, too!" he angrily shouts.

"Please, Jakim, just leave here in peace."

"Nah, you're *my* woman. How that niggah gonna disrespect me like that?"

I stop myself from saying what I was just about to say, and I calm my nerves because I want him to leave here in peace. He's really beginning to upset me, talking that shit about I'm still his woman. He just can't get the fact that it's over through his head.

"Yo, Shana, just think about us...my proposal...."

I just look at him. *Didn't I already tell him no?* "Jakim..."

"I'm not leaving here till you tell me that you'll at least think it over," he says very firmly.

"Okay, I'll think about it. Now can you please just leave?!" I say, frustrated that he's still here.

Jakim leaves the apartment and proceeds toward the elevator. I stand in the doorway, still clutching my mink, watching him. He glances back at me and cracks a halfway smile. The elevator doors open, and my worst nightmare comes true: Tyrone steps off the elevator and sees Jakim standing right in front of him. They stare at each other for a moment without saying a word.

Tyrone sees me in my mink coat and stilettos. *Oh, my God. Why is this happening?*

"So what's up wit' this?" Tyrone asks. "My girl's halfway naked in the doorway with you standing here...."

"*Your* girl!" Jakim finally says.

"Yeah, *my* girl, niggah. She wit' *me* now."

"Fuck you, you fuckin' thief!" Jakim shouts. "You a bitch-ass nig-gah!"

"Yo, you don't even have to hate like that, Jakim. I ain't steal your bitch. Niggah, she came to me."

"Yo, I thought you was my boy. How you gonna dis me like that? You know how I feel about her."

"*Feel* about her! Niggah, you cheated on her so many fuckin' times I lost count. Besides, if you was fuckin' her right, then she wouldn't have come to me."

"Oh, word, it's like dat?"

"Yeah, niggah, it's like dat!" Tyrone shouts.

They argue and shout at one another like I'm not even standing here listening. I just want this to stop. "Tyrone, can you please just come inside and let it be?"

"What? Shana, you gonna take his back...both of y'all just gonna stab me in the back like that?!" Jakim says.

"Yo, just fuckin' bounce, niggah, so I can go inside and fuck my bitch right," Tyrone says sarcastically. "It's my pussy now!"

That busted the bubble. Jakim walks up on Tyrone and snuffs him against the jaw, causing him to stumble and fall back against the wall. He then hits him with a hard right. I scream as they start to fight in the hallway. They grab at and fling each other from side to side until they both just fall to the floor. Tyrone is on top of Jakim now.

"Get off of him!" I scream. "Stop it! Please, stop it!"

Tyrone is stronger and quicker than Jakim. He gives him a staggering hit across the cheek, then another.

"Get off of me! Yo, get off me!" Jakim hollers, as Tyrone has him pinned down tightly, whipping his ass.

Neighbors are starting to peek through their doors now, some coming out to see what all the commotion is about. "Cut it, with all that fighting," an elderly lady says in her red housecoat. I'm embarrassed and in tears, as some of the neighbors gawk at me like I'm at fault.

Jakim manages to get back on his feet, gripping Tyrone by his collar. His lip is bleeding and his cheek is bruised. Tyrone has put a serious hurting on him. But Jakim won't stop; he punches Tyrone twice in the face.

"Yo, niggah, what I tell you before, huh?! If you ever touch me again!" Tyrone shouts, grabbing Jakim by his jacket and throwing him up against the wall.

Security has made its way up to our floor, stepping between Tyrone and Jakim and breaking them apart. The three black guards grip their black walkie-talkies while keeping both men on opposite sides of the hallway. Jakim is screaming and threatening Tyrone. By now it seems that everyone from each apartment is out in the hallway, catching a glimpse of the excitement.

I run to my bedroom to throw on something decent. I caught a few eyes staring at me with excitement and lust. After all, I *was* in the hallway half naked. I throw on a light blue, over-sized T-shirt that comes down to my thighs. When I make it back to the doorway, I see that security has Jakim subdued down on the floor; he just wouldn't calm down. And he's *still* hollering and cursing. Tyrone is just standing there looking pissed. He's holding his right jaw, massaging it with the tip of his fingers. I guess Jakim hit him pretty hard there.

The police come also. It's total chaos. They ask who the occupants of the apartment are. I tell them just Tyrone and me. Then they ask what happened. At first no one says a word. I can see in the officers' faces that they're getting upset.

"Nothin', officer, just a little misunderstanding here," Tyrone finally says.

"Misunderstanding?! It looks like y'all were ready to bash each other's heads in," one of the security guards says.

"Everything's cool, fuck it," Tyrone says, his face screwed up like he's just sucked on an onion. He starts walking toward me, still soothing his jaw.

The police officers raise Jakim to his feet. He's now quiet and calm. Blood trickles from his lip, and the muscles in his face appear tight. He gives me a very eerie and cold stare as the officers take him by both arms and tightly hold him in custody. They haven't handcuffed him. I guess because they don't know what went down yet.

"Sir, is this your place?" a white officer asks Tyrone. He's heavyset and pale, with short, blond hair.

"Yeah, didn't my woman already tell you that!" he rudely replies.

"Do you want to press charges against this man?" the heavyset officer continues.

"Man, you don't even know what happened, and you already want me to press charges against a brotha. Fuck no! I ain't pressing no charges. I don't need y'all fuckin' help!" Tyrone chides, grilling each cop.

The officers don't look too pleased; they look about ready to take him in. They start asking the neighbors standing around if they saw what happened. But all anyone can say is that they heard yelling and then saw fighting.

"Well, we're gonna escort him out of the building and off the premises," a slim, young-looking cop says.

"Fuckin' bounce then!" Tyrone yells. "And yeah, take that faggot niggah outta here right now!"

"Fuck you!" Jakim screams.

"It's on, dog."

"That's a threat?"

"That's a fuckin' promise!" Tyrone shouts.

"Please, sir, can you lower your voice? And please, no threats...goddamn, we're standing right here, for God's sake," another middle-aged officer says.

"Fuck you, too, and bounce from my door!" Tyrone screams. I can see that the officers are really upset with Tyrone and they want to take him down bad. But he's done nothing but defend himself in the hallway near his apartment. He's not at fault since Jakim started it.

The hallway starts to clear as the cops and security guards all make their way into the elevator, leaving a few baffled neighbors still standing outside their apartment doors. They observe Tyrone and me as we stand in front of our door. "What? Is there somethin' wrong? All y'all need to mind y'all fuckin' business!" Tyrone yells at them before slamming the door.

Of course I know he has some words for me, as I have some explaining to do. He asks me why I was butt naked under a mink and wearing heels, with my ex-man coming out of the apartment. I tell him that Jakim just stopped by unannounced, and he caught me by surprise. It's kind of hard for him to believe. We yell at each other for a few minutes. I know he's upset, and I can't blame him for being so. If I came home and saw some butt-naked bitch in my apartment, or saw her leaving and caught him ass naked, shit, I would yell and curse him out, too; so I give him that. He has a right to be upset.

I finally calm my man down and tell him every detail of what happened. Then I tell him I couldn't keep Jakim from coming to see me here; he already knew where we lived. Shit, he came here all the time when they were best friends. Tyrone understands that. The only thing I don't tell him is that Jakim proposed to me. He doesn't need to know about that.

About an hour has passed, and I'm on the couch giving my man a back rub while he watches TV. Despite everything that's happened, I still want to go out, and I still want some dick. I figure that going out isn't happening, but sex, well, that's something different.

"I love you, baby," I whisper in his ear, while sliding my hands down his chest as he sits on the floor between my legs with his back propped up against the couch. "And you know I wouldn't give this pussy away to anybody except you."

He smiles and looks up at me, and then gives me a kiss. "I'm sorry I flipped out today, but you know you're my boo, Shana."

"Yeah, I know."

"So, it's definitely over between y'all two, right?"

"Now, how you gonna ask me that. Of course it's over. I'm in love with you, Tyrone," I state, massaging his chest gently.

"Aiight, cool."

I don't like his tone. "What you thinkin' about, baby?" I ask him. He appears to be scheming about something.

"Nothin', Shana."

"You ponderin' *somethin*'," I say. Then I start to think. "Tyrone, don't you do nothin' to Jakim...."

"Jakim, that pussy niggah ain't even in my thoughts right now," he replies.

"Promise me that you won't do nothin' to him then."

"Why, y'all ain't together, so what do you care?"

"Tyrone, promise me. Y'all used to be boys."

"*Used* to be," he makes clear.

"Tyrone, if you touch him, I swear—"

"You swear what, Shana? Yo, I ain't gonna touch the niggah, so don't get your panties in a stir. That's *my* job."

"You promise?"

"I promise," he says. "Come here." He turns around and faces me. Still in between my legs, he presses down on top of me and begins kissing me. "I'm not even sweating that niggah no more. It's forgotten," he assures me, pulling off my panties. "It's only about you and me."

A huge smile appears across my face and I hug him. I feel so blessed.

"I'm about to make up for last night," he says, stripping off his clothes as I lie on my back, legs spread, waiting for some dick. I grip his shit and slowly push it into me. Surprisingly, he pulls out of me and says, "Nah, turn dat butt over doggy style, and let me fuck you in the ass."

Damn. We try it once and it won't fit, but Tyrone is adamant about fuckin' me in my ass.

"You sure about this? Remember, we had problems last time," I remind him.

"You owe me this, Shana, after what went down today," he says. He grabs some baby oil and Vaseline, and he starts lubricating my asshole for easy entry. I position myself doggy style on the couch, gripping the armrest tightly. He has a big dick, and my asshole is tight. Last time we tried it, he got only four inches in, and I couldn't take it. I made him stop.

I stare ahead, waiting for his entry. I feel him grab my butt firmly, spreading my cheeks apart. I feel the tip of his dick nearing the center of my ass. He rubs baby oil on his dick, and then he slowly inserts the tip of it inside my asshole. My butt cheeks tighten involuntarily, and I start to squirm.

"Ah...shit...shit...ah!" I cry out as he pushes about five inches of dick into me. My nails dig into the couch, and he thrusts in another two inches. "Aaaaaahhh....God....ssshhhh...shit! Damn...oh...mmm...please do it slow." The lubrication is beginning to make it a bit easier for me.

He fucks me in the ass slowly. I now feel every bit of his dick pushing inside me. Tyrone must have a spell on me, because I never allowed Jakim to fuck me in the ass. He would always ask, and I'd be very adamant about it: No! And it was always no. A bit of me feels that I'm playing myself tonight, allowing Tyrone to do it.

"You love me, Shana?" he asks as he slowly moves more dick into me. His legs are apart on the edge of the couch behind me, and one of his hands is on the small of my back. I know this looks like a porno scene.

"Yes! Aaaaaahhh...ah...yes, I love you. Oh, shit!"

"Does it hurt?" he asks.

"Yes, a little," I reply weakly.

"You'll get used to it. I wanna come in your fuckin' ass."

He continues pushing dick into my tight ass for ten more minutes before pulling out. He tells me to stay in this position, and then I feel him shove his big black dick into my pussy...now that's more like it. I pant and cry out. He grips my hips on both sides and goes to work on me something lovely. I know our neighbors hear us; I'm loud and can't shut the fuck up, as he rapidly pounds about nine and a half inches into me.

I cum and I cum, and after we're done, Tyrone leaves me passed out and naked on the couch. I said it once, and I'm gonna say it again: Tyrone is nothing but right in my life. And there are too many haters out there wanting to fuck up my shit.

JAKIM 15

I place the .45 in my mouth, and I'm tempted to pull the fuckin' trigger. I hate living right now; the pain is too much for me to bear. Every fuckin' second I'm thinking about that bitch, and it's driving me crazy. I loved her, and she dissed me. She dissed me for a fuckin' loser. I got down on one knee and proposed to her, and she fuckin' dissed me and stayed with Tyrone.

I'm parked in a supermarket parking lot in Rochdale. There are no cars around, so nobody can bear witness to my attempted suicide. I'm overwhelmed with tears. I take the gun out of my mouth and place it against my temple. Maybe a shot to the head would be easier for me. I press my index finger lightly on the trigger. I so badly want to squeeze. I pant loudly, overcome with emotion. I want my suicide to be on that bitch's conscience. I want her to suffer every day for the rest of her life, knowing that she caused this. I want Shana to hate herself every day.

Do it, Jakim. Kill yourself, my mind is telling me. I should have killed her first, but I was too afraid to shoot her down like that. I should have gone after Tyrone. He humiliated me. He didn't care. He was selfish.

Do it, niggah. It won't hurt. It'll end the fuckin' pain. There's a round in the chamber...I'm ready. I stare out the windshield as tears trickle down my face. It's silent...just me and my thoughts, and soon I'm going to splatter my brains all over this car. I want her so much, and it hurts so bad not being able to have her and be with her. I have women chasing me every day, like Milk, Latish, Lisa and a few others. But yet I'm trippin' over Shana. Love is a very dangerous emotion.

I miss her...I can't live without her. We've been through a lot. But she doesn't want me anymore. I cry louder and harder. I feel like a fuckin' bitch! And the more I think about my feelings and the way I'm acting, I want to squeeze the trigger.

Go ahead, niggah. She doesn't want you anymore. You couldn't kill them, so kill your fuckin' self, bitch! My mind is racing as a million and one things run through it. I grip the gun tighter and press it to my temple. *Get it over with.*

I take one last breath. I'm ready to squeeze, but my cell phone rings, distracting me. I glance down at the number and see that it's Latish. Seeing her name appear on my screen triggers something in me. *You gonna let that bitch Shana get the best of you? Handle your business, niggah. You can play games, too.*

I take the gun from my head and dry my tears. No one will ever know how close I just came to killing myself. I get myself together and give Latish a call back.

About an hour later I'm knocking at Latish's door. I thought I'd never find myself here again. But here I am... maybe it's fate. But my plan is to get even, and I know the best way to do it. I'll make Shana jealous, even furious.

Latish comes to the door in a white robe. She's not mad at me. She accepts me with open arms. I step into her apartment and waste no time. I take her in my arms and we begin to kiss passionately. We hurry downstairs, hungry for each other. Latish tears at my clothes, and I relieve her of her robe. She's completely naked now. "I miss you, Jakim," she says as she pulls away at my belt.

"You want this dick?"

"Hell, yeah," she answers.

"I got a surprise for you," I say. "You gonna like it, too."

"Fo' real? That's what I'm talkin' 'bout."

We make our way to her bedroom. I kick open her door and push her down onto the bed. She looks up at me with a lustful smile, massaging her pussy as I get undressed. I eagerly get on top of Latish and thrust my dick into her. She screams out, gripping my back and straddling her smooth legs around my waist. I fuck her vigorously. I'm on a mission. Latish nibbles at my ear and scratches my back, enjoying every minute of the sex. "Fuck me, niggah! Take the pussy!" she screams out.

I pant and huff, and then I say to her, "I want you to have my baby."

"Yes, Jakim, I wanna give you a son. Do dat shit, niggah. Oh shit, I love you."

I knew she'd be with it. And I know that getting her pregnant will really upset Shana. Shana and Latish are friends, but there's always tension between them. And once Shana finds out that I'm about to become a father with a baby on the way by Latish, it's going to fuck her head up. And I want it like that.

I continue to fuck Latish like tomorrow will never come as sweat pours from my brow. I grip her legs firmly and dig deeper and deeper into her. Her pussy is wetter than ever. I guess the thought of me trying to get her pregnant has really excited her.

Latish pulls me close to her and whispers in my ear. "Yes, I wanna have your baby, Jakim. Cum in me, niggah."

I'm used to pulling out when I cum, or wearing a condom. But tonight I'm wilding out. I feel a sudden rush below. I know it's coming. I thrust harder.

"I'm cummin', I'm cummin', I'm cummin'," I chant.
Latish gyrates her hips against me and holds me tight. Her sheets are saturated with sweat from both of our bodies. She kisses me on the neck and then nibbles on my ear. I feel myself about to explode. I grip her bed sheets, grunting and panting as I continue to thrust myself into her.

Fuck me! Fuck me!" She grips my ass and pushes me even harder into her.

"I'm cummin'!" I shout, and a minute later I explode inside her, clutching the bed sheets and quivering between her legs. I remain on top of her for a minute or so and then roll over on my back, panting and looking up at the ceiling.

Latish nestles against me. I hold her in my arms like she's my girl, which is new for me. She savors the moment. We talk for a while, and I tell her about my fight with Tyrone. I apologize to her for slapping her when she first told me the news about him and Shana.

About a half hour later, she straddles me again, riding me like a jockey. I come in her a second time. We rest up, order some pizza, and two hours later we're fuckin' again.

The next morning I wake up to Latish sucking my dick. This is my first time ever staying the night at her place, and I don't regret it.

"Good morning, baby," she says laughing. "You like the way I woke you up?" I'm speechless. I nod and lay my head back against the pillow, allowing her to continue. She sucks on me for about fifteen more minutes, and then she straddles me again and fucks the shit out of me. I came in this bitch like four times in less than twelve hours.

I leave her place around noon. What we just did hits me a few hours later. *What the fuck were you thinking, trying to get that bitch pregnant?* I say to myself over and over again. Latish is a ho. She's cute, but to make her the mother of my child—oh my God! I try not to panic. Just because I wilded out doesn't mean she's pregnant. I thought with my dick and I was upset. I was definitely in a vulnerable state of mind.

I try to forget about my actions with Latish and the shit I went through with Shana and Tyrone by going to a bar on Supthin Boulevard.

The place is empty. I sit at the counter with a Corona in my hand and look up at the mounted TV over the bar. I want to get shit-faced drunk and forget about my problems and my life.

I take pleasure in this solitude. No one knows me in the bar. The bartender is a heavyset black man with a thick, black beard and menacing features. He's quiet; all he does is watch the game. I don't complain.

I order a second beer and continue to think about my day. I lay my head down on the counter and try to keep myself from crying. Even though the place is empty, I'm still afraid to shed tears over a woman in public.

I continue resting my head on the counter top until I hear a female voice say, "It looks like you've had a hard day."

I look up, and I'm surprised to see Naja standing behind the bar.

"What you doin' here?" I ask.

"I work here," she replies. "What are *you* doin' here, moping and looking like you lost your best friend?"

I sigh. She pauses for a moment and then answers for me. "Let me guess—Shana."

"Fuck dat bitch!"

"So you know about Tyrone."

"You see my face? We had a fight yesterday at his apartment. And she gonna side wit' that muthafucka! You believe dat, Naja? I poured my heart out to that woman, and she turned around and fucked my best friend behind my back. And then the bitch had the audacity to move in wit' da niggah. You believe dat shit?" I feel myself getting emotional again. I take a quick breath and continue. "Naja, you believe I went over there yesterday to propose to her? I had the ring and everything. I got down on one knee and asked her to be my wife. She told me no. She told me she loves Tyrone."

"Well, I think you're better off without her, Jakim. You're a good brotha. And Shana is not the woman for you," she says wiping off the counter top.

"How long you knew about this, Naja?" I ask.

"Listen, I warned Shana about it. But that girl don't listen to me. Shana is gonna be Shana, and you know it, Jakim. I told her on numerous occasions that she needed to leave Tyrone alone or tell you about it. But she didn't listen to me."

"How long has it been going on?"

"About three months," Naja says. I have no words. "Listen, Jakim, you're a fine brotha. And any woman would love to have you in her life. You have potential. You have your music. You're caring. And we all know you're not perfect, and you've made your mistakes. I feel that you do deserve a second chance, though. But sometimes, life doesn't happen that way. Now, Tyrone, he's a loser. You and I both know how he treats women, but Shana thinks he's the man for her. Let her find out the hard way. She fucked up with you. Now what you need to do is pull yourself together and stop trippin' out over her. I know plenty of women that would love to get with you. Now that you're single, the sistas are probably ready to eat you up."

"You think?" I say laughing.

"Please, you know you're fine. *I* even had a little crush on you at one time," she admits.

"Fo' real?"

"Don't get gassed, boy. That was a while ago, when we were in high school."

"I know. We're cool, though," I say.   I look away from her for a moment and take a deep breath. "I miss her, Naja. I love that woman, and she fucked me over."

"Jakim, let me give you a little hint about women: ignore them sometimes."

"Why you say that?"

"Because we hate to be ignored. And when y'all men do that, it intrigues us. We wanna know why. We want the attention. But at the same time, give her enough attention where she wants more. If a man keeps me intrigued and guessing, I gotta know more about him and what's going on in his life. But don't ever try to figure us out, because you never will."

"You think?"

"We're more complicated than y'all think," she says giving me a sly smile. "You need to free your mind of Shana, Jakim. What's done is done;

there ain't no use crying over spilt milk. Forget about her and move on. You never know, she might come back to you. And if that happens, you need to be wise about it and ask yourself: am I willing to accept her back and is it worth it, knowing the shit she put me through."

"I know."

"You're a strong man, Jakim. I know it hurts now, but you'll get over it. It could be worse; you could have married the bitch," she jokes. I laugh. "You want me to get you another beer?"

"Yeah, another Corona."

Naja goes to get my beer, and suddenly my smile turns into a troubled frown.

"What's wrong now, Jakim?" she asks popping open my beer.

"Naja, I fucked up," I admit.

"What happened?"

"I was wit' your girl, Latish, last night."

"Latish?"

"Yeah, I really fucked up. We've been doing our thang for a while now. I was only with her for the sex and to get my mind off of Shana. But last night I was so devastated after seeing her and Tyrone at his apartment that I went over to Latish's and fucked her with the intention of getting her pregnant, to make Shana jealous."

"Niggah, is you serious?" she asks staring at me. "Damn, do every niggah think only with his dick? Out of everyone you could have been with—Latish? We're cool and all, but I feel sorry for any man that has Latish for a baby mama."

"I know," I utter, burying my forehead in the palm of my hand.

"Well, what's done is done. You just better pray that she's not pregnant, because if she is, you just made the situation worse on yourself."

"Please, don't remind me."

"That beer is on the house, Jakim. You need it," she says.

"I need a miracle."

"You need *something*." Naja is definitely a true friend.

We go on talking. The bar is mostly empty, beside the few stragglers who come in from the cold for a quick drink and leave. We reminisce on old times, and she even has a few drinks and watches the game with me.

"I swear, Naja, you think you know people, and they end up stabbing you in the back," I say.

"Tell me about it."

"I mean, Tyrone and I grew up together. We've been friends since the seventh grade. I know everything about this niggah, and–" I suddenly stop. I've just come up with a brainstorm on how to get revenge on Tyrone for taking Shana from me... I know everything about him.

"What is it, Jakim?" Naja asks.

"Yo, I'll be right back. I gotta make a phone call." I walk outside and take out my cell phone. I call information to get the number for the 113th precinct. I know it would be snitching, but he's not a friend and I feel he deserves to get his. He took Shana away from me, and now I'm gonna take him away from Shana–an eye for an eye.

I get the precinct and ask for the narcotics division. "Narcotics, Detective Kennedy speaking," I hear a male voice finally say.

"Yes, I'm calling about drugs," I say.

"Yes?"

"Well, I have some information about a well known drug dealer in Queens. His name is Tyrone Sorbs."

"Go on."

"Well, I know a lot about his operation and how he conceals and transports drugs back and forth from state to state. I can give you the names of the women he uses for drug mules and certain locations where he stashes kilos of cocaine."

"And how do you know all this?" the detective asks.

"I used to work for him, and he used to be a very good friend of mine," I state. And with that, I tell everything else I know about Tyrone. For fifteen minutes more, I run my mouth to the detective.

I hang up and try to feel good about myself, but overall I feel dirty. It was certainly a fucked up thing to do.

I head back inside the bar. Naja looks at me and asks, "Jakim, what did you do? Why did you run outside so quickly?"

"I had to make a phone call—nothing important." She looks at me with uncertainty. "I'm serious. I called a girl," I lie.

"Uh huh, whatever—and I'm Beyonce," she says. "Jakim, don't be so bent up on revenge because your feelings are hurt. All it's going to do is drive you crazy and make you sick. My mother once told me, if you love something, let it go. If it's meant to be, then it will come back to you. You got a lot to look forward to in life, Jakim. I don't want to see you caught up in nothing—especially drama over a woman."

"I feel what you sayin', Naja."

"Just let it be, and I guarantee that at the end of the day, you'll feel better about yourself," she assures me.

I admit, she *has* made a few good points. But I know it's too late, because I've already blabbed my mouth off to the police. But it's a good thing that I didn't give them my name or identification.

I'm going to take Naja's advice and move on and let it be. From this point on, Shana, Latish and Tyrone are erased from my mind. They can all have each other. "Naja, I'm out," I say.

"Come here," she tells me.

"What up?" She grabs me by my jacket and pulls me over the counter top toward her. She places a warm and friendly kiss on my lips. "You be careful out there. I don't want to see you in no shit. You hear me?"

"Yeah, I hear you."

"We need to go out one night and have a few drinks."

"You know I'm all for it."

"It's a date then."

"Bet."

I say goodbye to Naja and walk out of the bar a better and happier man than when I first arrived. Naja cheered me up, and it's so good to have a friend like her.

16 SHANA

Pregnant! I can't be pregnant. I've tested myself twice already with a home pregnancy kit, and both times the results were the same—positive. For the past few days I've been nauseous, my breasts are heavier and I'm constantly using the bathroom.

My mother is the one who's supposed to be pregnant...this shit can't be happening to me. I can't deal with having kids. But then again, when I think about Tyrone and me having a family.... I know it's his child. He's the only one who's been running up in me for the past few weeks now.

I sigh and throw everything in the trash. I need to be really sure, so I make an appointment to see a doctor.

A few days later, I find myself sitting in the doctor's office waiting for my results. She comes out and takes a seat at her desk. She's wearing a white lab coat and wire-rimmed glasses. "Ms. Banks, you're definitely pregnant," she informs me while looking over my chart.

I bow my head and let out a huge, stressful sigh. "How far along am I?" I ask with serious concern in my voice. "Three, four weeks?"

She looks up at me, baffled. "Ms. Banks, you're eight weeks pregnant."

"What? You got to be shitting me!" I shout, startling her. "Are you sure that test is reading right?"

"Yes, and the test shows that you're eight weeks pregnant."

I want to pass out. This can't be happening to me. If I'm eight weeks pregnant, that means I conceived some time in November. That's not good, because there are three different men who could possibly be the father: Tyrone, Jakim...and Danny.

"Ms. Banks, when is the last time you had your monthly period?" I think about it it was November, but I didn't stress missing my period in December because my aunt missed hers due to stress, and she wasn't pregnant. I figured I had the same problem, since I was dealing with a lot of stress during that time.

The doctor reaches across the table and takes my hand, trying to comfort me, as I start bugging out. "Look, there are options, you know, like adoption, abortion.... I suggest you think about it, give yourself time."

I feel my eyes watering up. This just can't be happening. I'm definitely pregnant, but the only question is, by whom?

I go home and take a nice, hot bath. As I sit in the tub, a lot of shit goes through my head like, *what if the baby turns out to be Jakim's or even worse, Danny's? How would I deal with that—me and my mother being pregnant by the same guy?* Just the thought of it makes me jump out of the tub and throw up in the toilet. I get back in the tub and think, *what if it turns out to be Tyrone's?* I wonder how he'll take it. Will he leave me if it turns out to be Jakim's? No matter how I look at it, I'm still in a fucked up predicament. I soak in the tub for about an hour more before getting out and drying myself off. I go to bed and cry all night.

I wake up for the third day straight with no Tyrone in bed with me. Frustrated, I call his cell phone, but there's no answer. I page him twice, but he doesn't call back. For the first time in weeks, I'm starting to have doubts about my relationship with him. His negative behavior toward me for the past two weeks has me thinking. When he's home, all he wants to do is fuck me. He doesn't want to go out anymore, at least with me. He doesn't talk to me, and he's forever on the phone whispering secretly to someone late at night when he thinks I'm asleep. What makes me really upset is when he stays out for nights at a time—like now—not even giving me a courtesy phone call to inform me that he's all right, or to check and see if everything is okay with me. Now here I am pregnant, and I'm not even sure if it's his.

And I thought things couldn't get any worse, but I was wrong. I'm even starting to get threatening calls from Chinky. She isn't trying to let bygones be bygones. She calls me at all times of the day, be it three in the morning or three in the afternoon. She rings my phone and says things like, "*It's still on, bitch! I'm gonna fuck your ass up! Tyrone's my fuckin' man; you ain't nothin' but some cheap, in-house pussy!*"

Arguing with her is pointless, so I always just hang up on her. But she usually calls back again minutes later. I'm starting to see that I'm going to have to go to war with that bitch!

This is the fourth night that Tyrone hasn't brought his ass home, and I decide to go and spend the weekend over at my mother's. I need someone to keep me company, and I don't care who it is. Besides, I have to tell my mother the news of me being pregnant. I'll just leave out that there are three possible fathers, including her man, Danny.

I catch a cab to my mother's house. I lug my suitcase up the front steps when I spot Danny's truck parked out front. The first thing that comes to my mind is that he and my mother could have made up by now. Then I start to feel nauseous when I think about the possibility of me carrying his child, as well as my mother. I pause halfway up the steps, trying to get my head and my emotions right. I want to look strong. I haven't seen my mother and aunt in weeks. I have to walk up in there and let them know I'm doing well for myself, no matter how fucked up things are looking for me.

I walk through the front door and drop my suitcase to the side. The place still looks the same, but I realize that I haven't been gone for that long. It's quiet, and I assume they're fucking in her bedroom, making up for lost time being apart. I walk past my mother's bedroom. Her door is open, and there isn't anyone inside. Then I start to hear noises coming from my aunt's bedroom. Curious, I slowly walk toward her room.... *Oh, no she isn't*, I say to myself.

The closer I come to my aunt's door, the louder the sounds of ecstasy that are coming from her room get. I peer inside the slightly open door and can't believe my eyes. My aunt, with her back to me, is riding Danny like there's no fuckin' tomorrow.

Stunned, I cup my hand over my mouth. *No, this niggah didn't! And no, this bitch didn't!* "Oh, hells no!" I scream, startling them as I fling open her bedroom door all the way and storm into her room.

"Shana!" my aunt shrieks, jumping off the dick, while Danny quickly gets up and plants his feet on the floor. He stands there naked.

"Yo, what's up wit' this?" he says looking at me.

"What the fuck is the matter with you? You got my mother pregnant, and now you fuckin' my aunt!" I yell.

"Shana, I can explain," my aunt says with the bed sheets pulled up to her chest.

"You're wrong, Aunt Tina," I say to her shaking my head in disbelief.

"Bitch, you got some nerve trying to criticize me when you was riding this same dick a few weeks ago. Don't be acting like it wasn't good to you," Danny says blowing up my spot in front of my aunt.

"What the fuck is he talking about?" my aunt asks.

"I fucked your niece, too. That's what I'm talking about," he vulgarly says. His words send chills down my back.

"Oh, you nasty bitch!" my aunt shouts.

"Nasty?! You're the one busted, Aunt Tina."

Danny just stands there with this fuckin' smirk on his face, like he's mocking us. Yeah, he ran up in all three ladies in the house, and we're the stupid ones to have given it up to him. He played all of us. I just want to run over there and fuck his ass up.

"Look, I'm out," Danny says pulling up his pants.

"Niggah, you think you just gonna come up here and fuck everyone and be ghost like that?!" I shout running up in his face.

"Y'all bitches need help."

"What? Niggah, you're the bitch. You ain't shit, Danny!" my aunt yells, trying to play like she's on my side.

"Whatever! I did y'all a favor."

"Fuck you, muthafucka! Fuck you!" I scream, slapping him across his face so hard that my hand stings. I'm not just raving mad at him; I'm mad at life period. Tyrone is acting up, showing his ass, after I thought we had something special. Then there's Jakim. He showed his ass a long time ago when he cheated on me, and now he wants me to give him a second chance and marry him. He thinks I'm being hard on him, but he doesn't' understand that I took it hard, the shit he did to me. And this muthafucka, Danny, he wasn't no good in the first place. I now see that all he ever cared about was a piece of pussy. He didn't give a fuck about my mother and her feelings toward him. I also had no regard for her feelings, because if I did, I wouldn't have fucked her man and be worrying about whether I'm carrying his baby or not. That's where that hard slap came from. Life just isn't fair.

"Bitch, are you crazy? Don't you ever put your mutha-fuckin' hands on me!" Danny shouts as he returns the slap I gave him, pimp-slapping me hard across the face and knocking me down to the floor.

My aunt is hysterical. She jumps on Danny's back, scratching and digging into his face, and he knocks her back down onto the bed. I remain on the floor, crying my eyes out. *Why is this happening?* I'm hurting more mentally than physically.

"I'm out. Y'all bitches are crazy." Danny fastens his jeans and throws on his shirt. "Y'all some fuckin' hoes anyway."

"What about my mother? You just gonna walk out on her, too? She's carrying your baby, and you just going to walk out on her like that?!" I shout, still on the floor looking up at him with tears in my eyes.

"Fuck that ho, too. She's the stupid one who got herself pregnant. Tell that stupid bitch to get an abortion, because I ain't takin' care of no got-damn babies," he says before exiting the room.

I start to breathe heavily. I feel like I'm about to have a panic attack. My aunt kneels beside me and cradles me in her arms. "It's all right, Shana. Fuck him! That muthafucka is definitely going to get his. I promise that shit," she assures me.

"We ain't right, Aunt Tina. We ain't right," I say, my words filled with pain.

"It's going to be okay, Shana. It's going to be okay," she says continuing to comfort me, despite everything that's happened.

"No, it's not, Aunt Tina," I utter. "I'm fuckin' pregnant! And I don't even know who the father is."

"What?"

"I'm pregnant, Aunt Tina," I repeat, sobbing.

"Oh, God, Shana. You know by who?"

"I told you, I don't know by who."

She looks at me closely, reading my pain. She's not stupid when it comes to situations like this. "You think Danny is one of the possible fathers?" she says. I don't answer her. I just keep crying, diverting my eyes to the floor. "Oh, Shana, how can you be so careless?!" she exclaims. This is coming from the woman who just got caught fuckin' the same guy. She helps me to my feet and over to her bed. "What are you planning to do, Shana?" my aunt asks as she gets dressed.

"I don't fuckin' know, Aunt Tina. What am I *supposed* to do?"

"Do you plan on telling your mother?"

"That's why I came."

"Shit," she mumbles to herself.

A few minutes later, we hear the front door shut. It has to be my mother. I agree with my aunt to keep her and Danny a secret. This family is already going through enough shit. But I have to tell my mother about my pregnancy. She's already three months into hers. *How will she react to the news?*

I dry my tears and go into the living room to greet my mother. She's holding the day's mail in her hand, sorting through it. "Hey, Ma," I say, greeting her with a phony smile plastered across my face.

She looks up from the mail and smiles when she sees me. "Shana, it's about time you came by, girl; it's been weeks. So how are things between you and Tyrone?"

"They're cool," I lie.

"Is he treating you right?"

"I'm pregnant!" I blurt out.

She just stands there looking surprised.

"Yeah, I'm pregnant, Ma."

"I see. By Tyrone, I hope." I nod my head yes, but I can't tell her the whole truth.

My mother was sixteen when she had me, younger than I am now, so she can't bitch about me being too young. I was born two days after my mother's sixteenth birthday, so that means she got pregnant when she was only fifteen.

My Aunt Tina is no saint either. She's already had two abortions, and my mother told me she had a miscarriage when she was fifteen; so she also isn't in any position to criticize me. This is my first pregnancy.

I have a long talk with my mother. She asks if I plan on keeping it. I tell her I'm not sure, but there is a good possibility that I just might. She makes me a cup of hot chocolate and we have something that we haven't had in a while—a mother-daughter talk. Deep down inside, I really want to tell her the whole truth—that Danny could also be this baby's father along with Jakim—that I'm a slut and fucked her man behind her back many times. But I hold my tongue. I do tell her about the problems I'm starting to have

with Tyrone, about him not being home half the time, the marriage proposal from Jakim and the fight between them in the hallway. She eases my pain
by telling me that I can always move back home whenever I feel like it.

It's been two weeks since that talk with my mother, and the problems with
Tyrone haven't stopped. We argue and bicker with each other almost every
other day. Moving in with the muthafucka was a bad idea.

Sometimes he'll call home and tell me to clean up the apartment,
because he's bringing some of his boys over to watch TV and chill for the
night. Other times the phone will ring or his cell phone will go off in the middle of the night and he'll quickly answer it, leaving out the door minutes
later.

Chinky isn't making things any better for me. She's constantly calling here, harassing me and trying to curse me out. I beg Tyrone to change
the number, but he tells me no and to just stop answering the fuckin' phone.
I feel that he's stopped loving me. I have a very strong feeling that he's
fuckin' some other bitch out there. Besides Chinky, some other ho is calling
here; when I answer the phone there's nothing but silence, and then she
hangs up. I know it's a woman, because his boys always call him on his cell
phone.

I'm procrastinating on telling him I'm pregnant, because like I said,
I'm not even sure if it's his baby. And by the way he's acting, I'm not so sure
if I want this baby to be his anyway. We rarely see each other, and when we
do, we're either arguing or fucking. I'm starting to believe what Chinky and
Jakim said—that I'm nothing but some in-house pussy."

It's Friday night and I'm in my apartment, but I'm not alone. I'm spending some time with the girls—Naja, Sandra and—I hate to say it—even Latish. She came with Naja. Tensions are definitely high between us, though. I still owe her an ass-whooping for that stunt she pulled with my uncles.

We order Chinese food and rent a few movies for the night. It feels good having my girlfriends around. I haven't told any of them about my pregnancy yet. I will tonight.

Naja puts in one of the movies we rented, and we all start digging into our Chinese food. I can't eat or enjoy the movie; I have too much on my mind. I haven't seen or heard from Tyrone in three days. It's pissing me off. And I'm starting to hear rumors about Jakim being with another woman. I know it shouldn't bother me, but it does big time! I can't blame him for getting on with his life. He needs to. I just never thought it would be so soon.

"What's wrong, girl?" Naja asks me.

"Nothing, I'm cool."

Naja has known me since elementary school; she knows how to read me, and she knows when I'm upset about something. "How's everything going with you and Tyrone?" she says.

I let out a sigh, knowing that I have to be honest; maybe Naja knows something that I don't. "Fuck Tyrone!" I shout, feeling the tears coming to my eyes.

"Damn, girl, it's that bad between y'all two?" Sandra asks.

"What's wrong, Shana? Talk to us," Naja says with concern.

"I haven't seen or heard from his trifling ass in three days. He hasn't called and he hasn't come home to see if I'm all right. Now that bitch,

Chinky, is calling here harassing me, trying to threaten me and shit. I would-n't be surprised if he's still fuckin' that bitch," I say in one breath.

By the way Naja and Sandra glance at each other, I know some-thing's up. I wait to hear Naja say *I told you so*, but she keeps her mouth shut.

"Look, Shana. I ain't the one to say, and I ain't trying to be all in your personal business," says Sandra, "but I know a girl who lives in Forty Projects, and she told me that she been seeing that niggah Tyrone's BMW parked there almost every night for the past three weeks now—right in front of that bitch's building. She told me he be spending the night there, because that muthafucka don't be leaving there till early the next morn-ing."

What Sandra just said hurt me more than a slap across the face. And I know what she said is true. Why would she lie? I can't bear to think about Tyrone screwing that bitch. He told me that it was definitely over between them—told me that bitch was lying. He even said that's not his seed she's carrying. I'm so devastated and distraught, and the tears start rolling down my face. Naja comes and sits down next to me, placing her arm around my shoulders. "Fuck him, Shana, he ain't no good for you anyway," she says trying to comfort me.

"Why don't you just leave his bitch ass," Latish says.

"If I were you, girl, I would just pack my bags and leave. You don't need to be taking that shit from him. And from what I'm hearing, Chinky ain't the only ho he's fucking. I heard that niggah got two kids in Jersey, and he got one more on the way from some ho out in North Carolina," Sandra says with attitude in her voice, causing me more pain.

"That niggah can't keep his dick in his pants. Yo, you better leave him before he gives you something," Latish warns. *Look who's talking; she can't even keep her legs closed.*

"Or worse, if he gets you pregnant, you'll be carrying his seed like all these other hoes he done already knocked up," Sandra says. I cut my eyes at her.

"Shana, are you sure you're okay?" Naja asks.

I take a deep breath. "I'm pregnant," I blurt out. They all gasp and stare at me like I just told them the world was ending.

"What? Girl, you're kidding?" Sandra says.

"No, Sandra, I'm so for real," I drag out.

"By who?" Latish asks. I don't answer her. I'm trying to get my thoughts together.

"It's Tyrone's, right?" Naja asks.

"I'm not sure," I tell her.

"Don't tell me it's Jakim's baby," Latish says, with her ignorant self.

"It could be his, too, or it could be..." I pause with the name of the last possible father stuck in my throat. They're all looking at me like I'm about to tell them the key to life. "It could also be Danny's baby, too," I finally say.

"What?" says Sandra.

"You fucked your mother's man?" Naja says, stunned.

"You slut!" Latish spits

"It just happened," I say cutting my eyes at Latish.   "Yeah, he slipped and his dick just happened to fall into you, right?" Naja replies sarcastically. "What the hell were you thinking, Shana?"

"Damn, girl, you ain't been using any protection with any of these guys?" Sandra asks. "Watch yourself, Shana."

"Do any of them know yet?" says Naja.

"No, I didn't tell 'em yet."

"Don't you think you need to tell at least one of them," Naja says.

"I'm scared. What if I tell Tyrone and it turns out to not be his?"

"What about Danny?" Latish asks.

"Does your mother know about you and Danny?" says Sandra.

"Shit, does your mother know that you're pregnant?" Naja asks.

"WOULD Y'ALL SHUT THE FUCK UP, PLEASE?!" I shout, fed up with being bombarded with questions. They all look at me with screwed up faces.

"Damn, bitch, you ain't gotta curse sistas out," Latish says. "It ain't my fault you can't keep your fuckin' legs closed."

"What, bitch?" I say. She has some nerve trying to play me out like that, like I'm the ho sittin' up in here. She's fucked more niggahs than Heather Hunter.

"Latish, chill," Naja says.

"Shit, don't be getting upset with me; I ain't the one pregnant with three possible fathers. The bitch needs to get an abortion or something," Latish continues.

I raise up out of my seat. Now is the time to give this bitch a proper ass-whooping. She stands up, too. The bitch got heart. I step to her, but Sandra and Naja come between us.

"Bitch, you don't come up in my muthafuckin' house disrespecting me like that! I'll tear that fuckin' weave out your muthafuckin' bald-head ass!" I yell.

"Do it then, bitch!" she warns. "Pregnant or not, I'll fuck your ass up."

I lunge at her, but Sandra holds me back. I'm sick of this bitch.

She's been smiling up in my face, trying to be my friend and shit, knowing she fucked Jakim. And she had the nerve to try to fuck my uncles in *my* fuckin' bedroom. Now she gonna sit here in my place and try to pass judgment on me, calling me a slut when she done fucked twice as many niggahs than any one of us sitting in here. I'm about to kill this fuckin' bitch–*with* a baby on the way.

"This bitch thinks she's too pretty to get hurt. I'm sick of her trifling ass," Latish chides. "Bitch, that's why I *did* fuck your man, Jakim. And I might be pregnant with his baby."

"Bitch, what!" I shriek, trying to free myself from Sandra's grip. "Sandra, let me go. Let me da fuck go!"

"No, it ain't worth it!" she says.

"Latish, what the fuck is your problem?" Naja asks.

"*She* my problem," Latish replies. "She out here playing games with my man's head, thinkin' dat shit is cute. He don't want you no more, Shana. He wit' me now."

"Your *man*?" I inquire. "Oh, you think Jakim is your man now? Fuck you, bitch!"

"I know it's fucked up to hear the truth, but dat niggah came to my crib one night with the intention to get me pregnant. He wants a family with me, you dumb bitch."

"Oh, you think he wants a family with you, you stupid bitch! He don't want you. You was just some rebound pussy, because I turned down his marriage proposal. Look at you! Don't no niggah want your used-up ass–black bitch! Pussy probably wider than the Grand Canyon."

"Fuck you, Shana. Everything ain't always about you. You think every niggah wants you...please. You wanna play games with that niggah's head and think you can have him back like that," she says, her words filled with emotion. I see a few tears begin to trickle down her face. She continues. "So what if everybody thinks I'm a ho; at least I'm real wit' mine. You constantly walk around like your shit don't stink, putting up a front and constantly lookin' down on me like you so much better. Bitch, you ain't better than me. I know who I am and what I'm about. So what I fucked a lot of niggahs, but I ain't the one pregnant, not knowing who the daddy is. And you got the nerve to call me a ho when you fucked your mother's man. You better check yourself, bitch!"

I glare at her without responding. The truth does hurt. I start to cry. But what hurts me the most is knowing that Jakim fucked Latish with the purpose of getting her pregnant. I know he did it out of spite toward me, though. "Fuck you!" is the last thing I say to her before making my way to the bedroom.

"Latish, just leave!" I hear Naja say.

"Fuck all y'all. No wonder Sasha fucked her ass up. Stupid cunt!" I hear Latish shout before leaving my apartment.

Moments later, Naja and Sandra comfort me in the bedroom and try to give me advice on what to do about my situation. What Latish told me about Jakim hit a nerve and hurt me bad. I want to hate him.

Naja says I need to tell all three guys about me being pregnant. She says I need to be straight up with them. I don't know if I can. I already know that if the baby is Danny's, he isn't going to take care of it. He dissed my mother, so why should I be any different? If it's Jakim's, I think because he's so hurt, he would probably neglect his own child just to get back at me. I ponder about Latish bearing his child. The thought is sickening. And Tyrone, he's another headache altogether. If he's got all these children by different women like I'm hearing, then I wouldn't be anything special to him. I'd just be another one of his baby mothers on the side.

Sandra tells me not to even bother with the headache of carrying this baby, and worrying myself about who the father is. She straight up tells me to get an abortion, since I'm still in the early stages of my pregnancy. She says that two out of the three men I might be pregnant by ain't worth shit, so why chance it and carry the baby around for nine months. She's more on the pessimistic side of things.

All night we talk. They cheer me up a little. We reminisce on the good times, and we also talk about the bad ones. We finish up the Chinese food and continue to watch the movie. I'm not even thinking about my pregnancy anymore, or stressing over that stupid bitch, Latish, and what she told me about her and Jakim. My homegirls have put me in a good mood for now.

When Tyrone finally brings his ass home two days later, he and I have it out. I confront him about Chinky. He argues with me and denies that he's seeing her. I tell him that one of my girlfriends saw him with her a good number of times, and he calls her a lying bitch. I'm so fed up with his bullshit that I almost want to go to blows with him. We continue to argue, and we're so loud that our neighbors bang on their walls and threaten to call the cops if we don't shut up.

I'm so hysterical and out of control that I tell him I'll commit suicide by jumping off the terrace with his baby inside me, which is how he finds out that I'm pregnant. He goes mad and calls me a crazy ass bitch. For a few moments, I actually do think I'm crazy and feel like I really do want to kill myself. This shit is getting to be too much for me to handle.

I start walking toward the terrace and he yokes me up from behind, throwing me down to the floor and threatening me, saying that if I keep acting up, he'll kill me his damn self. He hasn't even said anything about me being pregnant. It's like he doesn't care—probably because he has so many damn kids already.

Afterwards he just leaves, slamming the door so hard that a few pictures fall down from the wall and shatter. I remain on the floor crying, thinking nothing but suicide. Life is hard. I can't take this shit anymore.

When it rains it pours. After my blowout with Tyrone, things ease up a little between the two of us and he apologizes for his actions. Of course I forgive him. He charms me with his gift of gab and works his sweet way into my panties to get some pussy. He gasses me up, telling me that our baby is going to be special and smart because it has his genes. He even promises me that he'll take care of us. When I bring up Chinky, he warns me not to go there. He doesn't want to hear that bitch's name in his home. He says he's going to be home more often—no more staying gone for days at a time. I want to believe him. I have to believe him for my baby's sake.

For the next few days, there's nothing but sweet-talking and wicked lovemaking. Tyrone says if I have a boy, he wants to name him Tyrone Junior, which I think is sweet. Then the thought comes up again: *what if it ain't his baby?* This puts me in a depressed state. I can't afford to have this baby be anyone else's.

It seems like things are quickly turning to shit again. Tyrone's been gone for three days straight, and I haven't even gotten a phone call from him.

I am now four months pregnant. My mother will sometimes come by and spend the day with me. And both of us being pregnant helps us comfort one another. She's due in early August, and I'm due in late August. It's ironic, my mother and me giving birth in the same month. If things get any more ironic—and more fucked up for me—our babies will be by the same guy.

Sandra and Naja stop by to check up on me on a regular, too. Sandra usually tells me what's going on around the way, while I stay cooped up in this apartment. I'm getting fat, and I see my beautiful shape disappearing more every day. My self confidence is dropping to an all-time low. *Don't nobody wanna hang out with pregnant Shana,* I sometimes say to myself. I've gained twenty pounds in the last four months, and that's twenty pounds too many for me. I've gone from one hundred and twenty pounds to one hundred and forty pounds.

Everything comes crashing down on me by the time Spring rolls around. While taking a shower, I hear a hard knock at the door; it sounds like someone is trying to knock it down. I hurriedly turn off the shower and wrap myself in a towel. I step out of the bathroom stall, dripping wet, to go answer the door. "I'm coming, wait the fuck up!" I shout, annoyed.

"Tyrone Sorbs, this is the DEA. We have a search warrant for your apartment," a man announces through the door.

"Wh-what?" I stammer, quickly unlocking the door. Eight cops in flight vests, plain clothes and uniform storm past me and rush inside the apartment. I stand by the door soaking wet, holding onto my towel tightly, as a small puddle of water forms on the floor. "What's going on? Do y'all have a warrant?" I angrily ask.

"Yes, we do," a tall, slender cop says as he shows me his warrant to ransack the entire apartment. "I'm Agent Childs. We believe your boyfriend is concealing controlled substances in this apartment," he informs me as the others go through everything and anything, making a mess everywhere. "Do you have any knowledge of his whereabouts?"

Getting emotional, I answer. "No. I have no idea where he is. That niggah comes home whenever he feels like it."

I hear the other officers rummaging through my bedroom, bathroom and kitchen, where pots and pans are being tossed from the cabinets onto the floor. The apartment is being torn apart.

"Would you like to have a seat?" Agent Childs says.

"I would like for y'all to fuckin' leave so I can get dressed."

"That's not happening. Your boyfriend's a wanted man," he states flatly.

I sit on the living room couch, still in my towel, as the cops continue trying to find something. For the next forty minutes or so, they go through everything from room to room. They even violate me by searching through some of my personal belongings, like bras and panties, lingerie and even my tampons. It's a mess.

They come up with nothing. Tyrone's not stupid; he's been hustling for years, so he knows the game.

"Nothing?!" Agent Childs shouts, frustrated with the results.

"This place is clean," someone answers.

Agent Childs turns to me and says, "We'd like for you to come down to the station and answer a few questions."

"What? Muthafucka, don't you see I'm pregnant?" I bark.

"We're not asking you; we're telling you," he replies nonchalantly.

"We'll give you ten minutes to get dressed."

I can't believe this shit. These muthafuckas ain't got shit on us—or should I say, Tyrone's ass—and yet they insist on taking me in. I get dressed, throwing on whatever I can put together, seeing that my bedroom is in complete disarray, with clothes tossed out of my closet and dresser drawers. My mattress is turned over, and the television lies on its side on the floor. These muthafuckas ain't got any respect for people's personal shit.

I put on a pair of blue jeans, a sweater and a pair of white Nikes, and throw my hair up in a ponytail. The cops escort me out of the apartment. It's embarrassing; everyone is stepping out into the hallway to see what's going on.

It's the same way outside; a small crowd gathers around to watch me being led to one of the cars. It looks like a crime scene outside, with red and blue lights flashing from a small convoy of squad cars.

I get bombarded with questions down at the precinct and I'm given some disturbing details. I also find out that Chinky's apartment was raided two weeks ago, and the police came up with a shitload of drugs. She's in custody, but Tyrone's nowhere to be found. They want her to testify against him, but she's willing to take the rap for him. The shit they found at her place—four kilos of cocaine, three pounds of marijuana, twenty thousand in cash and a small arsenal of weapons—could have her looking at twenty-five years mandatory. They brought me here hoping I would squeal him out and inform them about anything I know that they don't. But I know nothing.

They've had Tyrone under surveillance for months now, but they don't have any real evidence to put him away for the number of years they want to. The charges they have pending against him will only allow a judge to sentence him to three, maybe five years maximum, and the D.A wants him to get more time than that. With Chinky not cooperating, their case looks bogus. *What the fuck is wrong with that bitch?* If I got caught with the amount of shit they busted her with, I'd be telling it all. I'm not doing any time for any man. I don't love a muthafucka that much. And I know Tyrone doesn't love Chinky. If he did, then she wouldn't be in the position she's in right now.

After spending hours in the precinct, I just want to go home and forget about all of this. My life is really turning into shit. As I get up from my chair, a familiar face enters the room; Detective Rice comes over and greets me. "How you doing, Shana?" he asks.

"What the fuck do you want?" I say with a heavy sigh.

"Look, put the hostility somewhere else. It was only a personal greeting—nothing to do with law enforcement."

I know he likes me, but I got this thing about cops. I don't date them or fuck them. "I gotta go," I say walking past him.

He grabs me by the arm. "Shana!"

I turn around and lift up my sweater, exposing my protruding stomach. "I'm fuckin' pregnant, so just fuck off!" I chide. He lets go of my arm, and I storm out of the room crying.

I catch a cab outside the precinct, but I can't think of anywhere to go. There's no way I'm going back to that apartment after what the cops did to the place. And I'm not trying to go to my mother's in the condition I'm in. Who can I see at a time like this? I think and think about it, and the answer comes to me—Jakim.

It's funny; after all we've been through, I somehow now know that he'll still accept me in his life, that he'll still be there for me no matter what.

He was always a caring boyfriend. And he's the only one who I think I can really find comfort in now, despite learning about him and Latish. And I've put that past me. I take a deep breath, dry my tears and give the cabbie Jakim's address. I believe he still loves me...at least I pray that he does.

17   JAKIM

One thing I've learned from my experience with Shana is that you have to be strong, have faith and cannot let a woman destroy you. I'm hurt and devastated about her being with Tyrone. And I know I needed help the day I was about to kill myself in my car.

I've been praying more often, and I've found things to do with myself to keep busy. I've even started going to church–not every Sunday, but whenever possible. I talk to the pastor on a regular and he advises me. He told me that some people are meant to stay in your life, and some are meant to come and go.

I know that I can't let a woman change me. I know I'm better than that. I've made my mistakes in the past, but I want to become a new and better man for myself. And my pastor says when the right time comes, the right woman will come into my life. God will take care of that. He said that sometimes men and women go looking for love in the wrong places. We confuse lust and infatuation with love. Love should be unconditional, and love is not perfect.

I've stopped drinking so much. And I've stopped having sex a lot—especially with different women. It's unhealthy, and after that night with Latish, I knew I was wilding out. But I thank God that Latish wasn't pregnant. I came in her four times in one night, and when she didn't get pregnant after that, I knew it was a sign from God telling me to leave her alone. She was very disappointed and tried encouraging me to keep getting her pregnant, but I broke it off with her for good. She was very upset, to the point where she threatened to have me fucked up. I just blew it off.

Naja and I have a very close friendship. We don't have sex; it's just platonic between us. She helped me out a lot through my ordeal; we go out for drinks and just talk. I need that.

I've even gotten involved in church activities, and I met a young man named Jamal. His friends call him Spanky. He's a cool dude, and he has a beautiful wife named Adina. I've become very good friends with them.

Sometimes when Spanky and I be chilling alone, we talk about our problems and our lives. He talks to me about marriage and how he fell in love with his wife. He admitted that he wasn't even attracted to her at first.

I told him about my ordeal with Shana and Tyrone. And he's the only person that I've told how close I came to killing myself one night. We've really bonded.

I love myself, and I'm happy now. Gradually, I'm getting my life back in order. The pastor asked me one day if I could forgive Shana. I believe that I already have; I'm not holding any grudges or contempt for her. And I feel that she helped me open my eyes to a lot of things. It may sound strange, but I thank her for putting me through trials and tribulations, because it's made me a better and stronger man today. I've moved on, and I'm still standing. I'm no longer bent on getting revenge, because in the long run, I'd only be hurting myself. I've followed Naja's advice and let it be. Shana has her life, and I have mine.

The pastor also asked me if Shana were to come back into my life, would I accept her and be able to start all over with her. I didn't know the answer to that question, and I'm still unsure. I know I'd be nervous, scared even, because I opened my heart to her once before and it ended in pain. I almost committed suicide over Shana, so would it all be worth it a second time? It would be hard for me to trust her again, and trust is a big issue when it comes to marriage and being in a relationship with someone. I know everyone should get a second chance, but it comes with risk. We can't predict the future. Love is not always certain, and if she were to break my heart again, what would my outcome be the next time around? I don't know, and I'm probably too scared to find out.

It's been a week since the pastor asked me that question, but I'll get back to that later; I think I hear someone out front.

SHANA 18

I arrive at Jakim's house and contemplate if I should go ring his doorbell. My heart is vigorously pounding against my chest. I take a deep breath and exhale. I feel my emotions get a little out of control as I wonder if he has company. I'm starting to have visions of Jakim loving another woman. I mean, he has the right to. And I can't blame him if he curses me out and slams the door in my face, shutting me completely out of his life. That would hurt a lot. But right now I just want him to hold and comfort me. I want to apologize and tell him that I still love him, and that he was right about all of the things he said about Tyrone.

I remember when he asked for a second chance with me. It's so ironic how I'm now standing in front of his house about to ask him for a second chance.

I take another deep breath, calming my nerves, and then slowly walk up to his door. I ring the bell and wait....

I hear the door being unlocked. It seems like everything is going in slow motion, and I feel like my life is at a standstill. I lower my eyes and when I focus them back on the front door, I see Jakim standing in his doorway. Neither of us says a word. I wait for something vulgar to escape his lips.

Suddenly all of the pain and agony I suffered over the past weeks starts to build up. My eyes dampen, and I feel cold and start to tremble. I want to scream, but a lump is stuck in my throat. A tear escapes from my eye and trickles down the side of my face. "Jakim, please hold me," I beg.

I realize that my love is still here with him. I've been away from him for far too long, doing the wrong things with the wrong men. Now I'm pregnant, scared and hurt.

I'm crying so hard that I feel like I'm going to pass out. "I'm so sorry, Jakim, I'm sorry." I apologize over and over.

Jakim wraps his arms around me. His embrace is strong as he nestles my head against his chest. "It's okay, Shana, everything's going to be okay," he assures me. I feel his forgiveness as he comforts me in his arms. This is true and unconditional love, and I plan on being here for a long time.

TWO MONTHS LATER

Jakim and I are officially back together. I'm six months pregnant and starting to look like a fuckin' mountain. I've gained thirty-five pounds, my face is fat, and my ankles and feet are so swollen that I can't fit into any of my old shoes. After taking three sonograms, the doctor assured me that I'm having a boy. I'm bringing a little boy into the world.

Not knowing who my baby's father is still haunts me. Jakim knows that Tyrone could also be the father. I haven't told him about Danny; I don't have the courage to. But he says he'll still be there for me no matter whose child it turns out to be.

I pray every night that this baby is Jakim's. He says it doesn't matter, but I know that deep down inside him, it does. I mean, it wouldn't look right for him to be raising Tyrone's child, being that they're enemies now. They can't even walk down the same block without an argument and some kind of fight ensuing between the two of them.

Tyrone is out on twenty-thousand dollars bail, and living life like he's not looking at serious time. Chinky is being held in Rikers with a fifty-thousand-dollar bond hanging over her head. Tyrone isn't even man enough to go and try to bail her out, and it sickens me to think that I actually thought I was in love with him. I now see that he does nothing but use and abuse the women in his life. And whenever the thought comes up that I might be pregnant with his baby, I cry so hard that I get a headache.

Right now I feel like I'm about to have a serious breakdown. Jakim tells me to keep my head up and stay on the positive side. I try and try, but until I finally find out who the father of my child is, I feel that I'll never be at ease. And truth be told, if it wasn't for Jakim sticking with me from day to day, I wouldn't have come this far. He's truly been there for me mentally and physically. We're even attending Lamaze classes together.

But you know, in this age—and in my neighborhood—when something positive finally happens in your life, or *with* your life, there's always some fool out there crashing your walls down on you, or at least trying to.

It's the first week of June, and the temperature has hit a high of ninety-eight degrees. I have two burdens: the unbearable heat and being seven months pregnant.

I've moved back in with my mother, and we're both moody, gassy and fat. My Aunt Tina finally moved out a few weeks ago. She shacked up with some old boyfriend of hers, who's out of prison and hustling again.

I've been up in the house for the past two weeks, and I can't wait to see Jakim tonight. He promised to take me out to a movie and dinner at this new restaurant in Valley Stream. He's still at work at FedEx, where he's been employed for about a month now.

I'm in my room with the stereo tuned to WBLS, rubbing my belly and trying to keep my thoughts positive and my head up high. It takes me a minute to realize that my phone is ringing. I quickly rush over to answer it, hoping that it's Jakim calling. "Hello?"

"What's up, Shana?" It's not Jakim, but I recognize the voice instantly.

"What do you want, Tyrone?" I ask, nervous about him calling.

"What, you don't call no more? You out there carrying my child and don't even check me?"   I get quiet. Just hearing him mention that I'm carrying his seed starts stirring up my emotions again. "I'm hearing stories that you're back with Jakim. What, you think you just gonna leave me for him that easy? Bitch, you fuckin' owe me!" he angrily shouts.

"Owe you? Fuck you, after the shit you done put me through...fuck you!" I shriek.

"Oh, so it's like that? After I done looked out for you, had you staying up in my crib, and bought you tons of shit, you think you gonna just play me like that?"

"You looked out for me!" I angrily reply. "I'm sorry that I ever got with your trifling ass! You were nothing but trouble from the day I met you!"

"Bitch, you *are* sorry, and you ain't nothin' but a ho! I'm gonna see that ass soon—you and that punk niggah, Jakim."

I get scared, knowing the things he's capable of doing. "Tyrone, why can't you just let us be?"

"Nah, that's my seed you're carrying. I told you—we're forever. What, you thought I was gonna get locked up 'cause cops raided my crib? Bitch, I'm gonna check you soon. You best believe that!" he hollers before hanging up.

Still holding the phone to my ear, I feel like I'm about to break down in tears. I'm frightened, and I don't know what to do. I slam the receiver down and drop to my knees. *What am I going to do?*

Later on in the evening, Jakim proposes to me for the second time. I feel like the luckiest woman on earth. He says that everyone deserves a second chance. Then he hits me with something I never heard him say before. "Let's leave here," he says.

At first I think he means 'leave here' as in just leaving Queens, but he wants to leave New York for good. He wants to move me and the baby down South. His cousin has a two-bedroom apartment in South Carolina that we could rent out for dirt-cheap. He also has a job lined up that pays up to fifteen dollars an hour. I'm all for it. I tell him we should go for it; it's definitely a good idea.

Sometimes I wonder why certain things happen to certain people. Why are some people blessed with good looks and charm, and others are cursed with disfiguration and ugliness? Why are some folks born wealthy and others are born so poor, living in the most dilapidated places, growing up in neighborhoods where some folks wonder how they can call it their home? Why do some women find *Mr. Right*, and other women are cursed with being abused and mistreated throughout their entire lives? Why are some men blessed with big dicks, and the other less fortunate ones can't keep it up any longer than five minutes? Why are some children growing up today without a mother or father to shield them from so much harshness, hate and bitterness? And my million-dollar question is: why can't something good happen to me for once without pain and suffering being soon to follow?

It's Thursday night. Naja calls me as I rest in bed. By the somber tone of her voice, I know I'm not ready for what she's about to tell me.

"Shana...Jakim's been shot." I swear my heart just stopped, as I lay there holding the phone tightly to my ear. I start to breath heavily, and I begin gasping for air. *No, this is nothing but a bad dream,* I try to tell myself. "THIS IS NOT H-A-A-A-P-P-E-E-E-N-I-I-I-I-N-G!" I scream at the top of my lungs. I pass out and go into early labor.

EPILOGUE

I gave birth to a premature, four pound, two-ounce baby boy two months early. I named him Jakim Junior. He's my world. The doctor assured me that he's going to be fine, though.

My mother visits me in the hospital frequently along with my aunt and some of my friends, including Naja and Sandra. They bring me flowers, balloons and cards. But nothing can cheer me up after Jakim's death. He was gunned down.

I'm taking his death real hard. I tried to imagine him being by my side when I was in labor, but that made it more difficult for me to get through the delivery. After pushing my son out, I cried for hours and hours. The nurses tried to cheer me up; they bought me gifts, made me visit my son from time to time, and they even broke hospital rules by sometimes letting visitors in after hours.

Having Jakim Junior sometimes eases the pain of Jakim's death. At times I'll hold his tiny, frail body in my arms, comforting and talking to him, and I convince myself that Jakim is the father. I search for similarities in their features, but Jakim Junior is really too young to determine that right now.

They've arrested two guys in connection with Jakim's murder. Naja somberly gives me the details of what happened the night he was killed.

She says they were at a club having a good time, and Jakim was buying them drinks at the bar. She says Tyrone walked in with his entourage of thugs, and then a confrontation took place that resulted in them all trying to jump on Jakim. But the fight was quickly broken up, and Tyrone and his crew were thrown out.

Jakim was really upset and Naja suggested that they leave. They did, and they ran into Tyrone and his crew, who'd been waiting for him to come outside, where three guys instigated the beef again. A scuffle broke out on the street and Naja says she tried to help him, but they beat on her, too. Then she heard shots fired and saw Jakim sprawled out on the ground. "I'm sorry, Shana," she says crying uncontrollably. "I'm so sorry...he's gone, he's gone."

When I first heard that Jakim was dead, I wanted to die, too. I contemplated suicide. Luckily for my son, I had the strength to move on, even though I was still hurting deep down inside.

The thing that made me furious was when I heard that Tyrone wasn't being charged for Jakim's murder; the D.A didn't have a stable case against him to charge him with homicide. I didn't understand how that could be. Tyrone had a motive. But then I realized that he's manipulative, conniving and has the gift of gab. He's smart; he gets other people to do his dirty work for him.

It's hard to believe that I was once head over heels in love with the man, ready to spend eternity with him. Now I hate him with a passion, so much, in fact, that I actually think about buying myself a gun to go and blow his muthafuckin' brains out. I really want to, for Jakim. Tyrone had him killed, and now he's getting away with it.

I build up enough strength to attend Jakim's funeral. Doctors warn that I shouldn't, but I have to. Naja picks me up from the hospital, and I get dressed over at her house. "Are you sure you're up to this?" she asks me. I nod. I have to be. I have to pay my respects to Jakim.

The funeral home is packed. I can tell by all the vehicles out front. Jakim's mother flew in from California. She's overcome with grief and sorrow. And as soon as I step into the building, I, too, am overcome with grief and sorrow. Naja takes notice and asks me again if I want to go through with this. I nod, and we proceed on to the viewing.

Naja grips my hand tightly as we slowly step toward the cedar coffin. My eyes are partially closed, and I start to tremble as I get closer to Jakim's lifeless body.

First Terry, and now Jakim. How many boyfriends and exes will I lose in my lifetime? I say to myself. Terry's murder is still unsolved, and that bothers me. I'm suspicions about Tyrone again, even though he gave me his word that he didn't do it. But he also once gave me his word that he wouldn't do anything to Jakim. Obviously his word doesn't mean shit!

I stand over Jakim's coffin and slowly open my eyes. Upon doing so, I see him—his shell anyway—lying there so peacefully. He's wearing a gray three-piece suit, his arms are gently folded and his eyes are shut.

As I peer down at him, I suddenly feel a surge of guilt. It's because of me that he's dead. I had to go and mess with his best friend, knowing the type of man he was. I let my sexual feelings get the best of me, and because of that, my true love is dead.

I start to tremble even harder, my bottom lip quivers and my knees buckle. I throw all of my weight against Naja, who holds me up and supports me. "JAKIM!!!" I scream out. He didn't deserve this.

Naja tries to comfort me, but I start to get wild and out of control. I feel a few more arms drape around me, then pick me up and carry me off down the aisle.

"It's okay, Shana," I hear someone say.

Then from the corner of my eye, I see her. She's slowly coming my way. She's dressed in a black blouse and skirt. She's cut her hair short, and her eyes stay on me the whole time as she approaches. "How you holding up, Shana?" Sasha asks with concern.

I don't answer. I just stare at her. She hands me a card and some flowers. I slowly take them. *Why is she here?* It's been months since we've last seen each other, and I haven't heard anything about her. It was like she just disappeared.

"Shana...look, I'm sorry. You have my condolences. Jakim was a good man. And I'm sorry about what happened between us and the way I acted. We were foolish, and I just want to put it behind us," she says, not once averting her eyes from me.

Jakim forgave me. He still took me into his life after all we had been through. He was ready for us to start a new life together. He was even willing to raise a child that might not have been his. Jakim forgave me, so there's no reason for me to not forgive her. "I'm sorry, too, Sasha," I say giving her a hug, and Naja even joins in on the embrace.

I'm ready to start a new chapter in my life, a better one, I say to myself as I look around. I know Jakim would want that; I have our son to raise and take care of.

SIX MONTHS LATER

It pains me to be here tonight at the Midnight Lounge. But it needs to be done, though. I look for Tyrone and see him in the VIP section having a good time. He has a bottle of Moet in his hand, and he's flanked by two beautiful women. He hasn't yet noticed me. He's too busy being the man and showing off.

I have some news to tell him. He has a son. I cried when I found out that the baby is his. Jakim's mother and father took DNA tests to see if Jakim Junior was their grandson, but the tests came back negative. Danny also got tested, too, which was a shock to me. He was charged with first degree murder and sentenced to life in prison. But he willingly took the DNA test to see if it was his child, and it was negative. I knew then that Tyrone was my son's father.

Unfortunately, my mother found out about my brief affair with Danny. We had a quarrel over it, but she eventually forgave me and we became the best of friends. She gave birth to an eight-pound, nine-ounce boy on August fifteenth. My aunt also gave birth—to a baby girl—five months after my mother. She slowed her life down after that, and now she's engaged to a sanitation worker. She's decided to leave the thug life to the thugs. She's done with them.

Sasha and I have become the best of friends again. We see each other almost every day. And with Naja around, we're like the *Dynamic Trio*. They really help me out a lot with the baby, and I love them so much for that. Sasha is watching my son tonight. She encouraged me to confront Tyrone at his club. She wanted to come along, but I need her to be with my son. Naja is in school full time trying to get her bachelor's degree, and holding down a full time job, too. She's doing her thang.

That ho, Latish, has surprisingly turned her life around, too. She found a stable boyfriend and has been faithful to him for a few months now. We speak here and there, but we're not cool like that. I keep my distance from her most of the time.

I've started going to school myself. I'm attending York College to get my Bachelors degree. I also got a job at a clothing store on Jamaica Avenue and have become very independent; I no longer look for men to take care of me. I'm making my own paper and providing for my son on my own.

We've all changed a lot since Jakim's murder. From family to friends, everybody's on the ball. Sasha dumped Cell a long time ago, and she's pregnant with her first child. The baby's father is a store manager at K-Mart. It's a drastic change for her, but she's getting used to it, as we are all getting used to the changes in our lives.

I stand by the bar watching Tyrone. I hate him. He wants his son, and he's going to have him; I'm going to hit that muthafucka with child support, back-payments and everything. He's gonna come out his pockets big-time. I haven't seen or heard from him since the funeral. He's still hustling in the streets.

"Can I buy you a drink, beautiful?" a tall, brown-skinned man asks me.

"No thanks," I gently reply.

"You sure? You lookin' good in that skirt, ma. What's your name?" I smile. He's cute, but he's not for me. He's dripping with jewelry and has that thuggish demeanor.

"Maybe next time," I tell him and casually walk off.

I move to the other side of the bar, and think about how I should approach him. I never once resented my son after I found out that Tyrone is his father; Jakim Junior was still the love of my life. And despite Tyrone being an asshole and more, I'm going to teach his son how to be a better man, more of a man than he ever was.

I take a sip from my Long Island Ice Tea and look over at Tyrone. He's finally noticed me standing by the bar. He smirks and gives me a slight head nod. Then he raises the bottle in my direction and starts guzzling down the Moet. One of the ladies sitting next to him kisses him on the neck and is then all over him. I sigh and roll my eyes at him in disgust.

He doesn't give a fuck, which is making it harder for me to do what I have to do. I sit my glass down on the counter...I'm about to go over there. I unexpectedly see Evay in the crowd. I haven't seen or heard from him in months. They say he was locked up.

Evay makes his way through the crowd, looking unaffected by the blaring music and revelers in the place. He has a cold, blank stare on his face as he walks toward the VIP section. He slowly navigates through the crowd. From where I stand he doesn't look right in his mind, but for some strange reason I can't turn away. I don't know what he's up to. He doesn't see me. I take a closer look at him and notice that he has something gripped in his hand. It's a gun. I'm in awe.

"Yo, Tyrone!" Evay shouts, standing a few feet from him. Tyrone looks up and sees Evay standing in front of him. I see Evay raise the gun and fire it at Tyrone. *Blam! Blam! Blam! Blam! Blam! Blam! Blam! Blam! Blam! Click. Click. Click. Click.*

Everyone instantly runs and scatters. The club is in chaos. Evay shot Tyrone nine times. Tyrone's body is slumped over in his seat, riddled with bullets. Blood is everywhere. His two female companions ran for safety along with everyone else, leaving him alone at the booth. All I hear is screaming and panicking. I never moved from my spot. I stand frozen by the bar with my eyes fixed on Evay. I watch his every move.

"That's for Jakim, you bitch ass niggah! And don't you ever put your fuckin' hands on me again!" Evay exclaims as he glares at Tyrone's contorted and lifeless body.

He turns and starts to walk the opposite way, passing me. He looks at me, and then he smiles and winks.

I'm still in awe. While everyone is running, screaming and looking for safety, I remain standing at the bar without moving.

Evay is gone. I look over at Tyrone. He's a mess. I feel nothing—no emotion whatsoever...he brought it on himself. And he didn't even get a chance to say one word. It happened so quickly. Just like that, his life ended at the hands of a friend.

AN URBAN NOVEL

NASTY GIRLS

ERICK S. GRAY

[LITERALLY DOPE]

GHETTO GIRLS (SPECIAL EDITION)
ANTHONY WHYTE

GHETTO GIRLS TOO
ANTHONY WHYTE

GHETTO GIRLS 3: SOO HOOD
ANTHONY WHYTE

THE BLUE CIRCLE
KEISHA SEIGNIOUS

BOOTY CALL *69
ERICK S GRAY

IF IT AIN'T ONE THING IT'S ANOTHER
SHARRON DOYLE

IT CAN HAPPEN IN A MINUTE
S.M. JOHNSON

A NOVEL BY
SHARRON DOYLE

A richly textured story of deceit; **If It Ain't One Thing It's Another,** is the most riveting tale of the decade. Every once in a while an author comes along with dazzling talents. In her debut novel, **It Ain't One Thing It's Another**, Sharron Doyle broke us off with this sensational tale of vengeance, thirst and hunger.

Streetwise, Petie is grinding on the road to infamy. His throne is toppled and his rule is coming to an end. He will not be kingpin, but he's bent on taking his family, his mistress, Share', best friend and fellow hustler, Ladell, through their most traumatic experiences. On lockdown, Petie is no snitch and does not cooperate with the justice department. After being released Petie's twisted method of exacting revenge on his enemies will shock and open the eyes of every reader. He comes armed to the nines ready to get rid of those who snitched or betrayed him. Only Share' stands in his way. His enemies soon find out that: **If Ain't One Thing It's Another** is revenge at all cost. Beef never dies, it multiplies.

If It Ain't One Thing It's Another brings you on a fast paced journey through the life of hustling where the grit of the streets and greed of the hustle are presented sumptuously in a magnificently convoluted plot. Mixed with zesty scenes, this clever, sexy tale from the streets you will not want to put down until it ends. Written from the inside out, Uptown's own, Sharron Doyle delivers brilliantly with a terrific drama. **If It Ain't One Thing It's Another,** will be forever etched in your mind.

"A fast paced hood chiller! This story is destined to be the talk of the town.
The story grabs you and just does not let go."

-Anthony Whyte (Bestselling author of **Ghetto Girls Series**)

S.M. JOHNSON

S.M. JOHNSON

It Can Happen In A Minute

It Can Happen In A Minute is a compelling story of love, deception, secrets, lies and making wrong decisions. From the beginning to a very explosive end, S.M. Johnson captivates, titillates and moves readers to tears. Take this journey with Samone who has been labeled the black sheep of her family. Slighted by the ongoing dynamic relationship between her mother and sister, Samone moves from Miami to D.C. But things aren't so good in the hood. She shares life with her father but discovers damaging and grave secrets about him while living in his home. Samone finds herself trapped in a perilous corner where her only escape is to look out for herself. Has she run out of love? And will it be too late to move on? It Can Happen In A Minute is an unforgettable quick ride through heavy drama.

ORDERFORM

NAME _____

COMPANY _____

ADDRESS _____

CITY _____ STATE _____ ZIP _____

PHONE _____ FAX _____

EMAIL _____

TITLES	PRICE	QTY	TOTAL
GHETTO GIRLS (SPECIAL EDITION) / ANTHONY WHYTE	14.95		
GHETTO GIRLS TOO / ANTHONY WHYTE	14.95		
GHETTO GIRLS 3: SOO HOOD / ANTHONY WHYTE	14.95		
THE BLUE CIRCLE / KEISHA SEIGNIOUS	14.95		
BOOTY CALL *69 / ERICK S GRAY	14.95		
IF IT AIN'T ONE THING - IT'S ANOTHER / SHARRON DOYLE	14.95		
IT CAN HAPPEN IN A MINUTE / S.M. JOHNSON	14.95		
	SUBTOTAL		
	SHIPPING		
	8.625% TAX		
	TOTAL		

**AUGUSTUS
PUBLISHING**

MAKE ALL CHECKS PAYABLE TO:
AUGUSTUS PUBLISHING / 33 INDIAN ROAD NY, NY 10034 / SUITE 3K
SHIPPING CHARGES
GROUND ONE BOOK $4.95 / EACH ADDITIONAL BOOK $1.00

AugustusPublishing.com
info@augustuspublishing.com

MEMBER OF SCABRINI GROUP

Québec, Canada
2006